A TANGLED
INHERITANCE

OTHER COVENANT BOOKS
BY CHALON LINTON:

An Inconvenient Romance

Christmas Grace (contributor)

ACKNOWLEDGMENTS

I WANT TO EXPRESS MY gratitude to my publisher, Covenant Communications, for the opportunity to share my stories. It's been a joy working with and learning from Kami Hancock—thanks for your patience with my grammatical shortcomings. Thank you, Michelle Pipitone, for the amazing cover and additional graphics, because I really love a pretty book. Here's a huge shout-out to Stephanie Lacy for sharing her genius. She held my hand through my debut launch, and I'm so grateful she's here for round two.

Lots of love to my faithful beta readers: Jen, Kodie, Laura, and Melissa. Your feedback and support is invaluable. Thank you for your friendship. I also want to express my gratitude to Gary Underwood and Stephen Tyler for sharing their expertise.

Thank you to my parents, siblings, and in-laws.

And once again, hugs and kisses to my children. They've been my cheerleaders from the beginning. Go, Team Linton! All of my love to my husband, who indulged a math teacher with a sudden desire for a career change. You are a true gentleman, a devoted father, and my best friend. I'm looking forward to eternity.

CHAPTER 1

Mr. Devlin Fausett, Derbyshire, England—1818

LOVE IS A BEAUTIFUL THING, even if watching the new Mr. and Mrs. Dashel step into their carriage was slightly nauseating. They'd been grinning at each other stupidly all day, and more than once I'd realized I was tremendously jealous.

Charles Brumley, my friend from Cambridge, invited me to his country estate, Riverton Park. I'd intended to only impose for a week or two, but my stay had become an excursion just shy of five weeks. My visit had provided a refuge, a place to escape the *ton*, my creditors, and my father. An added bonus was helping Brumley secure a bride of his own. Knocking some sense into his stubborn head had been a much-needed diversion, and thankfully, Brumley wised up and asked Miss Leah Hastings to be his wife.

As Miss Leah's elder sister was now married, Brumley only needed to postpone his nuptials until the new couple returned from their honeymoon trip. I had no doubt Brumley and his fiancée would make each other happy. I watched as they stepped together into the lane to wish farewell to the newlyweds. Brumley looked at Miss Leah with pure adoration. I watched the happy couple, lost in my musings, until a firm hand slapped across my shoulder. I turned to see Ferrin Hastings, Miss Leah's older brother.

"Fausett! How long do you plan to remain at Riverton Park?" he asked.

While my visit to Brumley's estate served as an escape, I knew the time had come to return to London. I was unable to pay my current debts until the living allowance my father granted was distributed. The money would arrive the following week, and the entire sum would be needed to satisfy my creditors. I'd appealed to Father for an advance, but he had rebuked me without hesitation.

I turned and shook Ferrin's hand. "I'm afraid I must return to Town."

We both watched Miss Leah laugh at something Brumley said.

"It must be a relief to see them both settled well," I said.

"Indeed," Ferrin said. "But now the pressure turns to me."

I scoffed. "Your father does not strike me as the pressuring type, unlike my own."

"True, Father would never force my hand." Ferrin lifted his fingers to his chin and mused, "If there's pressure from my family, it would be from Sarah. She's long insisted that I should take more seriously her admonishment to settle down. She's constantly introducing me to eligible young ladies, but the pickings are slim here in Paddington."

"Is Miss Ansley still listed among those eligible young ladies?" I asked. Upon my last visit, Ferrin seemed particularly interested in the quiet beauty.

"Unfortunately, she's not. Once Brumley announced his engagement to my sister, Mrs. Ansley whisked her daughter away to Bath." Ferrin's shoulders rose and fell. He pressed his lips up in a smile and turned back towards me. "Be grateful you don't have a younger sister to pester you. They take far too much delight in their duties."

"No need to say more, old chap. I understand completely." And I did. My mother tried to hide her concern. Her weekly letters were filled with detailed descriptions of fashion and society news, but I did not miss the subtle references to marriages or the names of young widows and new debutantes she dropped between the bits of fact. I stood quiet until Ferrin broke the silence.

"Truth be told, I think the brunt of guilt I feel is self-imposed. I feel a certain duty to my family," he said.

I nodded my understanding, and we discussed the affairs of Astoria, the estate he would inherit. Eventually, Ferrin turned the conversation to Newmarket. He shared a tip he'd heard about a promising new mare as Brumley and Miss Leah approached. The lead seemed solid, and I wondered if betting on the races offered the same rush I felt at the tables.

I refocused my thoughts and offered my congratulations to Miss Leah. "What a lovely day for your family. Please know how fortunate I feel to be included in the invitation."

"Come now, Mr. Fausett," Miss Leah reprimanded me. "After all you've done for my family, for me personally"—she slipped her arm through Brumley's—"I would not hear of you missing this happy event."

"With all of the festivities ended, I can resume my naps. Paddington is bound to be dreary now," Ferrin said with a teasing smile.

"Oh, hush!" Miss Leah playfully swatted her brother's shoulder. "You know you must turn around and do it all again. Otherwise I'll think Sarah is your favorite sister."

Ferrin winked at Miss Leah. "When Fausett leaves me stranded with you two love birds, I think I might have to get a dog and declare it my favorite," he said.

"Mr. Fausett isn't leaving," Miss Leah answered before I had the chance. "Charles would not hear of him leaving. Isn't that right?" she asked and turned to her fiancé.

Brumley shrugged. "We hadn't discussed the particulars," he said and then turned towards me. "But you know you are always welcome."

"I do." I tipped my head to my friend. "And I thank you. However, there is some business I must attend to in Town."

Miss Leah's face fell. "Surely it can wait a few weeks. Then you can return to London after our wedding."

"I can stay a few days, but then I have some pressing business I must conduct. Once all is concluded, I promise to return," I said, somehow pleased by the smile spread across Miss Leah's face.

"Very well," she acquiesced. "But the wedding plans have kept me so busy, and we've hardly had time to catch up, and . . . well, there's so much to talk about. You must spend some time at Riverton Park before the wedding."

Ferrin narrowed his eyes at his sister. "What are you playing at, Leah?"

Miss Leah's cheeks turned rosy, and she looked down at her shifting feet. "Aunt Phyllis and her daughters will be coming to assist with the wedding. I was hoping to introduce them to our dear Mr. Fausett."

Ferrin laughed aloud. "It's just as I told you, Fausett; it's Sarah's job to harry me, and Leah must have felt left out." He slapped his hand on my shoulder again. "It looks like you've been officially adopted. Welcome to the family."

CHAPTER 2

Miss Nora Ellsworth

TWO YEARS AGO, MY MOTHER took me to London. My first official Season came the following year. My first impressions of Town remained fresh in my mind. Every rumor I'd heard about the city proved true. London was unreal, unlike anything I had previously experienced. The buildings were tall and cramped so close they seemed to lean on one another for support. Soot hung in the air constantly, and people crowded every street and pathway.

I preferred my childhood home in Northamptonshire to the bustling London streets. Ellsworth Meadows stood upon a vast acreage with sprawling hills, meadows, wild grass, and even a copse of trees large enough to get lost in. I found the number of London citizens packed into the same amount of space both suffocating and fascinating.

Thankfully, our house in London was large enough to spread out in. We even boasted four solid walls, a small stable, and a decent-sized garden in the rear of the house. I'd found the majority of Town's diversions pleasant enough, but in the quiet of the night, when my hair was wrapped in curling papers, I longed for a diverting conversation about something other than the latest fashions or whispered accusations of debauchery. But life in the *ton* revolved around gossip, dresses, incomes, and dowries. Without a doubt, physical appearance factored in as well.

Our carriage pulled up to a large arching doorway set beneath an ornate balustrade. The footman handed us out of the carriage, and my sister, Claudia, Mother, and I followed Father into the Mortimers' foyer.

"Lovely evening, Mortimer," Father said and shook Mr. Mortimer's hand.

Mrs. Mortimer looked at our party, and when her eyes settled on me, a smile spread across her face. "We are so delighted Miss Ellsworth has accepted our invitation to perform this evening."

The truth was that Mother had accepted the invitation in my stead. We stood in the Mortimers' foyer at her insistence. While I enjoyed singing, I found the musicales in London to be an exercise in patience. I curtsied to our hosts but said nothing.

Mother touched a hand to her heart. "Nora does have a lovely voice. You will certainly not regret including her in the program."

"After I heard her perform at the Matthewses', I just knew she would be the perfect addition to our small gathering," Mrs. Mortimer said.

Small was not an adequate descriptor of the Mortimers' gathering. Claudia covered her mouth with her hand to smother her laugh.

Mother nudged me with her elbow. "Oh." I gasped. "Yes. Thank you for thinking of me. It was very kind of you. I hope my performance does not disappoint."

The evening paralleled the monotonous entertainments I'd come to expect in Town. Flowery compliments were tossed around as frequently as rain in England. Flattering words about hairstyles, dresses, and musical talents filled the room.

At the conclusion of the performances, Mr. Mortimer motioned Claudia and me towards a group of men, and when we stepped near, they were commenting on the reports of pirates pilfering ships along the trade routes.

Mr. Mortimer made the appropriate introductions, and after the gentlemen acknowledged me, I thought to share my opinion on the subject. "Perhaps England's efforts would be better spent if we hired the pirates as mercenaries to guard the trading vessels. The shipments would arrive to their destinations, and the pirates would receive their pay."

My suggestion was met with laughter. "You need not worry your pretty head about such things, Miss Ellsworth," one of my new acquaintances, Mr. Howe, said. "Issues of governance are best left to the men." My cheeks burned with resentment at the blunt dismissal. Why could I not have a conversation about the growing trade with India or share ideas about how to help the impoverished families living just across the river? Heaven forbid I try to discuss the exile of Napoleon or the expanding colonies in America. I would relish a discussion on any controversy so long as it did not include a maligned piece of clothing.

Mr. Howe leaned near. "You've an adorable blush, Miss Ellsworth." My hands clenched at my side. "Might I persuade you to join me for a turn about Hyde Park tomorrow?"

I declined with a forced smile, faked a headache, and then listened to Mother lecture me on propriety the entire drive home.

"It is not a lady's place to share her opinion," Mother said.

"But it was a good idea," I argued.

"I'm not debating that fact. Your brain trumps the combined intelligence of the Mortimers' guests," Mother said with a sly smile. "I'm simply saying that a proper lady does not flaunt her strengths."

"You would have me flaunt my beauty," I said with a heavy sigh.

Mother reached over and touched my cheek. "Your beauty is something we could not conceal even if we tried," she said.

We could not return to the country soon enough.

The following morning, Mother sought to console me with a promise that the man she intended me to marry was well versed on a great many things and he would surely satiate my appetite for meaningful conversation in addition to appreciating my beauty.

Her selection was made the moment the midwife had revealed my gender. I was told Mother had looked at the midwife and declared me betrothed. One month after my birth, Mother confirmed the arrangement with all parties involved. No sooner had her confinement been lifted than she scuttled to the home of her childhood friend, Mrs. Rosamond Browning, and the two women decreed that I would be the wife of Mrs. Browning's son, Jonathon.

The plan was not a bad one. Mr. Browning and I were both from notable families. Our mothers got on well, which seemed a rare thing for mothers-in-law. And he was nine years older than I, to the very month. The problem was that I had never met Mr. Jonathon Browning, at least that I recalled. All of these details were relayed again and again by my mother while she talked of delightful Jonathon and the delightful Browning family, although she had not seen them herself for more than sixteen years.

Our estate in Yorkshire, Payton Place had neighbored that of the Browning family. But when I was two years old, a careless servant toppled a bucket of hot ashes on the stairs to the servant's entrance, and fire engulfed our home. We stayed at Lily Glen with the Brownings until Father had settled his affairs, and then we relocated to Ellsworth Meadows in Northamptonshire, where we have since remained. I, of course, could not recall Payton Place, or Lily Glen, or the Browning family. My childhood home, my memories, all belonged to Ellsworth Meadows. It was there I first learned to skip and convinced Claudia to try with me. Unfortunately, her little legs could not keep up, and she returned to the nursery with bloodied and skinned knees. My first swing still hung from the largest oak tree, the seat now worn with use. I knew every stone, hedge, and rosebush, including the hollow log where I'd once tried to hide an extra biscuit, only to realize the ants discovered it before I could sneak away from my lessons to enjoy it. Ellsworth Meadows had become my home, and it had claim on my heart.

After we left Yorkshire, Mr. Browning had felt adventurous, and his entrepreneurial spirit carried his family to India. According to Mrs. Browning's correspondence, her husband's business pursuits had amassed quite a fortune. But alas, their residence in India denied me the opportunity to become acquainted with my betrothed. Mother, however, remained certain our engagement stood.

A week after the Mortimers' musicale, Mother came rushing into the sitting room.

I set my embroidery aside and exchanged a look of curiosity with Claudia.

"Oh, they are coming!" Mother squealed and flapped her hand near her face in a vain attempt to fan herself.

"Who's coming?" I asked.

"The Brownings, of course," she said with a tsk of her tongue.

"Oh, of course," I said with a hint of amusement.

Mother raised the letter and traced the words with her finger. "*My Dear Mrs. Ellsworth, I hope this letter reaches you quickly, for we shall shortly be departing for London. Mr. Browning hopes to depart in early September and promises we shall arrive before the end of the Season. I admit I am quite anxious to return to Town and enjoy those frivolities I have so long missed. I do hope we may meet in London and solidify the arrangements agreed upon all those years ago.*" Mother punched the paper with her finger. "See. There it is."

"There what is?" Claudia asked.

Mother turned her happy smile to Claudia. "The Brownings are coming home from India." She lowered the letter to her waist and sighed.

"I thought India was their home," I said.

Mother tsk'd again and waved a hand at me. "Oh, you know what I mean." Mother turned in a circle, and we watched her parade around the sitting room. "Girls, there's so much to do." She walked to the bell pull and called for a servant.

"Mother," I said calmly. "I understand your excitement to see Mrs. Browning again; however, you've made a promise to Cousin Leah. We are to leave in four days."

My dear cousin, Leah Hastings, would be getting married the following month. Her mother had passed away, and her Aunt Evelyn Clem had relocated to Bath for her health. Cousin Leah had asked if Mother and I would assist in her preparations for the wedding. Claudia would, of course, come along.

Mrs. Hastings and my mother were sisters, and as little girls, Leah and I were the best of friends. The Hastings family came on several occasions to visit Ellsworth Meadows, but more frequently, we visited Derbyshire and stayed at their beautiful home, Astoria.

When I was seven and Leah eight, our families drifted away. It may or may not have had something to do with a certain Christmas incident in which I accidently painted Leah's new white dress with a beautiful blue stripe. Leah's rebuke had been furious, and my mother refused to let me associate with her further. I missed my cousin, and gratitude filled my heart when I received a letter from her roughly seven months ago, describing her newly acquired understanding of repentance. She confessed to having held her grudge for far too long and asked if I would be willing to forgive her and if we could try to resume the friendship we had shared almost a decade ago.

I readily consented and found our correspondence to be delightful. I eagerly awaited the arrival of the post, for within our letters we conversed on a variety of topics without censure. It was enabling, and I relished each exchange of ideas.

My enthusiasm soared when Mother had agreed to Cousin Leah's invitation. We would journey to Astoria and spend a month in the beautiful country. I'd waited to meet Mr. Jonathon Browning for sixteen years and felt content to wait another month. I hoped Mother would not change our plans.

"Of course, don't you see?" Mother asked. "We shall travel to Astoria and assist Leah with the wedding plans. It will be the perfect preparation for your nuptials. We'll return to London after Christmas, primed and ready to meet Mr. Browning."

I smiled and shook my head. Mother was certainly determined. "Very well," I said, glad our plans would remain in place.

Traveling to Astoria brought back memories from all those years ago. Leah and her father met our carriage and welcomed us with enthusiasm.

"I'm so glad to see you, Cousin Nora!" Leah said. She held my hands and squeezed tightly. "You have grown into such a beautiful thing, though you always were lovely. I can't tell you how much I have enjoyed our correspondence."

I instinctively cringed at her comment, but as I looked into her eyes I could see that Cousin Leah's words were genuine. I squeezed her fingers in return. "Thank you for the invitation. I can't wait to see your Mr. Brumley. I remember how he used to tease when we were younger. I thought him rather insufferable," I said and gave her a wide smile.

"As did I," Leah said with merriment in her eyes. "Come, let's get you settled. I'm sure you're tired from your travels, so I planned a quiet dinner tonight with the family. Then tomorrow, I've invited the Brumleys to join us, along with Mr. Brumley's dear friend."

We walked up the front steps. "Please tell me this friend is ugly and penniless," I said and slipped my arm through Leah's.

Cousin Leah laughed. "You will have to meet him tomorrow and determine for yourself. I'm personally very fond of Mr. Fausett."

I stopped mid-step as the breath drained from my lungs.

"Cousin Nora? Are you all right?" Leah asked.

I swallowed and nodded then swallowed again. "Mr. Fausett, did you say?"

"Yes, Mr. Devlin Fausett, of Holbrook." Leah smiled. "Do you know him?"

"I believe I've made his acquaintance," I said, wondering if the burning I felt in my chest had moved to my cheeks. Mr. Fausett's lean figure, black hair, and deep-gray eyes were hard to forget. The man possessed a maddening, merciless grin that I adored as much as the intriguing conversation that fell from his lips.

I first met Mr. Fausett at Miss Cassandra Duff's coming-out ball. Thankfully the introduction was made early in the evening, so there was still an available slot on my dance card. When Mr. Fausett came to claim my hand for the quadrille, I was in rather a frump due to several forward advances by my previous partner, Mr. Glenn, who thought if he insisted I needed fresh air, I would allow him to escort me outside without my chaperone. When he ignored my protests, I whipped my fan open directly into Mr. Glenn's face. I feigned innocence, but when Mr. Glenn excused himself to secure another handkerchief for his bloody nose, I quickly returned to my mother's side. Mr. Fausett appeared shortly after, and while we danced he did not talk about the weather or the décor or my attire. Instead, he asked me if I knew the best remedy for a bloody nose. I certainly blushed, but with my chin held high I told him the ailment was best avoided by not upsetting witty young ladies. He laughed heartily then turned the conversation to an interesting discussion about the training of medics in the military.

Mr. Fausett gave me hope that a man could engage in and enjoy a charged conversation with a woman. In the time since the Duff's ball, I'd seen Mr. Fausett at various events in Town, and I'd hoped to converse with him again. However, circumstances had not allowed us the opportunity—until now.

My heart lifted with happiness as I followed Cousin Leah to my room. This new discovery trumped my enthusiasm to be away from London. I would have a month of inspiring discussion with Mr. Fausett, and him all to myself, and I was delighted.

CHAPTER 3

Mr. Devlin Fausett

I SAT IN THE COMFORTABLE armchair and watched Brumley grin while his valet adjusted the knot on his cravat.

"You realize you could show up in half-pressed breeches, with an ill-matched waistcoat and crumpled cravat, and Miss Leah would not care one wit?" I pointed out. "From the moment you enter her presence, she cannot take her eyes off you."

Brumley chuckled. "All the more reason to look my best. Just you wait, Fausett. Your time will come, and then you'll understand."

"Understand your fascination on being perfectly presentable when you no longer need to impress the girl? She's already accepted your proposal." I pulled my pocket watch from inside my coat pocket. My maternal grandfather had bequeathed the gold-gilded timepiece to me. From my early years, Grandfather Russell had watched me with a guarded eye. I believe he knew of my father's unrealistic expectations, and somehow he also knew how inadequate I felt. Grandfather Russell always found time to teach me the basic things a boy should know—how to whittle a stick, the proper way to hook a worm, and the perfect angle to throw a skipping stone. He'd passed from my life too soon, and I cherished the memento he left behind.

I verified the time. "I think Miss Leah would rather have you arrive on time with a slightly crooked cravat than to have to wait on you for dinner."

Brumley admired his valet's work in the tall mirror, shifting his chin in different directions as he made his inspection. "Right you are," he said, turning towards me. "Leah was glad to hear of your return from London. She's anxious to introduce you to her cousin."

I rolled my eyes. "I adore your fiancée, Brumley, but perhaps you could persuade her to stay out of my personal affairs."

Brumley laughed. "Shall we be off?"

Our party consisted of Charles, his mother, Mrs. Brumley, and Charles's younger sister, Miss Rachel Brumley. When we arrived at Astoria, the Hastings family butler, Jensen, greeted us and directed us to the drawing room.

I followed behind the ladies and heard Miss Leah's happy voice welcome our group. She complimented Miss Brumley on her dress, and I lagged behind to wait for my chance to offer a greeting.

"Mr. Brumley, Mrs. Brumley," Miss Leah said. "Do you remember my dear aunt, Mrs. Phyllis Ellsworth, and her daughters, Miss Nora Ellsworth and Miss Claudia?"

My head snapped up, and I searched the room. Miss Ellsworth smiled and walked to her cousin's side. She curtsied low and addressed the Brumley family. "It's so nice to see you again. I'm sorry to hear about Mr. Brumley's passing." Her voice softened, and her face fell into an adorable pout.

Brumley bowed to her mother, then to her. "Thank you, Miss Ellsworth. And may I say how grateful I am that you and your mother have come to offer your assistance for the wedding. It's all Leah's talked about for days."

Mrs. Ellsworth waved her hand. "'Tis a pleasure, sir, and may I offer my congratulations. It will prepare me for when my own daughter follows her cousin's example." She placed her hand on Miss Ellsworth's arm. "I've a nagging suspicion that she too will be wed within the year."

"Do you have a beau, Cousin Nora?" Miss Leah asked.

Miss Ellsworth's cheeks turned rosy, and she lowered her eyes. "No, I assure you, Mother's speaking in generalities."

Miss Leah once again took control of the conversation. She spied me behind the group, and when our eyes met, she motioned me forward.

"Mr. Fausett," she called. "Please, come meet my aunt and cousins."

Brumley turned around and must have seen the hesitation in my eyes, because he gave me a look of confusion. It wasn't that I felt any ill will towards Miss Ellsworth. She was delightful. I recalled the first dance we had shared. From her appearance to her intellect, I had enjoyed the interaction immensely. I purposely tried to discomfit the haughty ladies of the *ton*, and I found a discussion of politics, medicine, or trade agreements generally put them off. My partners' eyes would widen, followed by a demure look and a gentle nod, which really meant they either had no interest in the subject or did not follow along at all. They would then turn the topic to current trends or gossip. Several ladies were even so bold as to ask after my inheritance. It was a pleasant shock when during my dance with Miss Ellsworth I suggested that medics serving with the regiments did not receive enough training and she heartily agreed with me. She then offered several thoughtful recommendations on how the men could receive a more comprehensive education.

Miss Ellsworth had entertained me so thoroughly I discovered I wanted to dance with her all the more, and that fact scared me. She had not been thrown off by my antics, and I found she truly intrigued me. However, once I returned home and recalled the sorry state of my life, I determined I would not pursue any further connection with Miss Ellsworth. From our one interaction, I knew she deserved better.

Miss Leah called for me again, and I stepped beside Brumley and bowed to the women.

"Mr. Fausett," Nora's mother said stoically. "I don't believe we've seen you since Miss Duff's ball. I didn't realize you were lodging in Paddington."

"Fausett and I were schoolmates," Brumley offered.

"Well." Mrs. Ellsworth offered Brumley an appeasing smile. "What a pleasant surprise, don't you agree, Nora?"

I turned my attention to Miss Ellsworth. When our eyes met, she held my gaze with a mischievous sort of look. It was only for a moment, but long enough to know she was not as startled as her mother by my presence. She lowered her lashes and curtsied low.

"Mr. Fausett," she said. "I don't believe you've met my sister, Miss Claudia Ellsworth."

I bowed to the younger girl. Miss Claudia's features mirrored her elder sister's, with blonde hair and bold, wide eyes, yet she had softer lines in her face. She was indeed pretty but not in the immediate way her elder sister drew awareness.

"I did not realize you were acquainted with the renowned Mr. Brumley," Miss Ellsworth said with a smile.

"Renowned?" Ferrin laughed from where he stood near the fireplace. "I'd classify Brumley as notorious. I've still got the scar from when he pelted me in the head with a rock while I was peacefully trying to fish." Ferrin pushed his hair back on his forehead and pointed to a place near his hairline.

"I warned you to move," Brumley said with an unrepentant shrug.

"What news is there from London?" Mrs. Brumley asked the Ellsworths.

"Our trip was uneventful, but before we left I received news that my dear friend Mrs. Rosamond Browning would soon be returning from India," Mrs. Ellsworth said. She glanced quickly at her eldest daughter and clasped her hands in front of her bosom.

"What a delightful reunion," Mrs. Brumley said.

"Indeed," Mrs. Ellsworth agreed.

"And since Nora will be in London to meet the Brownings, Mother said I may have a Season as well," Miss Claudia said. She looked at me with anticipation, and instantly her cheeks turned a bright crimson.

Miss Ellsworth looked sideways at her sister, and I could not tell if the small smirk on her lips was from agreed excitement or exasperation with Claudia's boldness. I sifted through the options and did not come to an answer before Mr. Hastings joined the party.

"Please excuse my tardiness," Mr. Hastings said. He leaned over and kissed Miss Leah's cheek. "Did you accomplish all you wished today?" he asked his daughter.

"Yes," Miss Leah said with a smile. "Aunt Phyllis is so very thorough. She's infinitely more help than I was for Sarah."

"Nonsense." Mr. Hastings offered his arm to his daughter. "Sarah's wedding was perfect for her, and yours shall be perfect for you." He nodded to the servant standing near the door. "Shall we eat?" he asked, and off he walked.

Ferrin and Brumley assisted the matrons, and I was left to escort Miss Ellsworth. Her nearness crippled my usually loose tongue. I turned around to glance at Miss Brumley and Miss Claudia. Miss Claudia giggled as her companion followed the procession into the dining room, marching in a stiff cadence.

"Well, they are not dissuaded by propriety," Miss Ellsworth said near my ear.

The frivolity of the younger girls' mannerisms brought a smile to my lips. "I remember when I was young how dreary these sort of events seemed. I'm glad they've found a way to make it a little less so."

Miss Ellsworth stood straight and leveled me with the directness of her gaze. "Do you find this evening dreary?" she asked.

I smiled freely and held Miss Ellsworth's chair. After she took a seat, I bent closer, inhaled a quick breath of her sweet citrus scent, and replied, "Not in the least."

CHAPTER 4

Miss Nora Ellsworth

MR. HASTINGS LED US IN a conversation about the newly appointed Church Building Commission, and I watched in astonishment as Cousin Leah, Mrs. Brumley, and even my mother freely stated opinions on the matter.

Parliament established the Church Building Commission to provide a proposal on monies needed to establish more broadly the Church throughout England. The Commission was due to report on their findings and suggest a monetary allotment in the coming months. Mr. Hastings expressed his support of the idea that the government should provide suitable buildings and parishes for all classes. Mr. Brumley agreed, and my jaw dropped open when he turned to ask my opinion. The topic was not as familiar to me as some others, and I admitted as much, but contentment pricked my heart at being included in the conversation.

After dinner, Cousin Leah persuaded me to sing while she played.

"You have such a melodic voice," Cousin Leah said. "I wish I could play something worthy of your talent. My simple selections fall short of your ability."

"Perhaps Mr. Fausett could play for Miss Ellsworth?" Mr. Brumley suggested.

My chest tightened at the thought. "I did not realize you played, Mr. Fausett," I said. I'd noted Mr. Fausett's attendance at several musicales in Town during my first Season. His dark charcoal eyes would watch me with unwavering attention. Singing had always come easily for me. I thoroughly enjoyed the diversion, especially when it wasn't being touted to the masses. But to sing while Mr. Fausett played, working together to keep time and rhythm, seemed much more intimate, and my heartbeat quickened.

A teasing grin played at the edge of Mr. Fausett's mouth. "I would be delighted to accompany you, Miss Ellsworth." His handsome face held me spellbound. "Would you do me the honor?"

I stumbled through my response. "I . . . It would be my pleasure."

Mr. Fausett took his place at the pianoforte, and, watching his long fingers caress the keys, I became entranced until he looked at me and asked, "Are you familiar with this one?"

I nodded mutely.

"Begin whenever you're ready," Mr. Fausett said.

I shook my head clear and listened for the cue that signaled the beginning of the verse. I didn't have to think long on the words. If I could ignore the handsome distraction sitting next to me, the melody would flow as a natural extension of my being. I focused on Cousin Leah's smile and noticed her betrothed admiring her. Their connection pulsed real and strong, and I drew upon the emotion as I sang.

When the song ended, Mr. Fausett immediately began another. Before long, one song had turned to two, then three and four. I let go of my apprehension and sang with a freedom long absent from the music rooms in London.

The small company applauded the end of the song, and I took a playful curtsy and swung my arm wide in recognition of my accompanist.

"Shall we sing a duet?" Mr. Fausett asked with a wide, enticing smile.

Mother answered in my stead. "It's been a very long day. I believe the girls and I should retire."

Mr. Fausett's smile remained fixed, but his eyes flickered with . . . disappointment? Or maybe relief? "Another time then," he said and stood to offer a bow while Mother took my hand and led me from the room.

My emotions were depleted. I'd not allowed myself to sing from my soul in a very long time, but when I'd opened my mouth to sing with Mr. Fausett's accompaniment, the restraint snapped and I couldn't contain the passion the music stirred within me.

Mr. Fausett had given me a gift, and I planned to treasure it for a long while.

CHAPTER 5

Mr. Devlin Fausett

I FELL INTO BED A very contented man. The first time I heard Miss Ellsworth sing, I knew her voice rivaled the heavenly host. But after sitting beside her tonight, I knew she epitomized heaven itself. And while my insides warned me to stay detached, my senses did not listen.

I knew my contentment must begin and end with listening to Miss Ellsworth sing. It was selfish for me to keep her beside me for the evening. But greed had always been my weakness, not knowing when to say no, when to walk away. Miss Ellsworth was especially accommodating tonight, but she deserved far more than the ruined man I'd become.

The invitation to remain at Riverton Park for Brumley's wedding was a godsend. When I'd returned to London the previous week, I'd only met briefly with my creditors to satisfy my most pressing debts. I held no doubt that my losses and humiliation had spread through the clubs and drawing rooms of the *ton*. I returned to Riverton Park as soon as I was able, hoping that upon my return to London at the end of summer, my disgrace would be old fodder.

My last trip to the gaming hells had been the worst. After spending a degrading visit with my father and mother, I'd returned to London determined to break the deplorable habit and with every intention of walking a new path. My resolve lasted for five months before I broke.

I assumed the Chesterfields' dinner party would be an innocent diversion, but Mr. Chesterfield enticed me to join a game of cards that somehow shifted to an intense game of whist. I'd won the first three hands easily and thus justified remaining at the table after losing the next two rounds. I resolved to leave with the remainder of the guests, but when they offered their goodbyes, I possessed a hand I knew would prevail. I'd guessed wrong, and three hours later I wandered back to my rooms without even a penny to hire a hack. I ventured to the gaming hells in the next days and weeks, determined to restore what I had lost, yet returned with further debt. The inspiration to visit Brumley occurred while I contemplated how I would pay for my next meal. Brumley readily welcomed me, and the invitation to remain for Miss Hastings's wedding became an added blessing.

I rolled over in my bed and let my mind wander back to Miss Ellsworth's melodic voice. A match with Miss Ellsworth would solve my worries, at least my financial ones, but 'twould not be fair to the poor girl. Doubtless, there were numerous men vying for her affections, and she could have her pick of the lot. She need not settle for a penniless, worthless addict.

Besides, she was the cousin of my dearest friend's betrothed. And while Brumley currently remained unaware of my situation, it was only a matter of time before he discovered my ruse.

I turned the calculations over again and again in my head. My recent trip to London offered a temporary reprieve from my creditors. I'd satisfied most of them with a partial sum and a promise to pay in full by the end of September. The plan now included relinquishing my London rooms and sending my belongings to Holbrook, my father's home in Essex. Unfortunately, he too would then be alerted of my desperate situation. With my generous monthly stipend, I could almost pay off the debt within sixty days, with the exception of Higgins. Unfortunately, he wasn't known to show mercy.

I turned again in my bed. Without question—I was in a muddle.

I woke early, desperate to find a way to repay what I owed without making my situation known. I mounted Raven, my black mare, and pounded through the meadow with renewed determination. The brisk morning air washed my head clear, and my concentration centered on remaining astride my horse. At the edge of the meadow, I reined her in and patted her neck while I caught my breath. The freedom found on the back of a horse was unparalleled, and the exhilaration easily matched the haughty pleasure induced from a winning hand of cards.

While I'd dismissed Ferrin's talk of Newmarket, perhaps there was something to be discovered at the races. Horseflesh was often the conversation at the club. Perhaps if I wagered only a small sum . . .

"Fausett!" Brumley yelled from atop his horse. He cantered near then pulled his mount to a halt. "You're up early."

"I didn't sleep well," I said. "Figured I'd get an early start."

Brumley narrowed his eyes. "Ahh, a blonde debutante invaded your dreams?"

There was no need to burden Brumley with the true reason for my discomfiture. "Something like that," I said with a grin.

"Are you heading back to the stables?"

I shrugged. "That depends. Where are you riding?"

"Through the woods," Brumley said. His horse skittered beneath him, anxious to get moving again. "Leah's meeting with the dressmaker this morning and plans to go over wedding details with her aunt afterwards. She has banned me from Astoria until tomorrow."

I hadn't realized the happy anticipation I felt at seeing Miss Ellsworth again until it wasn't an option. "Then we can take our time this morning," I said quickly, in an effort to mask my chagrin. I turned Raven around and followed Brumley into the trees.

We spent a casual day riding over the acreage of Riverton Park. Brumley reminisced about our days at Cambridge and told me stories of his childhood mischief, many of which involved his soon-to-be bride.

His eyes lightened when he mentioned Miss Leah's name or recounted a story in which she was involved, and I found myself intrigued by the change that rolled through his entire demeanor.

Brumley's London townhouse was only a mile and a half from my rooms. In school, we'd grown close, and I knew Brumley well enough to recognize the depression that had encased him after his father's death. He'd rarely accepted invitations, and he never entertained anyone other than myself, so I'd visited him often.

Only a year ago, Brumley resembled a dour old coot, content to wallow in self-pity. The man riding beside me now glowed, and I welcomed the marked change. I craved a similar revolution. I recognized my addiction for what it was, but playing a numbing hand of faro supplanted facing my father and his derision. The habit came easily. It came fast. As did the danger, the rush—and the debt.

I viewed Brumley's depression to be of his own making, something that could be remedied with a change of attitude. My circumstance was of my own making as well, but events had quickly spiraled out of my control, and I wondered again if the peace Brumley now felt would forever evade me. I deserved no less than continual torment.

We rode out of the trees and moved back across the meadow. "Miss Ellsworth has a lovely voice," Brumley said, pulling me from my reflections.

"Yes, very lovely," I agreed.

Brumley maneuvered his horse beside mine, and I felt his eyes boring into the side of my head. When I could no longer take his silent scrutiny, I spoke. "I've heard her perform before, in Town."

"From your greeting, I gathered you'd been introduced. Why have you not mentioned her before?" Brumley asked.

I shrugged. "What was there to mention? Had I realized she was related to the Hastingses, of course I would have said something. You don't really expect a report on every eligible woman I dance with, do you?"

"No," Brumley said casually, sweeping his eyes up to the clouds overhead. "Not all of them. Just the ones who discomfit you."

I refused to let Brumley see how the mention of Miss Ellsworth's name or the reminder of her voice or her eligibility affected me. I let out a derisive huff. "Race you back to the stables," I said and kicked Raven into a run. "A guinea to the winner," I called over my shoulder, hoping I could maintain my lead.

Old habits died hard.

CHAPTER 6

Miss Nora Ellsworth

AFTER SPENDING THE PREVIOUS DAY with Cousin Leah and the dressmaker, I eagerly awaited the picnic Cousin Leah had planned for today. Mr. Fausett was, of course, included in the invitation, and I found myself counting down the hours and minutes until the Brumley carriage arrived.

When I heard the horses, I smoothed my skirts and quietly hummed a lullaby while awaiting the announcement of the party's arrival.

Jensen appeared in the doorway. "Mrs. Brumley and Miss Brumley," he said, standing stiff while the ladies entered the drawing room.

Cousin Leah greeted them warmly then asked the question consuming my thoughts. "Did Mr. Brumley and Mr. Fausett not join you?"

"Charles insisted on bringing Mouse. I think they were going to ride along the river," Charles's sister said with a happy smile.

"Mouse?" Claudia repeated with a giggle. "What a silly name for a horse."

"I agree," Cousin Leah said. She shielded her mouth with her hand. "But don't tell Mr. Brumley I said so."

"They should be along any minute," Mrs. Brumley added.

"Well then, shall we meet them outside?" Cousin Leah asked.

Miss Brumley laced her arm through Claudia's. It seemed the two of them were becoming fast friends. I stood and followed the women out of the drawing room to the back door.

"Jensen?" Cousin Leah called, and the man appeared immediately. "Will you please tell Father and Ferrin that our guests have arrived? We will begin walking towards the bridge and meet them there." Jensen gave a quick bow and left to deliver the message.

I could not account for the excitement swirling through me. When Miss Brumley turned to me for an answer, I pressed a hand to my chest and confessed my ignorance of her question. "Pardon me, Miss Brumley, I'm afraid I was woolgathering."

"She does that often," Claudia said with a conspiratorial grin.

"Claudia," I began, prepared to correct her, but Miss Brumley spoke again before my reprimand could be delivered.

"I simply asked if you like picnics," she said.

With a calming breath, I composed myself and smiled. "In fact, I do. But it's been a very long time since I've had the pleasure of enjoying one."

Miss Brumley practically skipped along, with Claudia in tow. Claudia was two years older than Miss Brumley, but the two possessed very similar temperaments.

"You should come to visit more often. We have picnics all the time," Miss Brumley said.

We stepped from the shadow of the house into the sunshine and instantly my spirits smoothed. Claudia and Miss Brumley skittered ahead of our group, and I saw the servants preparing for our arrival in the grassy clearing that marked our destination. The open space sat on the opposite side of a small footbridge. We covered the distance, with amiable conversation, and when I walked onto the wooden bridge, I paused to enjoy the babbling of the river running beneath me.

The sound of horses drew my attention to the tree line, where Mr. Brumley and Mr. Fausett burst into the clearing. My heart fluttered when I caught sight of Mr. Fausett. He looked rather dashing astride his mare. He leaned forward and rode with perfect posture, holding the reins lightly while urging his animal to sprint faster. He resembled a convoluted mix of reckless control. The men pulled to a stop downriver, and my eyes were drawn to Mr. Fausett's dark hair, tousled in various directions from his ride. We were too far away to greet one another, but I knew the moment our eyes met, because my entire person tingled in anticipation.

A groom met the two gentlemen to take their horses to the stable. The men walked towards us. "How are you lovely ladies faring this fine day?" Mr. Brumley asked with exaggeration.

Cousin Leah pressed her lips tight but couldn't reel back the smile that spread across them. She turned to acknowledge her father and brother approaching from the house.

"What a lovely sight," Mr. Hastings called as he crossed the bridge with Cousin Ferrin and joined the group. "Happy company, delectable food. I am indeed a contented man."

Cousin Leah directed us to the food, and we talked and laughed while indulging in the rich fare. The weather turned warm, and Mr. Hastings escorted the matrons back to the house. Cousin Ferrin excused himself as well. The remaining party opted to stroll downriver to the shade of the oak trees.

Claudia and Miss Brumley walked arm in arm, whispering their confidences to one another. Mr. Fausett walked up beside me at the same moment Claudia looked over her shoulder. She saw him address me and didn't waste a moment before she turned back around and giggled with Miss Brumley.

After exchanging basic courtesies, Mr. Fausett grew quiet. We walked side by side, and I admired the low-hanging bows of the oak tree kissing the water as it passed by. Birdsong rang from various trees, and the lull of the running water provided euphonious accompaniment. I inhaled the crispness, the cool reprieve offered only within the confines of the shade.

Mr. Fausett pulled a pocket watch from his coat and checked the time.

"That's a beautiful timepiece, Mr. Fausett," I said.

"Thank you. It was a gift from my late grandfather." Mr. Fausett handed the watch over to me, and I admired the intricate etchings covering the casing.

I returned the trinket to him. "What a treasure. Were you close to your grandfather, then?"

"Very. My father and I do not share a very close bond, but I hold my grandfather in highest esteem. He was an ideal role model and a good man." His fingers closed around the watch, and he held it for a moment before returning it to his pocket.

"Are you enjoying your time in the country?" I asked.

"Indeed, I am. Despite my differences with my father, he bought Raven as a gift at the completion of my studies. She's fast—bred to be a racehorse—and we enjoy a good run in the open air." He grinned. "Galloping down Bond Street in London is generally frowned upon. Thus, the country is a welcome reprieve."

I laughed. "I'd like to watch you and Raven take Bond Street by storm. Only, give me ample warning so I may take refuge in the milliner's shop."

"And you must tell me which milliner you prefer so we may stop and buy you a bonnet."

"That would not be necessary," I said. My cheeks warmed.

Mischief danced in Mr. Fausett's gray eyes. "I think emerald green would suit you well. Or perhaps blue? It would match your eyes."

I looked away from him and focused on the path before us.

After walking a few moments in silence, Mr. Fausett cleared his throat and said, "Tell me, Miss Ellsworth, which do you prefer: the simplicity of the country or the enticements of Town?"

With the change of topic, my heartbeat steadied. "There are many benefits to life in the city—constant engagements, the opera house, and the museums. There's never a dull moment, nor is there a moment of peace." I paused and turned to admire the clear water moving melodiously over the rocks in the riverbed. "I enjoyed my time in London, but I think country life suits me far better."

"You seem content here," Mr. Fausett said.

"I am." I smiled and turned to walk beside him again. "I only wish the papers reached Derbyshire as quickly as they spread through London."

Mr. Fausett faltered for a moment and fell a step behind. "You miss the society pages?" he asked.

I laughed at his question. "Not at all. I assumed you would appreciate a well-informed conversationalist. The truth is, I miss the actual news. At least, the reports that are unbiased and factual."

"Hmm," Mr. Fausett mused and began walking again. "I've never met a woman anxious to hear news of war or politics."

"Then perhaps you associate with the wrong kind of women," I said.

A smile split Mr. Fausett's lips. "I shall have to expand my circle of acquaintances," he said and offered his arm.

I placed my hand on his sleeve, and we turned back towards the house with the remainder of our party. As we approached the footbridge, a young servant boy came running from the house.

He approached Cousin Leah and bowed quickly. "Excuse me, ma'am. There's a gentleman come to see Miss Ellsworth—a Mr. Trenton."

The heat of the sun became instantly stifling, and my feet stopped moving altogether. Mr. Trenton was Father's heir presumptive and one of the most insufferable men of my acquaintance. The entailment on Ellsworth Meadows had been in place since my great-great-great-grandfather purchased the land. And while Father did not consent to the arrangement, he remained bound by it. Upon his passing Mother, Claudia, and I could no longer call Ellsworth Meadows home. I'd always felt that Claudia and I would marry one day, especially with Mother's insistence about Mr. Jonathon Browning's intentions. I could only hope that I would not be forced into an arrangement. However, I did need to secure some stability for Mother, should Father pass before her. It was a duty inherent with the entail and one I resented, for I would desperately miss my childhood home.

Mr. Trenton was a self-absorbed man. He donned the latest fashions, associated with the wealthy elite, and preened more than a peacock. He was also a notorious flirt. I believed he liked to think of himself as a favorite among the ladies more than the debutantes considered him one.

Mr. Trenton made it a habit to stop unannounced at Ellsworth Meadows. He would unabashedly assess our home, commenting on the furnishings or the repairs he insisted should be made. Dinner became his opportunity to brag about his connections, to comment on his wardrobe, or to waggle his eyes at Claudia and me. His visits were exhausting, and I wondered how he discovered us at Astoria.

Cousin Leah turned towards me but did not say anything. Mr. Fausett placed his hand atop mine, but Claudia spoke first. "Nora, you look like you've seen a ghost."

"You do look rather unwell, Cousin. Who is Mr. Trenton? Shall I send him away?" Cousin Leah asked.

Reason snapped, and I pushed away the awful memories of my previous interactions with the man. "No," I sighed. "Mr. Trenton is Ellsworth Meadow's heir presumptive. I'm afraid he's a bit bothersome. He's probably with Mother now. I will see him." I looked at the concerned eyes of those around me. "But will you all join me?"

"Of course," Cousin Leah said and led the procession over the bridge. We marched across the meadow, wound through the gardens, and entered Astoria as if storming a castle. Mr. Trenton was a nuisance but did not deserve such a ruckus. Mr. Fausett slipped my hand from his arm and gave my fingers a gentle squeeze before letting go. We handed our things to Jensen then proceeded to the drawing room as a unified front.

Mother sat on the divan, looking flustered. Mr. Trenton rose from his seat and caught my fingers. "Ah, Cousin Nora. How delightful to see you," he said. Before I could extract myself from his grasp, he bent low and delivered a slobbery kiss to my bare skin.

My stomach churned at the saliva pooled on my hand, and it took every ounce of strength I could muster not to gag. I fumbled to find my voice and looked to Cousin Leah for help.

"Mr. Trenton, how kind of you to call at Astoria," Cousin Leah said and motioned for our party to be seated; Mr. Trenton, Mr. Fausett, and I remained standing. "I'm Miss Leah Hastings—"

"Soon to be Brumley, I understand," Mr. Trenton cut in. When Mr. Trenton turned to address her, I brushed my hand forcefully against my skirt. I would have to insist that our maid wash my dress. "I assume one of these gentlemen is the lucky man?" He looked at Mr. Brumley and Mr. Fausett in turn.

Cousin Leah remained unaffected by Mr. Trenton's interruption, and she introduced her fiancé and then Miss Brumley and Mr. Fausett. Mr. Trenton hardly acknowledged Claudia or Miss Brumley, but he did evaluate Mr. Fausett thoroughly. "Mr. Fausett of Holbrook? It's good to finally put a face with the name so often bandied about Town."

Mr. Fausett stood tall, looking down on Mr. Trenton. Unfortunately, Mr. Fausett's height did not appear to deter Mr. Trenton.

I spoke quickly. "How very bold, Mr. Trenton, to stop by unannounced," I said.

A smirk continued to play on his lips. He casually walked to a chair near Mother and sat himself down. I looked at the others, and they seemed to want me to decide how to proceed. Mr. Trenton did not warrant a scene, so I lowered myself onto the nearby sofa. Mr. Fausett took a seat near me as Mr. Trenton spoke again. "My business led me to Northamptonshire, so naturally I called on your father." His skinny fingers flipped through the air. "He sends his regards, of course." His hand settled back into his lap, and he continued. "He told me you were all in Paddington planning a wedding and insisted I stop by on my way north."

I knew Father insisted no such thing.

"I hope I was not mistaken to assume I would be welcome. Miss Hastings, I realize we are not a direct relation, but seeing as I am family to the Ellsworths, I assumed you would not mind." Mr. Trenton's eyes shifted, and he directed his attention to me. "It has been such a long time since we've had a chance to . . . catch up." Something dark and deliberate brewed behind his eyes. I knew not how to respond.

Thankfully, Cousin Leah interceded. "The Ellsworth Family will always be welcome at Astoria, and I do thank you for stopping by; however, we surely don't want to postpone your journey."

Mr. Trenton held my gaze a moment longer before slowly turning towards Cousin Leah. I watched Mr. Brumley clench his jaw while Mr. Trenton addressed her. "'Twas no trouble at all. I'll be glad to be on my way right after supper."

The audacity! To invite himself to a meal with a family he had just met! I flushed in embarrassment that he was indeed related. Mr. Fausett pushed out of his seat and brusquely moved to the nearest window.

Cousin Leah scanned the faces in the room, desperate to find an acceptable solution to the problem that *was* Mr. Trenton. "Unfortunately, we've just enjoyed a lavish picnic, and our cook is not planning to serve a formal dinner this evening."

"Hmm," Mr. Trenton mused, looking unperturbed. "I suppose some finger sandwiches and a tea tray would suffice."

Mr. Brumley clenched his fist. "I—"

Cousin Leah quickly put her hand over his. "Of course," she said. She waited a decisive minute before moving to the bell pull. When a servant arrived, she made the request.

"Splendid," Mr. Trenton said when Cousin Leah returned to her seat. He settled farther back into his chair and turned his calculating gaze on my mother. "Mrs. Ellsworth, Mr. Ellsworth told me you expect to be reunited with an old friend."

"Yes," Mother said with more sturdiness than I expected. She disliked Mr. Trenton as much as I and usually avoided speaking with him, preferring to defer the conversation to Father. She looked at Mr. Trenton with determination. "Mrs. Browning and I grew up together. I've not seen her for many years, as she's been in India, but she will soon return with her husband and son." Mother enunciated the last word, and Mr. Trenton's smile widened.

Mr. Fausett turned from the window and looked from my mother to me, but I could not hold his gaze long enough to decipher the sudden distance in his eyes before Mr. Trenton spoke again.

"Of course—your trump card," Mr. Trenton said.

I looked between them and realized they were playing a game that I did not understand.

Mother blinked quickly. "I consider Mr. Browning more of a predetermined plan." Mother raised her chin, but her eyes skittered around Mr. Trenton's face.

"Trump cards don't always play out the way one might hope," Mr. Trenton said. "What do you say, Mr. Fausett?" he called over his shoulder. "Would you agree that a trump card in a hand of whist can make all the difference? For better or for worse?" His mouth stretched into a wide line, twisting upwards at the edges.

Mr. Fausett did not respond. His hands clenched at his side as the housekeeper entered, followed by one of the kitchen maids. Each placed her designated tray on the table in the corner.

"I'll pour out," Cousin Leah said, rising from her place on the sofa. "Mr. Trenton, how do you take your tea?"

"None for me, thank you." Mr. Trenton stood and made a spectacle of adjusting his jacket to precision.

Cousin Leah stood with her mouth ajar, and I hung my head in continued embarrassment.

Mr. Brumley stood, his eyes ablaze. "Miss Leah, please allow Fausett and I to escort Mr. Trenton out. I'm afraid we've overstayed our welcome, and no one likes to entertain an unwanted guest," he said. Before receiving a reply, he motioned to the door. "After you, Trenton."

The vile man bid us goodbye with hollow wishes for extended health and happiness. I didn't have the strength to reply, which was a blessing because the only thought that came to mind was, *Good riddance.*

CHAPTER 7

Mr. Devlin Fausett

I was grateful Brumley proved clearheaded enough to find a way to evict Mr. Trenton from Astoria and ensure he left its occupants alone. The means I'd considered to remove the man were much more forceful, and several were rather permanent.

While our horses were saddled much sooner than Mr. Trenton's coach was readied, we delayed our departure until we could see him definitively removed. Brumley also bribed one of the young stable lads sixpence to send word to Riverton Park if Trenton should return.

We waited in the lane until Trenton's coach disappeared towards Town and then turned west to Riverton Park. My anger stewed as Raven moved slowly down the road. Trenton proved that the title "gentleman" was given far too liberally.

Brumley slowed Mouse and turned to ride next to me. The fury in his eyes had abated, but his jaw was still set tight. "Everything about that man felt off. Arriving unannounced, imposing on the Hastingses the way he did. He was completely presumptuous and contemptible. What do you make of it?" Brumley asked.

"Mr. Trenton seemed comfortable in his role as abrasive guest. I assume there is more to the feud between the families than a disagreeable entail," I said.

"I suppose you're right." Brumley rode in silence before he spoke again, touching on a subject I'd rather hoped to avoid. "Have you met the man before? He seemed to be acquainted with your family."

"I've never seen the man before today," I answered honestly. Although he did address me with surprising familiarity, specifically in referencing my knowledge of cards. "Talk of Trenton wears on my patience. Let's run these animals and forget the wretched man."

"Agreed." Brumley kicked Mouse's flanks and bolted past Raven. It didn't take long for my horse to respond, and we galloped side by side until Riverton Park came into view. We slowed the horses to walk around the far side of the barn to cool them off before stabling them for the evening.

"I thought we had you beat," Brumley said with a smirk.

"Raven's got spirit. She won't give up without a fight." I leaned forward and rubbed my mare's dark mane.

Brumley watched me, a mischievous smile playing on his lips.

"What?" I asked. "Out with it."

"You, no doubt, heard Mrs. Ellsworth's reference to her friend's son. I was just contemplating what you are going to do about it." Brumley dismounted and stroked Mouse's nose. "Will you give up without a fight?"

With a roll of my eyes, I answered, "I don't plan to do anything." I swung down from Raven's back and led her towards the stables.

"Nothing?" Brumley said from behind me. "You're going to watch Miss Ellsworth be courted by some bloke from India and do nothing about it?"

We reached the yard, and two stable boys quickly emerged and took charge of the horses. I gave Raven a final slap on her hindquarters and turned to walk with Brumley towards the house. "What would you have me do?" I asked.

"You gave me some great advice not long ago. I believe your exact words were, 'Fight for her,'" Brumley said.

His quote was accurate. I'd admonished him to follow his heart and fight to win Miss Leah's hand. I looked towards him, fully prepared to combat his banter, but the sincerity in his countenance disarmed the sarcasm I had prepared to defend myself.

"These circumstances can hardly compare. You've known Miss Leah all your life. I've only recently met Miss Ellsworth," I said.

Brumley slapped me across the shoulder. "These circumstances are not so very different, my friend. Did you forget I've seen the way you look at her?"

"None of that matters if she's already spoken for," I said with a resigned smile.

"Go. Fight for her," Brumley repeated softly. "You told me exactly what I needed to hear. I'm only trying to return the favor."

Upon entering the house, I excused myself to clean up for a light supper. Brumley did not mention Miss Ellsworth again that night, but his advice swam through my mind continually. Even without my horrid debt and gambling addiction, Miss Ellsworth surpassed any of the genteel women I would be expected to court. I did not know her dowry, but by her grace and beauty alone, Miss Ellsworth qualified to wed a high-ranking member of the aristocracy.

How could I fight for her? The answer was simple: I could not. No matter how much I wished the opposite were true, I did not deserve her, and fighting was not an option.

The next few weeks passed quickly. While Brumley and his future bride found a few quiet moments together, both households were frantically preparing for the arrival of additional wedding guests and the ceremony itself. Brumley tasked me to work with his steward and assist with the needs of his tenants. He concentrated on finalizing his wedding trip and made the necessary arrangements for his mother and sister in his absence.

Amidst the chaos of planning and organizing, my proprietor in London forwarded a note from Higgins refusing my request for an extension on the balance I owed him. Upon receiving the letter, I collected Raven and took a bruising ride to clear my head. Higgins did not list specifics, but his missive left little doubt about the consequences he would inflict should I miss the appointed deadline. I kicked hard at Raven's side and tucked low against her neck as she accelerated across the field. Her speed always amazed me, as did her natural reflex to push to the front of a challenge. We neared the barrier of trees, and Raven veered in the final moment, pulling back only to avoid a collision with the branches. The rush, the exhilaration, clarified my solution. I would follow up on Ferrin's lead and place a bet at Newmarket with the hope that I might recover my losses and meet Higgins's deadline.

I made a quick trip to London to settle the lesser sums owed and returned to Derbyshire by week's end. I did not see Miss Ellsworth outside of a few family dinners. We talked about Napoleon's exile to Saint Helena Island, and she sang one more time, accompanied by Claudia. I soaked in the sweetness of her voice, knowing the memory of her song would have to be enough.

The day of the wedding arrived, and the ceremony unfolded exactly as prescribed. Brumley was the epitome of a lovestruck fool, and I was happy for my friend.

Heavy rain filled the sky on my return to London. I was grateful for Raven's steady nerves. I'd had to dismiss my valet on my previous visit. Quiet misery was the only welcome I received upon returning to my quarters.

I knew a match with Miss Ellsworth was unreasonable, yet I couldn't help but envy Brumley and his situation, and I resolved to improve myself. If I could eschew gambling, there had to be a kind, pleasant-looking lark who would be happy to marry me. Holbrook was not grand, nor was my income significant, but it was sustainable and generous enough to raise a family in comfort.

Contentment could be found in such a situation, and while it might not match the bliss or grandeur of Brumley's circumstance, it would be enough for me. It had to be.

My addiction did not rise from the need to have more. I didn't covet wealth or prestige. In truth, I couldn't pinpoint the exact reason for my draw to the tables, but I knew winning a fortune was not the determining cause. When I sat around the tables, my drive stemmed from somewhere deeper. A desire to prove I could win or maybe a resolve to prove I wouldn't lose, I wouldn't fail. The irony lingered with the proof of my debt. I had failed. I had fallen. Along with the money, I'd lost my freedom. But no more. I vowed to pay off Higgins and refrain from further failure.

CHAPTER 8

Miss Nora Ellsworth

THE DAYS SINCE COUSIN LEAH's wedding had been dreadfully dull. We ventured from Astoria to Ellsworth Meadows, where we spent a solitary Christmas holiday with our family. Mother wished to return to Town immediately after the New Year. However, Father did not want the associated expense, and since the Brownings were not due to arrive in London until mid-February, Mother was pacified to put off our arrival with the promise of new gowns before the Taylors' ball, for that was where I would finally meet Mr. Jonathon Browning.

My correspondence with Cousin Leah continued, albeit less frequently. She updated me on the pleasures and pressures of running her own household and oft repeated her blissful opinions of matrimony. I was happy to see her settled so contentedly and contemplated the day I might experience the same joy. I'd never given much consideration to the particulars of my future since that future had been attached to Mr. Jonathon Browning all my life. I hoped my union with Mr. Browning would provide Mother and Claudia with the security of a home upon Father's death. Mr. Trenton certainly would not provide for them, but if Mother's assertion proved correct and Mr. Browning truly was a respectable gentleman with the means to provide a comfortable lifestyle, they would be cared for.

Yet, I'd recently begun to wonder if romantic notions were as frivolous as I'd previously thought. Whenever Mr. Fausett was near, my stomach fluttered with excitement. His flirtatious smiles were harmless and welcome. Whether singing, walking, or simply conversing, Mr. Fausett seemed able to elicit emotions beyond anything I'd felt with other gentlemen of my acquaintance. I hoped my interactions with Mr. Browning would produce the same giddy sensations, because I found I rather enjoyed them.

The day of the Taylors' ball arrived, and I was ready. Ready to meet Mr. Jonathon Browning, ready to meet his mother, and ready to decide if he was a man I could marry. Knowing that my mother often embellished her stories made me question her assertion that he was handsome and well-spoken. It had been so long since either of our families had seen each other I was sure she based her account on Jonathon's appearance seventeen years ago. He was only nine.

Now six and twenty, he was bound to be vastly different from my mother's recollection. She often remarked that Mr. Browning, Jonathon's father, was extremely handsome. Perhaps she based her hypothesis on that knowledge. But I was not naïve. People change and are not destined to follow in their parents' footsteps.

A rap on my door alerted me to the hour. Cooper, who served as maid to both Claudia and myself, had completed her ministrations for Claudia and had been sent to help me. I waved her into the room, and the preparations began.

Mother insisted my ball gown be green. The shade she chose really did suit me. The dress was fitted, and at my insistence, simple. I refused to put on airs for Mr. Jonathon Browning. If this marriage was to take place, I wanted him to know the real me. I would not mislead him to capture his interest, no matter how rich or handsome he was.

Cooper secured the final pin in my hair, and I smiled at my image in the mirror. I felt beautiful and hoped Mr. Browning would take the opportunity to see beneath the mask and come to appreciate me beyond my appearance.

Thankfully, Mother was wise enough to acknowledge that we should not be the first ones to arrive at the ball. Waiting with Claudia in the drawing room provided ample entertainment. She paced the floor and fanned herself so excessively that Mother called for Cooper to tidy her hair.

Claudia had attended numerous balls in Rigdon, but this was her first London soiree. A fortune and a happily ever after with a handsome man—the idea was beginning to affect her equilibrium.

"Claudia, if you don't sit down, you'll be too exhausted to dance," I teased.

"I know." Claudia sank into a chair, and Cooper began to repair the damage done to her coif. Cooper released a startled gasp as Claudia jumped back up. "It's just that I'm so nervous!"

Mother walked over, took a firm hold of Claudia's arm, and lowered her back into her seat. "Now, dear, let Cooper tend your hair. Your father will be ready to leave soon, and you cannot show up to the Taylors' ball looking like you just ran through the pasture."

Claudia complied and sat still. All except her fingers, which continually twisted around in her lap.

"Now, Nora," Mother said as she motioned for me to stand. "Let me look at you again." She rotated her wrist in a twirling motion indicating that I should turn and let her evaluate me from all sides. I completed the circle and could tell by the grin spread across her face that she approved. "I knew that color would be perfect."

"Shall we depart?" Father entered in his formal black waistcoat with his white cravat tied in a perfect mathematical knot. He eyed each of us in turn with a look of pride.

Cooper finished repairing Claudia's tresses, and my sister rose from her seat. "What do you think, Father?" She gathered a handful of skirt in each hand and twirled.

"Claudia, be careful, or you will ruin your hair all over again," Mother chided.

Father smiled at Claudia. "You look beautiful, my dear. You shall take London by storm," he said and winked at me. I gave him a slight curtsy in reply. "But as always, I am drawn to my lovely bride." He held out his arm. "Shall we, Mrs. Ellsworth?" Mother clicked her tongue and swatted Father playfully as she took his arm. He always indulged her frivolity, and I envied their relationship.

The carriage ride was not long. We followed Father up the entrance to the house. Claudia came to a standstill as she gawked at the ornate carvings on the portico.

"Keep moving," I whispered and pushed her forward. I straightened my gloves and concentrated on keeping my back straight.

Father had secured the invitation to the ball through his acquaintance with the Taylors. I had seen them only once before, when we went on holiday to Brighton. Father had conducted business with Mr. Taylor, and Mother had hosted a small dinner for the two families. Claudia and I were too young to join them, so after a quick introduction, our governess led us away. I only remembered Mr. Taylor's happy eyes and Mrs. Taylor's exquisite beauty. I also recalled that Mrs. Taylor was her husband's junior by many years.

Father made introductions, and the Taylors gushed over how we had grown. I wanted to ask if the Browning family had arrived, and it took all of my willpower to keep silent. I dug my fingernails into the palms of my hands, grateful that my gloves would conceal any marks I would otherwise leave.

Father acknowledged the growing line of guests. "Very well, Taylor. We won't monopolize any more of your time. Thank you again for the invitation."

I glanced behind us and saw the line extending past the front doors. A swarm of impatient eyes returned my stare.

"Your decorations are simply divine," I heard my mother say, effectively halting our progress once again. Murmurs of disapproval wafted in with the night air, and I felt my cheeks flush.

My nails dug deeper into my palms, and I decided to plead with my father to pull her away, but as I turned towards him, a pair of dazzling blue eyes met my frustrated gaze. My mother was momentarily forgotten as I took in the gentleman. He was tall, but not slender. Rather he was sturdy and solid. His hair was dark brown, and his jaw was set so perfectly I wanted to reach out and touch it.

That thought sobered me. I blinked and realized he was walking towards us. At first, I thought he wanted to complain along with the others in line, but his smile brought reassurance. He maneuvered through the crowd, walking to where we stood in front of Mr. and Mrs. Taylor. I turned with his movement, and he quickly raised his eyebrows as if we shared some secret joke.

Mrs. Taylor placed her hand on my mother's arm, effectively stopping her chatter so she could address the gentleman. "Mr. Browning, did you find what you needed?"

"Yes, thank you, Mrs. Taylor. Mother left her wrap in the carriage, but I have retrieved it." He held up the shimmery material as proof.

Mother spun around. "Mr. Browning? Mr. Jonathon Browning?"

The gentleman did not look shocked at my mother's forwardness. His hands dropped to his side, and he bowed politely. "At your service, ma'am."

My mother fluttered her hand near her heart. "Oh, my! I am Mrs. Ellsworth, and this is Mr. Ellsworth." She pointed to my father. "Please, take me to your dear mother."

"It would be my pleasure." He turned towards Father. "May I?" Father nodded, and Mr. Browning offered his arm to my mother. We began to follow, and Claudia took Father's arm. Father was drawn away as another gentleman called to him. He stepped aside with Claudia, and she looked towards me for help, but I could only shrug. There was no way to extricate her from her predicament.

Another guest moved past and bumped my arm. The movement spun me around, and the stranger stopped to apologize and comment on the crush of people. I accepted the apology, and when I turned back to follow Mr. Browning, I could no longer see him. I moved beside one of the columns and surveyed the floor. The dancing had not yet begun, so the space was filled with colorful satins and crepes, dotted with formal black tailcoats.

Above the cacophony, I heard my mother screech and followed the sound to the far-left side of the room. Through the mass of people, I caught a glimpse of her bronze-colored gown and moved in that direction.

"Excuse me. Pardon me," I offered as I pushed through the fashionable crowd. I felt so small in the enormous space. The throng in the room reminded me of a hornet's nest. The hum of hundreds of people laughing and talking buzzed through the air, and I felt jumbled by the tumult of it all, until I saw a pair of familiar gray eyes.

Mr. Fausett leaned against one of the many columns circling the room. A smile filled his handsome face, and he stared at me so intently it stole my breath, and my feet stopped moving altogether.

He pushed away from the striated marble and walked towards me. I felt so silly, unable to control the smile dancing around my lips, but amidst the chaos of the night, his friendly face was a welcome sight.

"I wondered when we might meet again," Mr. Fausett said, bowing over my hand.

"It's a pleasure to see you tonight, Mr. Fausett," I said.

"I assure you, the pleasure is all mine. You look lovely, Miss Ellsworth. I knew green would suit you well." The sincerity in Mr. Fausett's compliment sent a flush through my cheeks. "Are you attending with your mother?" he asked.

"Yes. And my father and Claudia are here as well. I would like to introduce you to my father."

Mr. Fausett extended his arm. "Lead the way."

I happily wove my arm through his and pointed to where my parents stood, Father having rejoined Mother, across the room. Mr. Fausett navigated our course and led me directly to where Mr. Jonathon Browning stood beside a woman I assumed to be his mother. When we approached, a smile played at the edges of Mr. Browning's lips. His observations were not unnerving, because I evaluated him just the same. Our mothers chatted on and on, and it became clear they meant to catch up on all their years apart.

I knew I should not address a gentleman to whom I had not been introduced. So instead of speaking, I slipped my arm from Mr. Fausett's and stood there like a mute puppy, waiting for my mother to acknowledge the both of us. The moment dragged on until Mr. Fausett forcefully cleared his throat, causing Mother to turn at the obvious interruption.

"Oh? Oh, Nora! Well, yes, of course." She stepped to the side, and I got my first full glimpse of her dear friend. "Mrs. Browning, may I present my daughter, Miss Nora Ellsworth?" I offered my most elegant curtsy and tipped my head at the perfect angle.

Mrs. Browning was a handsome woman. She wore her age confidently. She had the same square jaw as her son, and it became obvious he had inherited his eyelashes from his maternal side.

"Miss Ellsworth, how you have grown." Mrs. Browning took my hands in hers and acknowledged me with a wide smile. "May I reacquaint you with my eldest son, Mr. Jonathon Browning?"

I dipped into a second curtsy.

"Ahem."

The sound came out like a little rasp from directly behind me. I stepped back to widen our circle and saw Claudia standing there with an expectant look on her face. I turned back to Mother, who stood flitting her eyes at Mr. Jonathon Browning. I thought she would acknowledge Claudia, but instead she kept making faces at the poor man in a sorry attempt to convey her approval of him.

To the gentleman's credit, his eyes remained steadily on Claudia, and he patiently ignored my mother's batting lashes. I was unsure how to proceed. Claudia obviously needed to be introduced, but Mother remained oblivious.

Claudia shifted nervously until Mr. Fausett spoke from behind me. "I'm Devlin Fausett of Holbrook, and may I introduce Miss Claudia Ellsworth?"

I breathed a sigh of relief and turned around to see Mr. Fausett give a proper bow while Mr. Browning lowered his head in return.

"And how are you acquainted with the Ellsworth family?" Mr. Browning asked.

"Oh, he's a family friend. An acquaintance of my dear niece's new husband," Mother said. Then she sighed dramatically and clapped her hands in front of her bosom.

I was afraid to look at Mr. Fausett, for I knew the disappointment I would see in his eyes. While we had not known each other long, we had conversed on a variety of topics and spent several evenings in one another's company. He deserved more than to be referenced as a distant acquaintance. When I dared a glance, his amused grin surprised me and settled my nerves.

"Dear Mrs. Browning," Mother said. "I believe we were wise to keep in touch all these years."

The musicians finished tuning their instruments, and Mr. Taylor led his wife out for the opening dance. Before I realized what had transpired, I was dancing with Mr. Jonathon Browning, and Claudia danced beside us with Mr. Fausett. Mother must have been extremely pleased to see the product of all her machinations.

"Is London so very different from the Indian colonies?" I asked Mr. Browning.

"Many of the diversions are the same, but the location varies. Last summer I had the privilege of attending the governor's ball. It was held in a large open-air rotunda."

"That is vastly different from our current surroundings. I have never had the privilege of attending a ball out of doors. I imagine it would be delightful to dance under the stars."

"The setting was ideal, but I think I might have enjoyed it more if the governor's pet tiger was not staring at me as if I were a piece of raw meat."

"Surely, you jest?" I couldn't help the smile that spread across my face.

Mr. Browning met my smile with one of his own. His straight teeth gleamed white. "Indeed, it is the truth, Miss Ellsworth. I never jest when it comes to things of import." We performed our bows to the couple to our side, and then I lay my hand atop Mr. Browning's arm. We walked towards my mother, and his voice dropped to a whisper. "Please forgive my boldness, Miss Ellsworth, but I would be remiss if I did not tell you how lovely you look tonight."

I felt a blush rise to my cheeks and paid little attention to Mother's reminiscing with Mrs. Browning. Mr. Jonathon Browning had been kind and proper. Granted, a minuet was not the ideal time to get to know someone in great detail; however, the night was young, and I had quite possibly just danced with the man who would determine my future.

It did not take long for Mr. Jonathon Browning to be the center of attention. It did not surprise me that he had made such an impression. He was handsome, to be sure, and for those debutantes who frequented the events of the *ton*, he was new, refreshing, and unattached.

I watched from the outer edge of the room as eyelashes fluttered and giggles erupted all around him. Outwardly, I smiled at the ridiculousness of it all. But inside, I felt quite jealous. It took a moment for me to sort out my feelings, but I decided that my jealousy was rooted in the fact that the man did not seem fazed by the ample addresses of the women surrounding him. He wore a stern expression but did nothing to dissuade the women from their false flattery. He merely bowed and offered a coy smile now and again. I wondered if he enjoyed the charade.

"Don't worry, dear Miss Ellsworth. Your Mr. Browning is simply the shiny new toy." I turned to find Mr. Fausett standing beside me. "You can see the boredom in his eyes. He is simply waiting them out and no doubt wishing you were one of the swooning masses."

"He is not *my* Mr. Browning." Heat touched my cheeks as I watched the spectacle across the room.

"Perhaps not yet," Mr. Fausett said. "But that is the intent, is it not?"

I remained silent and watched with wonderment as one woman orchestrated a timely fall right into Mr. Browning's arms.

With a shake of my head, I pulled my eyes away and turned to Mr. Fausett. "I must apologize for Mother's earlier introduction." I placed my hand on his arm. "You are more than an acquaintance of my cousin. I'd like to consider us friends. Please forgive me for not making a proper introduction."

"You never need to ask forgiveness of me," Mr. Fausett said, and there was a depth to his words, an undercurrent of conviction that I did not understand but desperately wanted to.

Mr. Fausett stared at me. His eyes were so deep, holding me in a trance that suspended time and silenced the commotion around us. My breaths became short and quick, and my heart tingled inside my chest.

I tried to take a step back but found myself pressed against the column behind me. A melting smile spread across his face, and he took a step closer. His nearness affected me in a most peculiar way. I wanted him to come closer. I wanted to feel more of the warmth he exuded, and at the same time, I wanted to push him away for causing this havoc within me.

Mr. Fausett extended his hand. "Could I entice you to dance, Miss Ellsworth?"

Surely, he had to know how enticed I was. How could I not be, with his charcoal eyes boring into my own?

I lowered my eyes and willed my heartbeat to steady itself before I responded. "I would be honored."

I placed my hand in his, and in one swift movement, Mr. Fausett had turned and settled my hand on his arm as he pulled me towards the dance floor.

"As a friend," he whispered but kept his eyes forward.

I startled and looked over at him, but he said nothing further. We reached an open position on the floor, and he turned me to face him once again. The music began, and we moved with the steps.

Mr. Fausett stepped back, following the sequence of the dance, and we did not speak again. Instead, we dared each other to look away. It became a game of sorts, to hold our eyes on one another as we moved and skipped through the motions of the music.

The trance was broken only when we were required to spin or acknowledge our neighbors. Then our eyes would return to find each other, and we would hold the position again until the next required break.

When the song concluded, Mr. Fausett once more tucked my arm into his. We walked towards my mother, who sat with Mrs. Browning, the two women giggling in the corner like schoolgirls.

Just before reaching them, Mr. Browning stepped in front of us. "Pardon me, Miss Ellsworth. May I have the honor of this dance?"

Mr. Fausett gave a slight incline of his head, and I missed his nearness the moment he stepped away.

I dipped into a curtsy. "Of course, Mr. Browning," I said, and Mr. Fausett disappeared into the crowd.

Mr. Browning's movements were once again precise, and he was attentive, and I wondered if he'd agreed to our mothers' matchmaking tactics. Mr. Browning did not cause havoc in my heart. Dancing with him was pleasant and comfortable, unlike the swirling emotions I'd felt during my set with Mr. Fausett. Both gentlemen were delightful, yet both stirred a variety of emotions. Mr. Fausett seemed an easy ally and a friend, but he'd given no other sign to indicate he was interested in more than friendship. My acquaintance with Mr. Browning was new, but he seemed kind and genuinely interested in pursuing a courtship. Confusion swarmed through me, and I considered that maybe Mother's scheming was right after all.

CHAPTER 9

Mr. Devlin Fausett

I COULD NOT COURT MISS ELLSWORTH, but I reasoned that a dance couldn't hurt. My reasoning was flawed. She was too perfect not to want more. The wager I'd placed from Ferrin's tip in Paddington returned a pretty sum. I'd paid Higgins enough that he agreed to grant an extension of my remaining debts, but he stipulated a hefty increase in interest. With the small remainder, I purchased a new jacket I'd hoped to don when I next saw Miss Ellsworth. But when I learned she would be attending the Taylors' ball, I decided to save the jacket for another time and dress for the formal occasion.

Mrs. Ellsworth's introduction as the acquaintance of her niece humbled me. It served as a solid reminder that she did not consider me a prospect for her daughter. I wondered if the family knew my propensity for the tables. Miss Ellsworth never mentioned my debts but instead apologized for her mother's awkward introduction. Her kindness further confounded me and muddled my intention to let her be. I couldn't help but ask her to dance, and that dance served as the climax of my evening. Staring into her blue eyes, touching her hand, and watching the smile she tried to suppress became another memory to be tucked away and treasured.

I'd managed to steer clear of the gaming hells since my return to Town. Most of my time was spent at the club listening to gossip and being grateful the news of my unscrupulous losses was no longer top fodder. I paid particular attention to the social events that I assumed Miss Ellsworth might attend. Several bachelors noted her return to London, and jealousy pricked at my heart.

I calculated my expenditures and decided to rehire Harris, my valet.

The morning after the ball, I received a letter from my mother. While news of my losses was no longer of interest in London, the information had reached Holbrook before the Christmas holiday. Father had made it clear I was not welcome until all of my debts were paid in full. In fact, he threatened to cut off my allowance entirely. Mother had persuaded him otherwise and dropped subtle hints of concern in her continuing correspondence.

Notwithstanding Higgins, the remainder of my debts had been paid by early December, but I'd allowed the holidays to pass and waited until my most recent letter to reveal that information. My intent was not to worry my mother, but I knew she could not hide anything from Father. I eschewed the gambling for my benefit, not his. Mother's latest letter effused the joy she felt knowing things had been sorted, and she begged me to return home for a visit, insisting Father was agreeable to the invitation. She also hinted that a visit home might soften Father and convince him to allow me more responsibility in the running of the estate.

Holbrook itself was pleasant. The green acreage sported a variety of ash and oak trees. Mother kept a flower garden, and Father's stable was supplied with sturdy, able-bodied horses. Father dealt fairly with his tenants, and the nearby town of Briarsdale offered plentiful diversion. Returning home would not be a problem. Returning to live under my father's thumb was an entirely different story.

The fact that I was the only child Mother had carried to full term meant that all of Father's abundant expectations fell to me. For years, I'd tried to appease him. I worked studiously at my lessons and followed every admonition he discharged. But it was always to no avail. When I attended Cambridge, Father once came to visit. I'd excelled in my courses and introduced him to each of my professors. When it came time for him to depart, I was certain he would finally grant the acknowledgment I'd worked so hard to achieve. I was no longer a lad, but his rebuke that my success only qualified if I were first in *all* of my courses stung as sharply as a switch across my bare back would have. It had always been all or nothing with my father, and I continuously fell short.

Mother's letter ended up in the ashes. I ignored Harris's silent warning and headed to the tables. The idea that my father was *agreeable* to a visit from his only child sickened me. I did not need his support. I needed an escape. I needed to become independent from his hold and able to sustain myself. Unfortunately, that could only happen if I had the funds to do so.

CHAPTER 10

Miss Nora Ellsworth

THE DARK-BLUE DRAPERIES IN MY room fought to filter out the morning light, but the sun refused to be deterred. It pulsed and pushed through any possible crack until Claudia entered my room, pulled the curtains wide, and let the sun free.

"Was it not splendid?" Claudia asked as she raised her hand to her forehead and collapsed onto my bed. "Mr. Fausett danced with me at first. He was so divine." Claudia released a heavy sigh and flipped around to lay on her stomach. "Then there was Mr. Hudson. He was handsome, was he not? Then Mr. Davis and Mr. Newton. It was the epitome of a fairy tale." Claudia rolled onto her side, draped her arm across her forehead, and sighed dreamily. I smiled at her contented grin. Then she added, "But no one was as handsome as your Mr. Jonathon Browning, except, of course, Mr. Fausett."

"He is not *my* Mr. Jonathon Browning," I corrected my sister as I had done with Mr. Fausett the previous evening. I pulled on my robe and moved to sit in a chair near the window to join Claudia's musing.

Mr. Jonathon Browning proved himself everything proper. He danced gracefully and demonstrated impeccable manners. All of the lavish compliments Mother had paid over the years held true. I credited it more to luck than to my mother's ability to judge character, but I was glad the pedestal she placed the Brownings on was deserved. Jonathon Browning—we'd finally met. And danced.

He was an exquisite dancer. Confident and strong as he led me around the floor, but a layer of tension lay hidden in Mr. Browning's smile. Not obnoxious, nor obvious, more a wisp of strain, a breath of pressure that he concealed with his formality.

It was the opposite of Mr. Fausett. Despite my bumbling introduction, his relaxed persona set me at ease. Dancing with Mr. Fausett was easy, natural, and when I recalled his hand on my back, or his gentle but firm touch, my cheeks turned up in a smile.

Claudia and I dressed and called on Cooper to complete our ministrations. Then we went to breakfast. Once Claudia had broken her fast, she became even more talkative. It was as if all of the resplendent memories from the previous evening flooded her at once.

"Wasn't Mr. Fausett dashing?" Claudia asked and then stuffed a large bite of bread into her mouth.

"Mr. Fausett was . . ." I paused, searching for the right word. What was he exactly? ". . . distinctive," I finally said.

Claudia sighed and propped her chin in her hand. "Mr. Browning and Mr. Fausett, most distinctive gentlemen."

While I had only described Mr. Fausett as distinctive, I did not correct Claudia. Instead, I laughed at her and continued to eat while I pondered the differences between the two men.

Mitchell entered the breakfast room carrying a buoyant arrangement of flowers. "A delivery for Miss Ellsworth." Mitchell bowed his head towards the blooms, a beautiful assortment of white roses and leafy greenery. Mr. Browning's card accompanied the arrangement, and I directed Mitchell to place the roses in the parlor.

I'd known the man less than twenty-four hours, and he already made me smile.

Mr. Jonathon Browning and his mother called the following day. Mother served tea and biscuits and made an admirable effort to include Claudia and me in the conversation; however, after only ten minutes, any attempt by either of us to interject was futile. The two matrons were like long-lost sisters. They gasped at the same things, scoffed in unison, and leaned forward in tandem when sharing a secret. They even laughed with a similar jovial cackle. In truth, I had never seen my mother so at ease. She often visited with neighbors and acquaintances, but she held back. She hid her true self in her societal knowhow. Talking with Mrs. Browning, Mother radiated beauty. Mrs. Browning was a true friend indeed.

Mr. Browning entertained Claudia and me with stories of his upbringing in India. Claudia paled and grabbed for my hand as Mr. Browning narrated his encounter with a tiger. One of the kitchen maid's children had wandered outside the protective walls of their estate. Mr. Browning had joined the household staff in their search for the child and was confronted by the large predator. His descriptions of the tiger's vibrant pelt, chisel-like teeth, and enormous paws were vivid and chilling. Thankfully, his father had happened on the scene and deterred the animal with several warning shots.

"And did you find the child?" I asked.

Mr. Browning's eyes softened. "Yes. In the course of my confrontation with the tiger, one of the footmen found the child and returned him to his mother. So you see, the story does have a happy ending."

Claudia still held my hand tightly and shook her head in disbelief. "You were very brave, Mr. Browning."

He laughed lightly, and it was a pleasant sound. "Not so brave, Miss Claudia. It was not an experience I am wont to repeat."

Mrs. Browning stood. "We should be going, Jonathon," she said. "Your father hoped you would join him this afternoon when he meets with his man of business."

Mr. Browning's forehead creased in response to his mother's words. But he stood and said nothing. We rose as well and offered all the appropriate niceties. Then Mother walked her friend to the door. Claudia returned to her seat and picked up her embroidery.

Mr. Browning placed a hand on my elbow and, turning away from my sister, asked if I would join him the following day to ride out in Hyde Park.

"Of course," I answered, and then he was gone.

Mother made a few more calls that afternoon and returned with an invitation for a musicale that was to be at the home of Mr. and Mrs. Blunt on Friday evening.

"I've made sure the Brownings were included in the invitation, and Mrs. Blunt has requested you as the final performance of the night," Mother said.

"You know I prefer not to sing in a large gathering," I said.

"But you have such a beautiful voice, my dear. It would be a shame not to share your talent. Besides, Mr. Browning has not yet heard you sing. Once he hears your voice, you will most certainly capture his heart." Mother beamed at her matchmaking.

"I don't want Mr. Browning to fall in love with my voice. I want him to fall in love with me," I said, surprised at the desperation in my voice.

Mother rolled her eyes and waved a dismissive hand. "Now you're talking nonsense. Love is love." Mother sat down beside me and took my hand in hers. "Just sing like you did at Astoria and you will have nothing to worry about."

I pulled my fingers away from my mother and held them silently in my lap. Astoria. Singing. Mr. Fausett. There was a reason my song sounded so beautiful that night, and it had nothing to do with my voice and everything to do with my accompanist.

CHAPTER 11

Mr. Devlin Fausett

IF I WAS A BROKEN man before, I was even more so now. My night at the gaming hells had swerved downhill quickly. In my anger over Mother's letter and Father's backhanded threats, I drank. I never drink. My weakness at the tables was enough of a handicap; compounded with alcohol, I'd become my own worst enemy.

I lost Raven that night. Consumed with rage and the urgency to walk away with a win, I bet my horse, and I lost. When they came to collect her, I was passed out in my room. Harris made the arrangements, and once I'd sobered, he reiterated it all again. Not that I needed the reminder. Raven was the one positive in my life. On her back, I found freedom. Yet, my selfish addiction won out again, and now my freedom was gone in more ways than one.

I had vowed to eschew the horrid habit, and I had failed. Raven's stall had been empty for two days, and I determined to rise above wallowing in self-pity. I opted for a stroll through Hyde Park, hoping to clear my head, although had I paid attention to the hour, I would have elected to walk along the river.

Open carriages and pairs of riders paraded through the park. Even the horses seemed to prance as if they knew they were on display. Hopefully, the extravagance of the *ton* would work to my advantage, for while others strutted and postured to attract attention, I hoped to quietly meld into obscurity.

My focus remained on the path in front of me, and I decided on a quick stroll around the Serpentine.

"Mr. Fausett!"

My chest froze. Her voice often filled my thoughts, but I could not face Miss Ellsworth now, so I kept my feet moving forward and hoped she would move on.

"Mr. Fausett!" Miss Ellsworth called again, and I heard the clomping of horse hooves behind me.

With a heavy sigh, I stopped. I didn't turn completely around, grateful that the brim of my tall hat partially concealed my face.

"Mr. Fausett, you remember Mr. Browning?" Miss Ellsworth said.

I definitely remembered the man she was due to marry. Sleep was one of my only reprieves, and the man's image ruined my dreams.

"Browning," I said and touched my hand to my hat with a small bow. "You've a lovely pair of chestnuts." If I stared at the horses, I didn't need to acknowledge the fine open carriage or Miss Ellsworth's sapphire-blue gown that illuminated the hue of her eyes.

"Thank you," Browning said. "A recent addition. My father's determined to build up our stables now that we've returned to England."

The irony might be laughable if I didn't feel so broken.

"Mr. Fausett? Are you quite all right?" Miss Ellsworth asked, and I suppressed the desire to groan in frustration.

"Quite," I answered and touched my hat again. "Good day to the both of you." I began to walk away.

"Wait!" Miss Ellsworth called. The urgency in her voice caused me to turn and look up at her.

She was beautiful, as always. The yellow flowers on her hat contrasted the deep blue of her dress. Bright matching ribbons were tied beneath her chin, and when I looked at her face, she was evaluating mine. I'm not sure what she saw, but the urgency faded along with her smile.

Miss Ellsworth moved her hand to the side of the carriage and leaned forward the tiniest bit. "There's to be a musicale on Friday. Mrs. Blunt has asked me to sing. She's Mother's friend, and I'm sure she would be happy to include you in the invitation."

I looked at her companion. He assessed our interaction but remained silent.

"I know you're a lover of music," Miss Ellsworth added, as if the enticement of hearing her perform were not enough. "Will you come?"

"If I can manage," I said.

I forced my eyes to turn from her hopeful face, forced my feet to move forward, and I did not look back.

CHAPTER 12

Miss Nora Ellsworth

I RETURNED HOME AND ASKED Mother to ensure Mrs. Blunt included Mr. Fausett in the invitation. She told me it was too late for such a request.

"He's a musician," I told her. Then I planted my hands on my hips. "Besides, I've already told him you would make sure he's invited."

"Nora," Mother said with a solemn voice. "I've heard rumors about Mr. Fausett."

"Rumors. What rumors?" I asked. My voice held steady, but my pulse immediately sped.

Mother took my hand and led me to the sofa. "I know you consider Mr. Fausett a friend, but he has deceived us."

I laughed aloud and sat down. "Deceived us?"

Mother raised her brow and after a calming breath spoke again, "Nora. Mr. Fausett is a regular at the gaming tables, and I've learned that he is in a great deal of debt."

My laugh quieted, and I shook my head. "Many gentlemen gamble. Father's even tried his hand a time or two."

Mother straightened in her seat and leveled me with a stare. "Your father knows when to quit. Mr. Fausett, it seems, does not."

I pulled my hand away from Mother's. "Where did you hear this? Surely you don't believe all of the mindless prattle spread throughout the drawing rooms of the *ton*?"

"I heard it from a reliable source. Mrs. Peabody," Mother said. Mrs. Peabody was not a regular gossip, but she did like to propagate a good tale.

"What does Mrs. Peabody know about it?" I asked, straightening the gathers of my skirt.

"She knows that Mr. Fausett lost his prized horse."

My head whipped up as my gut clenched. "Raven?"

Mother's head tilted to the side. Resignation crossed her face. "The new owner is hoping to turn a profit and is accepting bids on the animal now." She put a hand on my shoulder. "I'm sorry, Nora."

Mother was not trying to gloat, but the sting of truth settled uncomfortably in my mind. I stood and walked a quick circle around the sofa. Could it be true? Did Mr. Fausett really part with his beloved horse? He was walking this afternoon instead of riding, and he looked sad. So sad. I sank down into a wide wingback chair.

Mother spoke so softly I could barely hear her. "I don't think you should associate with a man who demonstrates such a lack of self-control. What will Mr. Browning think?"

My answer came quickly. "Hopefully, that I am a kind woman and that I don't desert my friends," I said forcefully. Then I added, "Please ensure Mr. Fausett is invited to the musicale, Mother. It sounds as if he could use a night of uplifting music."

When Friday arrived, Cooper thought she was very clever to collect small white roses to adorn my hair. She gushed at how the flowers would be just the thing to show Mr. Browning my gratitude for his roses and his attention. It was a bit bold, but I allowed Cooper to weave the delicate white flowers through my tresses.

Aside from my required performance, I looked forward to the evening. Good music was such a delight and, of course, Mr. Browning would be in attendance. Mother grudgingly secured Mr. Fausett an invitation, and I hoped he too would come. He had smiled before when I sang, and I longed to see him smile again. He was a strong man. A good man. Surely, whatever demon drove him to this state, he could find the strength to cast it out.

Mitchell handed me my wrap, and Mother gushed at my appearance. "My, my, dear Nora. It would not surprise me if Mr. Browning declared himself this very evening."

"Mother, you should not say such things," I chided.

When Father declared us ready to depart, Mother reached over and grabbed the flesh of my checks between her thumb and forefinger.

"Mother!" I pushed her hand away and took a step backwards.

"Oh, it's all working out so perfectly." Mother clapped her hands together and giggled while she led the way to the carriage.

Claudia sat quietly beside me on the bench. I meant to call her attention from the window, but Father spoke before I had a chance. "What have you prepared, Nora?"

"I thought I'd sing 'Bright Gems That Twinkle', by Dibdin," I said.

"Such a simple piece?" Father asked. "Surely you want to flaunt your talents more."

"You know I prefer the simpler songs to the operas. And I don't favor a large crowd." I glanced again at Claudia staring out into the night. She never remained this passive. I decided to corner her later and turned back to my parents. "If a gentleman wishes to marry me based solely on my voice or my beauty, then that is not the type of man I should like to be attached to."

Mother tsk'd and Father harrumphed, but neither of them said anything more.

When we arrived at Mrs. Blunt's musicale and alighted from the carriage, I reached for Claudia's hand and gave it a quick squeeze. She turned her petrified eyes towards me.

"What's the matter?" I asked on a whisper. Poor Claudia's pallor reflected the white of a ghost. Claudia's head shook and her eyes remained wide, but no words formed on her lips. "Claudia?" I asked again. "Are you all right?" I grabbed my sister's hand and pulled her to a stop.

She looked frantically at my parents walking up the front steps then met my eyes again. "They've asked me to play," Claudia said.

"Mrs. Blunt?" I clarified and Claudia nodded.

Was that all that was bothering her? I took both of Claudia's hands and swept her arms wide. "You are a natural on the piano, and you look lovely tonight. You have nothing to fear."

Claudia let a small smile touch her lips. She looked down at our clasped hands. "I don't like large crowds either."

We turned towards the house, and I pulled her stiff arm through mine. Leaning close, I whispered in her ear, "Just look at me and forget the rest of them. Imagine yourself in the drawing room at Ellsworth Meadows and you will be fine."

Her posture relaxed as we greeted Mr. and Mrs. Blunt and followed the gathering towards the music room. One gentleman in particular stood out. It seemed Mr. Browning did not need formal attire to showcase his natural good looks. He needed only to make an appearance. My cheeks warmed while I curtsied and admired his finely polished boots.

"Miss Ellsworth." Mr. Browning bowed his head. "You look enchanting this evening."

"Thank you," I said.

"I look forward to hearing you sing."

I suddenly wondered if I'd be able to follow my own advice knowing he sat in the crowd. Could I pretend to be in the drawing room at home?

Mr. Browning's eyes wandered to my hair. "White roses fit you perfectly." Warmth flooded my cheeks anew. "Come, your parents have already joined us." Mr. Browning offered his arm, and we wove through the party. He led me to a row of seats with a direct view of the ivory keys.

Mother conversed with Mrs. Browning and Mrs. Peabody. Mrs. Peabody's small mouth and her drawn face were inconsequential. She wore an intricate coif, perhaps to distract from her nondescript features. I wondered if she continued to slander the name of my friend.

Mr. Browning caught me staring. He leaned towards me and said, "She is curious, but harmless. I assure you." I straightened immediately, ashamed to be caught assessing Mrs. Peabody's features.

The performances began, and I lamented Mr. Fausett's absence. I knew his problems would not merely disappear, but I hoped a night of music might bring solace and the promise of a new beginning.

Claudia played her piece radiantly. Her fingers hesitated at first, but once she allowed her eyes to drift closed, the notes flowed and cast a happy spell throughout the room. Her efforts were met with earnest applause.

Most of the performers were women, but a few men joined in some of the duets. The vibrations and crescendos wafted through the air, and I inhaled each note, feeling the movement and rhythm of each song. The entire gathering was hypnotized as a sweet string of Italian words flowed from an ebony-haired beauty, ending on a note of desolation.

Then it was my turn. Nerves bunched through my stomach, and I pressed my fingernails into my palms as I walked to the piano. Mrs. Blunt had agreed to accompany me. We exchanged a few whispers to confirm the tempo, and the music began.

I looked over the heads of the audience and sang about the planets and stars. My stomach fluttered until my eyes drifted along the back wall and I saw Mr. Fausett standing in a corner of the room. His face remained impassive, but when our eyes met, I saw the sadness he harbored. I was so very touched that he made the effort to attend that my inhibition vanished, and I sang without restraint.

The song closed with reference to the rising moon, and on the final chord, Mr. Fausett nodded his approval. My heart soared as I turned to curtsy to the applauding crowd. Mr. Browning stood, and the rest of the audience rose as well. There was no reason the simple song should elicit such praise, and I found my nerves bundling inside once again as the applause continued.

Mrs. Blunt placed a hand on my arm and whispered, "You must perform an encore."

"Oh no, I couldn't." I shook my head.

"But they loved you," Mrs. Blunt insisted. "You've touched their hearts."

The only person whose heart I cared to touch was Mr. Fausett. I hoped to give him courage and the assurance of friendship. I looked to where he stood, and an idea came to mind.

"Would a duet be acceptable?" I asked Mrs. Blunt.

Her eyes widened. "Indeed." She raised her hands to her guests and made the announcement that I would sing another.

As the guests whispered and sat back down, I caught Mr. Fausett's attention and motioned him forward. His eyes narrowed, and he shook his head. I almost laughed aloud at his mulish behavior, but when I motioned again, he inhaled deeply and something in his countenance shifted. He held his head sure, keeping his eyes on me, and walked forward amidst whispers of rumors and fractional truths. When Mr. Fausett reached the piano, the room dropped into a dreadful silence.

I swallowed past the apprehension in my chest. "You owe me a duet," I said softly.

"I do," Mr. Fausett confirmed. Then, without reservation, he took his place at the piano. "Do you know Dibdin and Bickerstaff's 'Venus, Mother of Desire'?"

Before I could contradict his choice of songs, his hands began to caress the keys with docility. Mr. Fausett began his part, and I became immediately lost in the timbre of his voice. The words of the song did not help either.

> *By Venus, Mother of Desire,*
> *Your eyes have set me all on fire.*
> *There's magic in your touch,*
> *There's magic in your touch.*

My turn came, and I could not form a coherent thought, let alone sing the words required of me. I missed my cue, and Mr. Fausett artfully repeated the refrain. Then he slowed the music and looked at me. His smile was a gentle invitation, his eyes a call for help.

So I sang.

> *My eyes! dear Sir—a-well-a-day,*
> *Tears must have wash'd their power away:*
> *Indeed you say too much,*
> *Indeed you say too much.*

And then we sang together. Emotion broke through, leaving no doubt as to my friendship with the man. The duet became my gift to him, my promise that things could improve.

Mr. Fausett played the final notes of the song and slowly lifted his fingers from the keys. The sacred moment remained long and unbroken until the applause began, quiet at first, then building with the awakening of the guests.

They again offered a standing ovation, and Mr. Fausett and I accepted their praise in tandem. I looked over the crowd and found Mr. Browning watching me with an upward twist on his lips.

I received compliments heaped one upon another, and when I turned to acknowledge Mr. Fausett's contribution, he was gone. I didn't have time to consider where he'd disappeared to as a multitude of faces and words pelted me from every side.

Mr. Browning stepped forward with a large smile. "I wasn't aware of your abundance of talent, Miss Ellsworth." I blushed at his compliment, and gratitude swelled inside my chest that he did not question my selection of songs or singing partners. "May I escort you to a seat, and we can find some refreshment?" he asked.

I gratefully took his arm, and he led me to a cluster of chairs near the far wall. Mr. Browning left with a promise to return with food, and Claudia came to join me.

"Oh, Nora!" Claudia said wistfully. "It was beautiful! So romantic. Did you know Mr. Fausett had such a lovely voice?"

"I admit, I did not," I said.

Claudia sat still in her chair, her eyes pressed closed for a moment before she opened them again. "He played and sang from a place deep inside. I would love to hear him sing again."

I smiled my agreement, amused at the lulling effect Mr. Fausett's voice had on my sister. Claudia extracted her fan and sat in silent contemplation until Mr. Browning returned.

The conversation turned from the performance to a discussion of the Blunts' generosity. Claudia excused herself to find Mother; however, when she stood she wavered and grabbed the back of her chair for balance.

Mr. Browning immediately stood and held her elbow. "Are you all right, Miss Claudia?"

Claudia raised her gloved hands to her flushed cheeks. "I'm afraid . . . I am not quite myself this evening," she said and sank back into her chair.

I moved next to my sister and took her hand. Heat pulsed through her gloves. "You're burning up."

"I will inform your mother," Mr. Browning said with a bow and quickly turned into the crowd.

"I'm sorry." Claudia shook her head and stared at her lap. "So sorry," she said. "Perhaps I only need some fresh air."

Claudia began to rise, and I stood with her, bracing my arm around her back. My efforts were not enough. Claudia's eyes rolled back in her head, and I screamed for help as she collapsed to the ground.

CHAPTER 13

Mr. Devlin Fausett

I FELT A WEEK OF sobriety and abstinence from the gaming hells deserved a reward. Thus, I had accepted the invitation from Mrs. Blunt. The promise of Miss Ellsworth's performance was incentive enough, but when coupled with her personal invitation, the motivation had become even greater.

My position in the rear of the room allowed me to observe her throughout the evening. She happily smiled in conversation with Mr. Browning and applauded with exuberance at her sister's performance. Jealousy nipped through me, but I was pleased to see her content.

When she sang about gems and stars and the loss of day, it was the epitome of a lullaby. Miss Ellsworth mesmerized the entire crowd, and when they asked for an encore, the last thing I expected was to be included in the affair. I'd come to listen, not to perform, but I could not resist her simple request. Singing and playing with her beside me had been a balm to my maimed soul, and when it was over I was grateful to deflect the compliments to Miss Ellsworth and excuse myself entirely. Although, as I made my way to the door, I found I could not quit the evening. I wasn't ready to sever the connection with Miss Ellsworth completely and feared when I walked out the door, the contentment I'd found would exit with me.

I lingered near the front foyer and was approached by a gentleman I recognized, although we had not been formally introduced. "Quite a performance you put on, Mr. Fausett," the man said with a slight incline of his head. "Mr. Russell Browning."

I bowed back, my eyes remaining on the gentleman. "It's a pleasure to make your acquaintance, sir. I met your son briefly at the Taylors' ball, Friday last."

He grunted in reply and eyed me up and down. "I heard you lost your horse."

Anger, remorse, and distrust vacillated through me. A multitude of words jumbled with my coursing emotion, but I kept my tongue silent.

"I've been looking for a mount since my return to England. Do you think your mare's worth the price they're asking? Seems a bit steep to me." Mr. Browning's question was layered with insinuation. I clenched my jaw, and a slow smile crept across his face. "By the fire in your eyes, I'd say she's worth more," he said. "Well, I suppose that's what Higgins wants—to turn a profit."

A sudden commotion turned our attention back to the main room. I was grateful for an excuse to terminate my conversation with the elder Mr. Browning. We both moved towards the doorway to uncover the source of the tumult. Whispers and cries bounced off the walls, and men and women craned their necks for a glimpse at the far side of the room. I noticed the younger Mr. Browning pushing through the crowd towards Mr. and Mrs. Ellsworth. After only a brief exchange of words, the trio moved back through the crowd.

I stood up on my tiptoes, and looking over the masses, I saw Miss Ellsworth attempting to support her sister while guiding her through the throng of onlookers. I inwardly smiled at Miss Ellsworth's determination but instantly recognized the impossible task before her.

"Hurry, man," I called to the footman stationed at the door. "Call for the Ellsworth carriage. They will be departing at once."

I forcefully maneuvered through the crowd and came upon Miss Ellsworth trying to negotiate her sister's weight between herself and her father. I suppressed a rebuke to Browning, who stood mutely watching, and without asking permission, I lifted Miss Claudia into my arms.

"Lead the way," I said to Miss Ellsworth.

Her eyes glistened with moisture. Mr. Ellsworth took the lead, admonishing the guests to stand aside, and I followed along behind.

Miss Claudia moaned in my arms, and her mother bustled beside me. "Oh, my poor girl. My dear Claudia! Mr. Ellsworth you must have the doctor come at once," Mrs. Ellsworth said.

We waited only a moment on the front steps before the carriage pulled into view. Miss Claudia's eyes blinked open. "What happened?" she asked.

Miss Ellsworth took her sister's hand. "You were so moved by my song, you fainted," Miss Ellsworth teased.

Miss Claudia turned her sallow eyes and looked at me. "Oh, hello, Mr. Fausett," she said, and I smiled. "It was a lovely song."

"Thank you," I said with a chuckle.

Miss Claudia's eyes quickly widened, and she turned back to her sister. "But Mr. Browning," she said. "You can't leave now."

"Nonsense," Miss Ellsworth replied. "I will see you home and tucked into bed."

Mr. Ellsworth ushered us to the carriage. He climbed inside, and I handed Miss Claudia up to him. When I turned back around, Browning stood ready to assist Miss Ellsworth and her mother. He then climbed into the carriage himself. The footman lifted the step, and before I could offer any further assistance, Mr. Ellsworth gave the signal to depart.

I stepped onto the curb and listened to the wheels clattering away. In the moment before the carriage rounded the corner, Miss Ellsworth's face appeared in the window. A spot of warmth touched my heart, and I began the long walk back to my lonely apartment.

CHAPTER 14

Miss Nora Ellsworth

CLAUDIA SLIPPED IN AND OUT of consciousness until we arrived home. She kept rambling apologies for cutting the evening short, despite my insistence that it was not an inconvenience and I had no regrets.

It was mostly true. My one regret was that I never properly thanked Mr. Fausett for singing with me. I wanted to ask him about Raven, to understand how he found himself in a situation so desperate that he parted with his beloved horse. But I did not have the opportunity. Nor did I get to express my relief when he appeared and swept Claudia into his arms. The twinge of jealousy I may have felt seeing his arms wrapped around my sister was quickly replaced as I watched him maneuver with ease through the crowd.

My focus turned to my sister, and I determined to call on Mr. Fausett another time to offer the appropriate gratitude. I assured Claudia she only needed to rest and all would be better in the morning.

But it wasn't.

Not the next day, nor the one after that. Doctor Carrow did not seem overly concerned. He came every day, felt her head, and checked her vitals. She slept almost the entire time, waking only to sip a bit of broth or take a swallow of water. The doctor assured us that she would be fine. He said the illness must run its course and insisted these things take time.

Mr. Jonathon Browning called with his mother the day after the recital. He didn't stay long—only inquired after Claudia and promised to call again when she was well. Only Claudia didn't get well. She didn't get worse. There was simply no change.

The fever continued to ravage her strength and make her breath stick. Her lungs fought back, forcing the air in and out. I continued to help Cooper pour water and broth through Claudia's lips, but she would take only a few sips before she turned away and tried to cough out the bit we had coerced into her body.

Father did not handle Claudia's illness well. He would make a daily appearance and try to appear unfazed, but he was too easy to read. His routine became predictable. After breakfast, Father would stride through the door full of feigned confidence.

"Is Claudia better today?" he asked, directing the question to my mother.

Mother would shake her head or clutch her chest and mumble something dire.

Father would look to me to clarify the situation, and after I confirmed there had been no change, Father would appraise Claudia's inert form. His shoulders would fall, and moisture would begin to gather in the corners of his eyes. His eyelids quickly blinked away the sentiment, and he raised his chin in defiance.

"I'll be at the club," he said. Or sometimes he went to meet with his solicitor or elsewhere to conduct business. But it was always somewhere else. Anywhere else.

Mother fretted continuously over Claudia, pacing beside the bed, swiping a moist towel across my sister's forehead or adjusting her blankets. A white almost-halo shone around Claudia's face; it was unnerving. Her faded red lips turned up enough that if I didn't know better, I would think she was smiling. I hoped wherever she was, in dreams or out, she felt peace.

Mrs. Browning began to call daily, and I gratefully welcomed the diversion she provided for Mother. Of course, they would talk about Claudia's condition and the doctor's latest pronouncements, but then Mrs. Browning was wise enough to turn the conversation to other topics.

The garden was too small to allow me to outrun my constant worry, and I dared not leave the house for long. After a sleepless week, rain pelted the windows, prohibiting even my meager exercise.

Mitchell informed me that Mr. Fausett was waiting in the sitting room. A tinge of happiness fluttered through my heart.

I waited for Cooper to come sit with Claudia. She'd assisted in Claudia's care morning and night since she had fallen ill. I would try to take a turn, but she would shoo me from the room and insist I sleep. Any lassitude I felt, I knew Cooper suffered twofold.

Cooper appeared and pushed her tired eyes up with a forced smile. "I'll sit with her now, miss. You go have a nice visit." She waved me from the room.

"Thank you, Cooper," I said, and she gave me a tired nod.

Mr. Fausett stood and bowed when I entered the room. His eyes did not follow the incline of his head; instead they stayed fixed on me. I wished I could wash the exhaustion, the fear, from my face, but I could not hide my emotions.

"I'm sorry I could not come sooner," Mr. Fausett said. "I had some pressing matters, but you and your sister have been constantly on my mind."

I sat in a large yellow pinstripe chair near the door and motioned for Mr. Fausett to take a seat.

"May I offer you something to drink?" I asked.

"No, thank you," Mr. Fausett answered. "I only wanted to inquire after your sister."

I looked at my stilled hands in my lap and thought about Claudia lying still and lifeless upstairs. My eyes met Mr. Fausett's earnest gaze. "I'm not sure, to be honest. At first the doctor was not concerned. He said that fevers sometimes take a week or more to run their course, but . . ." I gulped down the lump that formed with my next words. They were the reason I feared the most. "Now that it's been ten days and there has been no change, I'm afraid I've lost confidence that all will be well. The doctor insists he needs to bleed her. I have convinced Mother and Father not to let him, thus far. I have heard terrible things about the practice." I swiped at the moisture in my eyes. "I'm sorry," I said.

Mr. Fausett moved in two quick steps and pressed his handkerchief into my hand. I accepted it with a small smile.

"Perhaps you could consult another doctor?" he suggested, sitting in a nearby chair.

"I suggested that to Mother, but she said . . ." I paused because I found myself confiding things I would not normally share. Yet, Mr. Fausett could be trusted, and maybe if I voiced the words aloud it would somehow help.

Mr. Fausett leaned forward, eager to hear my explanation. "I believe my father and mother are both in denial. They believed Claudia's malady to be temporary and refuse to consider that it could be more serious." I stood and walked to the window. Fear swelled within my breast, and the feeling matched the dismal weather. With a deep breath I turned around to face Mr. Fausett. "I fear for my sister. She has always been healthy and happy. Something is not right." I felt the truth of my words all the way to my bones.

Mr. Fausett sat stock-still, his eyes turned dark like a winter storm cloud. I wasn't sure what to make of his manner. I felt he could be trusted with this secret, this insight to our family, but perhaps I'd assumed wrong.

He opened his mouth to speak, and I swayed backwards, ready for the rebuke I felt certain he was going to give. However, his words surprised me. He did not chastise our family or critique my mother. It was a rebuke, just not the one I expected. He stood and walked near. "I wish you had come to me," he said.

More tears tumbled as the words floated on the air between us. Mr. Fausett deserved my trust. I wanted nothing more than to go back in time and honor his wish. Those moments were gone, but I could start anew.

"Mr. Fausett, can you, will you, help Claudia?" I raised my fingers in front of me as though in prayer.

His lips pushed up in a small smile, and he said, "All you had to do was ask." Lightness filled my chest, and hope bubbled within.

"Brumley and I studied with a Doctor Hadley. He specializes in conditions of the heart, but he received his training from some of the best physicians. Would it be acceptable for him to examine your sister?" he asked.

"Of course," I said.

"Then I shall go to him at once."

We walked together to the door. Before Mitchell handed Mr. Fausett his hat and gloves, Mr. Fausett turned to me and took my hand in his own. "I'm honored you would share your fears with me," he said.

"Come now, Mr. Fausett. Our friendship is beyond inconsequential conversation," I said.

His eyes lit and his lips suppressed a smile. He looked down at our hands, and when he returned his gaze to mine, he'd sobered. "Yes, but you trusted me, and that is not something I take lightly."

"Perhaps one day you will return the favor," I said.

"Perhaps," Mr. Fausett said. He squeezed my fingers, took his things from Mitchell, and then he was gone.

CHAPTER 15

Mr. Devlin Fausett

I REACHED INTO MY POCKET and wrapped my fingers around my grandfather's watch. It remained my one connection to him, the thing I valued most, and while I had sworn never to part with it, the time had come. It was the only way.

Doctor Hadley was a busy man. We had been friends at Cambridge, and I'd heard snippets about his career in the years since. Hadley was leading a research team studying rhythms of the heart. Common illness was not necessarily his specialty, but I hoped he would come see Miss Claudia and give a recommendation for her care.

Hadley listened patiently while I explained all I knew, urged him to come immediately, and told him all expenses should be directed to me. I planned to offer Grandfather's watch for his time and hoped Hadley would accept the timepiece in lieu of payment. Gratefully, Hadley returned with me to Ellsworth House.

In my excitement to prove myself to Miss Ellsworth, I did not consider the possibility of other callers. Mitchell announced us, and I entered the sitting room eager to introduce the doctor. Instead, I ended up looking the part of a fool. Browning sat with Miss Ellsworth and Mrs. Ellsworth. They started at my entrance, and I quickly cleared my throat and presented Doctor Hadley.

Miss Ellsworth's exhaustion remained evident behind her smile. "Are you able to see Claudia now?" she asked.

"Please, lead the way," Doctor Hadley said and then followed Miss Ellsworth and her mother from the room.

Thirty minutes later, the chiming clock interrupted the silence between Browning and myself. His direct stare was meant to intimidate me, but I refused to leave without first hearing Hadley's prognosis. When voices finally sounded on the stairs, Browning and I moved in unison towards the door.

Hadley reached the bottom step then turned back to Miss Ellsworth. "I want you to take her temperature and her pulse every hour and keep a record of each, along with the time." He ticked off the requirements on his fingers.

"Every hour," Miss Ellsworth confirmed.

Hadley waved his hand vaguely. "You may extend it to every two hours during the night," he said and moved towards the door. "I will be back tomorrow." And then he turned to me. "Ready, Fausett?"

I nodded and turned to follow him. Miss Ellsworth touched my arm. "Mr. Fausett, how can I ever thank you?"

"Tend to your sister. Her health is all I desire." I bowed over her hand. "Good day, Miss Ellsworth."

She clasped her hands in front of her waist, and Browning stepped behind her. I accepted my things from Mitchell and turned back to look at Miss Ellsworth one more time. She raised her hand in a final farewell, and I walked out the door. I placed my hand in my pocket over Grandfather's watch, feeling no regret.

CHAPTER 16

Miss Nora Ellsworth

MR. FAUSETT SURPRISED ME WHEN he returned so quickly with Doctor Hadley, but after the doctor's thorough evaluation of Claudia, I was grateful he had come.

Doctor Hadley listened long and intently to Claudia, measuring her breaths and timing the rise and fall of her chest. He felt for her pulse on her wrists and at her neck, even feeling her feet for the steady beat.

When Mother questioned his methods, Doctor Hadley simply looked at her and said, "Her rhythms are strong, but they are not necessarily consistent." He lowered Claudia's left foot then lifted the right one.

"What does that mean?" I looked at Cooper, wondering if she understood any more than I did.

The doctor repeated all of Claudia's symptoms and confirmed that Doctor Carrow had been attending her. I confirmed with a nod.

"Did you keep a record of her fever?" he asked, and I shook my head. Doctor Hadley glanced at me then returned to fingering Claudia's feet. "Has he not taken her temperature?"

My frustration escaped on a sigh. "He did, once or twice—"

Doctor Hadley cut me off. "Once or twice in ten days? And he left no record?" He covered Claudia's feet crudely with the blanket, and Cooper stepped in to assist.

I folded my hands in front of me, and I raised my chin. "No. I'm sorry. Doctor Carrow did not think the illness would last so long. He . . . he insists we should bleed her, but . . ." I didn't complete my thought.

Doctor Hadley mumbled something that sounded vaguely like *incompetent*, but I chose to ignore him and focus on my sister. Despite his grating and harsh manner, he was correct: we should have acted sooner.

He stood with his hand on his chin, his finger drumming against his cheek as he stared blankly across the room. The moment shifted, and I no longer felt I was on the defense. The stillness allowed me to prioritize my desires, the greatest of which was for Claudia to get better. Doctor Hadley was here to help. I could endure his caustic manner.

Mother spoke, breaking his reverie. "How is my dear girl? Can you help her?"

Doctor Hadley took a step back. He inclined his head the tiniest bit, and, ignoring my mother, he turned to me. "Do you know how to check for a pulse?"

"Yes." I nodded.

"Do you have a timepiece and a thermometer?" he asked pointedly.

Doctor Hadley's determination to help my sister made me want to acquiesce to his every command. But I could not. "My father has a pocket watch, but we do not have a thermometer."

"Hmm, I'll arrange to have one sent over from my office." He reached for Claudia's wrist and opened his pocket watch while counting silently.

Mother jumped with a gasp when Doctor Hadley dropped Claudia's lifeless hand back onto the blanket. Mother scurried to the bedside and stood protectively over my sister.

I followed Doctor Hadley from the room, where he gave me instructions for Claudia's care during the night. He hadn't given a prognosis or proclaimed that she would have a miraculous recovery. In fact, he hadn't given us any further information than Doctor Carrow had. Yet, despite his abrupt manner, a tiny seed of hope blossomed within me.

I expressed my appreciation to Mr. Fausett, and in the next breath they were both gone. Mr. Browning remained and asked if there was anything more he could do. He listened while I explained Doctor Hadley's instructions, then left with a promise to return the following day.

Doctor Hadley sent the thermometer that afternoon, as promised. I didn't let Cooper assume her station near Claudia that evening. Instead, I sat vigil and forced myself through a terrible novel with only the dim glow of a single candle.

Every recording was the same. Claudia's temperature hovered around thirty-nine degrees, and her heart rate was sixty-five to seventy beats per minute. As dawn yawned in the early hours, Cooper appeared and urged me to sleep. I didn't argue.

I slept soundly for the first time in more than a week and enjoyed a late lunch. Mitchell told me that Mr. Browning had called. His mother had as well, and she'd convinced Mother to join her for a short walk.

When I returned to Claudia's bedchamber, she was as I'd left her. But when I looked at Cooper's record, it did not make sense. "Are you certain this is correct?"

Cooper looked flustered and walked to the desk. "Yes, ma'am. I took her temperature and pulse every hour as you instructed me to." Her hands twisted in front of her while her eyes darted nervously across the sheet of numbers.

"Her pulse was one hundred eighty?" I asked in disbelief. "Are you sure?"

"Yes, ma'am. I . . . I did my best to count exact. Miss Claudia didn't want to hold still, but I told her I was followin' the doctor's orders. I even took it twice." Cooper shifted on her feet. "I was just trying to do right, Miss Ellsworth."

I set the paper back on the desk. "Thank you, Cooper. It doesn't make sense to me, but Doctor Hadley will be pleased that you followed his instructions." I tried to offer her a reassuring smile, but my effort fell flat. I wrapped my arms around my middle and stared at Claudia, longing to understand the meaning of the tabulations. They were numerals on a page, and I hoped they somehow revealed a clue that would lead to my sister leaving this disease behind and finally feeling whole.

Claudia woke again before dinner, and I witnessed firsthand what Cooper meant. Mother sat with me, and as soon as Claudia stirred, we forced some water down her throat. Her skin hung limp and pale from days of lethargy. She moaned and turned her head in protest, but there was no energy left for her to fight us.

As soon as she swallowed a few mouthfuls, I reached for her wrist to take her pulse. Her heartbeat sped, skipping and thrumming so fast I had to begin my counting twice. I turned the calculations over in my head and realized that her heart rate was more than two hundred beats per minute.

"I must summon Doctor Hadley," I told Mother. She stuttered something unintelligible as I quit the room and called for Mitchell.

Both Cooper and Mitchell met me in the entryway. "Cooper, please go help Mother with Claudia." Cooper rushed up the stairs, and I turned towards Mitchell. "Send immediately for Mr. Fausett and Doctor Hadley. They must come at once!"

"What is all the commotion about?" Father emerged from his study.

I grabbed his hands. "Claudia's heart is . . . it's . . . wild." It was impossible to describe what I had felt. "It's beating so fast. I don't know what to do." I squeezed his hands harder. "I've asked Mitchell to fetch Doctor Hadley and Mr. Fausett."

"I'll go," Father said, and he slipped free from my grasp at once. "Have my horse saddled straightaway." Mitchell nodded compliance and disappeared. "You're sure this doctor can help?" Father asked.

I told my father the truth. "I don't know what to do. I pray he does."

It was enough. Mitchell returned, and Father snatched his hat and gloves and was gone.

Doctor Hadley leaned closer to Claudia and pressed his fingers against her throat. "Hmm," he mused. "It seems her heart rate is steady now."

On my insistence, Mr. Fausett stood near the desk in Claudia's room. Father guffawed when I'd suggested he join us, but I stepped in front of my father and ushered Mr. Fausett inside. I needed another rational mind to help me decipher what the doctor would say. Mother still flitted about like an injured bird, and Father's face had blanched to match the milky clouds outside the window.

"It was well over two hundred, I assure you. I counted for ten seconds, and when it was so high, I counted again for the entire minute," I insisted. "Although it was difficult to count so quickly . . . it was beating so fast."

"Oh, I do not doubt you, Miss Ellsworth. I simply stated that her rhythms are steady now." Doctor Hadley clasped his chin and tapped his finger over his lips. "Hmm," he mused again.

Frustration boiled inside of me. "What does it mean?" I was desperate for answers that were not coming.

The doctor stared at Claudia a little longer. "Well, I have seen something similar before."

My heart hopped. "You have?" I took a step towards him.

"Yes. However, the patient did not have the persistent fever that has beset your sister. They experienced some fainting spells, a swooning of sorts, and a quickened heartbeat."

"What did you prescribe? How did you treat them?" I asked impatiently.

"I did nothing," the doctor said.

"Nothing!" Father roared from his perch in front of the window.

Doctor Hadley's eyebrows rose with my father's voice. Mother moved to Father's side and buried her head in his chest.

"Is there no cure for Miss Claudia's ailment?" Mr. Fausett asked. I reached across the space between us and dug my fingers into his arm, hoping and praying the doctor would be able to help my sister.

The doctor's lips twitched in a movement so slight, if I hadn't been staring at him, I would have missed it. With a stoic face, he answered, "Her condition is not fatal." I exhaled the breath I'd been holding. Doctor Hadley continued. "I cannot speak to the fever. I believe it should subside in another day or two, and the lack of nourishment has definitely taken a toll. But there are simple remedies for the unsteady rhythms of her heart."

Doctor Hadley sat in the chair that I had pulled up beside Claudia's bed. He crossed his legs as if he were cozying up for a good story. "Miss Claudia may or may not feel the irregular rhythms she is experiencing. However, when the flutterings get severe enough, she will begin to recognize their side effects. She may get lightheaded or dizzy. She may feel out of breath or suddenly fatigued. As she learns to recognize these patterns, she will be able to adjust her activity and with an hour or two of rest, her heart will return to its normal cadence, and she will be fine."

"What if it doesn't return, or what if she misses the signs?" I asked.

"What if you are wrong?" Father's voice filled the room.

Mr. Fausett looked down at my fingers still curled around his forearm. I quickly retracted my hand. He looked at me, straight into my eyes, leaving no doubt that he could read my fears.

Mr. Fausett turned back to my father and calmly said, "Hadley is a distinguished doctor. He is a recognized authority in his research and practice. We are very fortunate that he took the time to assess Miss Claudia. I'm sure we have no reason to doubt his diagnosis."

I looked between the men and my mother. "What about the fever? What is your opinion on that?" I asked the doctor, hoping that I did not disrespect Mr. Fausett by posing more questions. I knew Doctor Hadley was here because of him, and I did not wish to affront either gentleman.

"I believe your sister contracted a cold, and her heart is working extra hard to compensate." Doctor Hadley rose from his seat. "Tell Doctor Carrow no bloodletting will be needed. It's a vile practice."

Mr. Fausett stepped forward and shook Doctor Hadley's hand. "Thank you, Hadley."

Doctor Hadley nodded. "If the patient consents, I wish to visit again. Discussing her condition from her viewpoint would be fascinating. I would love to get some details for my research. It's a very curious case."

Mr. Fausett escorted Doctor Hadley out. I processed each new bit of information like a breath of clean air. Doctor Hadley predicted a full recovery. My dearest hope was manifest when three days later, Claudia's fever broke.

CHAPTER 17

Mr. Devlin Fausett

Miss Ellsworth summoned me to Ellsworth House, and I arrived with a pitiful handful of daisies I'd purchased for tuppence from a young street urchin. When Mitchell led me to the sitting room, Miss Ellsworth spied the flowers and smiled.

"Oh, Claudia will love these!" she said, taking them from my hands. "Thank you for thinking of her."

I didn't have the heart to tell her the flowers were meant for her, so I smiled and asked after her sister. With lightened eyes, Miss Ellsworth shared the happy news of Miss Claudia's improvement.

"She's still unable to leave her room, but her strength is improving every day," Miss Ellsworth said.

"I'm glad to hear it," I said and took a seat across from her.

"I wish there was some way to repay you." She quickly continued. "Doctor Hadley assured us all expenses were covered, but . . . ." Her voice drifted away.

I followed Miss Ellsworth's gaze to her hands in her lap. The fingers of one hand pressed deeply into the palm of the other. The nervous tick was endearing. When Miss Ellsworth looked at me again, I averted my eyes.

"You know I avoid the society pages," she said. "I detest gossip and do my best not to indulge in meaningless speculation." She looked quickly at my face then away again. "I would never press you to share, . . . but . . . I've heard things."

She began to blink rapidly, and I found myself in a strange conundrum. Despite my mild amusement at her bashful approach, I knew the question to follow and resisted shifting in my seat.

"Miss Ellsworth—" I began.

"Please," she cut me off, "let me finish."

"Very well," I said and forced myself to remain silent.

She moved her eyes to mine and held my gaze. She clenched her fists several times before she finally spoke. "I insist we pay for Claudia's care. 'Tis not right for you to assume the expenditure when you have debts of your own to settle." Her chin inched up half a notch, and she quickly continued. "I do not know particulars, nor do you need to share them, but if you truly lost Raven . . ." Her voice caught.

Miss Ellsworth's discomfiture caused an aching in my chest deeper than any remorse I'd previously felt. She understood the extent of my loss of Raven.

"I insist on compensating Doctor Hadley," she said.

I pressed my eyes closed and rubbed a hand over my forehead. When I opened them again, Miss Ellsworth jumped to her feet. "My father is very generous with my allowance. If it is a matter of pride, I can cover the cost myself, anonymously."

"As is evident from this conversation, my pride is no longer of consequence," I said.

Miss Ellsworth's hand flew to cover her mouth. "I'm so sorry, Mr. Fausett. I only meant . . ."

I held up a hand and stood. "Please, don't worry yourself. Any bruising to my ego is well-deserved and something I've entirely brought on myself."

Her hand fell from her face, and her head tilted to the side. "Is it that bad, then?" she asked on a whisper.

I let out a resigned chuckle. I'd not confided the desperation of my situation to anyone. Yet, for some reason I wanted to tell her. "It's bad," I said, but I could not hold her gaze long. I didn't deserve the sympathy I saw.

Miss Ellsworth walked to where I stood and placed her hand on my arm. "But we are friends, Mr. Fausett. When I heard news of Raven . . . well, I'm sure you've reprimanded yourself quite thoroughly. There's no way I can accept your contribution to Claudia, no matter how well-intentioned, if it means you will not have the ability to buy your horse back. You helped me. Let me help you."

My chest burned with emotion. The fiery sensation filtered through my limbs. Her kindness and empathy, given so freely, touched me to my core.

I nodded once, then again. "All right," I said.

"All right?" she repeated and smiled in relief.

"But Miss Ellsworth, you must know that Raven is gone. She sold at auction last week," I said.

"Then I'm too late." Her smile fell.

"For Raven, yes. But perhaps you can still help a friend who is broken," I said.

"I don't understand." Miss Ellsworth looked at me once again, and the steady measures of her breath brought reassurance.

"Raven is gone. Hadley's expenses are covered, and I'll soon settle the rest of my debt." Thankfully, Hadley had agreed to take my grandfather's watch in trade for Miss Claudia's care. Thus, only my debt to Higgins remained.

Miss Ellsworth clapped her hands in front of her. "What wonderful news," she said.

"Perhaps," I said.

"Perhaps?" she repeated.

I placed my hand on Miss Ellsworth's elbow and led her to the sofa. She sat, and I took a step back, clasping my hands behind my back. "Yes, everything will be settled. This time."

Understanding dawned, and Miss Ellsworth's exuberance melted away.

I paced back and forth in front of the sofa. "I didn't mean for it to go that far—I never do. And if I hadn't been drinking, I never would have wagered Raven. But somehow when I'm sitting there, I convince myself that the next hand will be different. I can't find the will to walk away."

The words sounded petty and juvenile, and humiliation for my weakness flooded anew. But I'd lived the reality too many times to deny the truth. There was a pull, an insatiable desire to win, to redeem myself. One big win would vindicate my actions, would prove the game was more than an addiction.

"You have the will, Mr. Fausett. I know you do," Miss Ellsworth said on a breath. "Now you must find a reason, a motivation strong enough to help you walk away."

I turned to her. "Will you be my reason? So that I will not disappoint you . . . Miss Ellsworth, my dear friend?" Desperation coated my words.

She raised her head and with the smile of an angel answered, "It would be my pleasure."

CHAPTER 18

Miss Nora Ellsworth

MY CONVERSATION WITH MR. FAUSETT did not happen as I'd expected, but I was pleased with the outcome. I wasn't above allowing him to help with Claudia's expenses, but knowing his sacrifice, I wanted to reciprocate.

Mr. Fausett accepted his hat and gloves from Mitchell as another knock sounded at the door. Mr. Fausett stepped aside, and Mitchell pulled the door wide to reveal Mr. Trenton standing on the opposite side.

He looked at Mr. Fausett and his brows peaked. Then he turned to me. "What a welcoming," he said with a smirk. "Or am I interrupting something?"

The last thing I wanted was a private audience with Mr. Trenton, so I ignored his comment. "My parents are not at home, sir. Perhaps you may call again later?"

Mr. Trenton stepped across the threshold. "'Tis fortunate I am not come to visit your parents." He began to pull off his gloves while his eyes made a sweeping inspection of the entryway. "I only came to inquire after Cousin Claudia's health."

"She has been tended well," I said and dared a glance at Mr. Fausett. "Thankfully her fever has finally broken."

"Tsk, tsk, you should have come to me. I have been conducting business out of town, but had you sent word, I would have come immediately. As I'm sure you're aware, I have many connections in London. I could have made certain my dear cousin was tended by only the best of doctors. It really is a wonder you did not consult me in this matter."

Consult him? I realized Mr. Trenton awaited my reply. Or more likely, he awaited my profuse apology for not deferring to his expertise in caring for Claudia. "Forgive me, Mr. Trenton, but Claudia is under my father's care. If you have suggestions or recommendations, you will have to meet with him."

Mr. Trenton's eyebrows dropped and his eyes lost some of their joviality. "Of course," he said, curtly. "Fausett," he said as he looked over Mr. Fausett's person. "You are looking surprisingly well." Mr. Fausett did not falter, so Mr. Trenton pushed again. "I heard word that after your recent exploits, you returned to Essex," Mr. Trenton said.

"Obviously, you were misinformed," Mr. Fausett said.

"Hmm." Mr. Trenton pressed his lips together. "Yes, I suppose travel becomes difficult when one has neither the funds nor a horse."

Mr. Fausett clenched his jaw then turned back to me. "Miss Ellsworth, we shall leave you to tend your sister. Please extend my wishes for her continued recovery."

"Thank you," I said.

Mr. Fausett motioned Mr. Trenton towards the door. "After you," he said.

With a straight face, Mitchell opened the door wide, and only once both gentlemen departed did he allow his lips to twitch in merriment at Mr. Fausett's dismissal of the odious Mr. Trenton.

Perched on the side of Claudia's bed, I pulled a brush through her long golden hair.

"I really wish you would let Cooper wash it," Claudia complained. "There is no reason I can't be properly dressed when Doctor Hadley calls."

"There are plenty of reasons, the foremost being that he insists you stay in bed for another day. You could very well set *his* heart in a frenzy if he sees you up and trilling about." I laid the brush to the side and sectioned off Claudia's hair to weave it into a braid.

"I don't think I'm quite up to trilling," she said in a teasing voice.

"No, you aren't. But I am glad that your breakfast sat well."

Claudia giggled.

"What's that for?" I asked.

"You should have seen Cooper's face when I asked for a third helping of eggs. You'd have thought I asked for her firstborn." Claudia laughed again.

I tied off the end of her braid, and she leaned forward while I straightened her pillows. After I finished she leaned back and settled against the headboard. "I'm ready to see him now," Claudia said, and I opened the door to allow Doctor Hadley entrance.

Doctor Hadley scribbled notes viciously during his discussion with Claudia. He asked her to detail everything she felt, from each breath she took to the tiniest tingle in her toes. As the doctor had guessed, Claudia could not yet recognize when the rhythms of her heart sped. But Doctor Hadley gave her some descriptions he had obtained from other patients and told her what to do if the palpitations should occur.

As he finished his inquiries, he turned to me and said, "When your sister has revived, I suggest a trip to the country. I believe Fausett mentioned you have a home in Northamptonshire? She will need peace and quiet and rest for several weeks before she is returned to her full faculties."

"We can go home. To Ellsworth Meadows," I said on a breath. But then I remembered my promise to Mr. Fausett; how could I support him from such a distance?

"Miss Claudia," Doctor Hadley said. "Would you be willing to continue a correspondence with me? Following your case would be ideal research."

"Of course," Claudia agreed. I walked Doctor Hadley out, and, after extending my profound gratitude, I bid him farewell.

While I was anxious to return to Ellsworth Meadows, I worried about Mr. Fausett. I'd promised to be his friend, to support him in his weakness. If I returned to Ellsworth Meadows, I wouldn't be much use to the man. I'd asked Mitchell to discreetly ask around Town to discover the extent of Mr. Fausett's debts. I'd also asked him to locate Raven's new owner.

Mitchell's inquiries uncovered a much more dismal picture than I'd expected. Mr. Fausett's finances were indeed dire. After his recent losses, his father had threatened to cut him off. Raven's buyer remained a mystery.

I wrote to Cousin Leah, telling her of Claudia's illness and included a line about seeing Mr. Fausett on a few occasions. I hinted at rumors in Town but intentionally left only a vague connection to Mr. Fausett. Our friendship was too new and fragile to fracture his trust, but I wondered if Mr. and Mrs. Brumley were aware of Mr. Fausett's situation.

The following week, Claudia sat in the chair beside her bed while Cooper dressed her hair and I packed her trunk. "No, not the blue one; put the brown one on the bottom," she said and pointed a finger at the multiple piles spread across the bed.

I huffed my obvious frustration but did as she asked.

"I'm glad you are feeling better, dear sister," I said on a low growl.

As she demanded and ordered Cooper and me around, the mantra remained in the forefront of my mind. I much preferred Claudia's over-ambition to the lethargic being she had been just three weeks prior.

Claudia had yet to take dinner with the family, but she had walked with me daily in the garden for the past week. Each day her fortitude increased and her pallor diminished.

The day before our departure, I had still not heard back from Cousin Leah. I assumed she and Mr. Brumley were unaware of Mr. Fausett's situation, and I would not be the one to inform them.

The Browning family joined us for dinner. Since Claudia's episode, Mother's insistence on a match with Mr. Jonathon Browning had faded. I knew her resolve would return, but it was nice to visit with the man without pretense.

"You look much improved, Miss Claudia," Mr. Jonathon Browning said with a smile. "But please, do not overexert yourself. Doctor Hadley was very specific in his instructions. You must ease back into your activities. A relapse is to be avoided at all costs," he finished.

"Every day I feel abundantly better," Claudia said. "Nora is taking good care of me."

"Splendid. I have an announcement I would like to make," the younger Mr. Browning said, and my stomach tangled. "Father has agreed to host a house party at Lily Glen to mark the end of the Season." He turned to address Father. "We considered an earlier date, but we wanted to give Miss Claudia adequate time to recuperate. We would be honored if your family would join us."

"I'm confident there will still be good hunting to be had. The pleasure would be ours," Father said and raised his glass in a toast.

Claudia fairly bounced in her seat. "What fun!" she said and clapped her hands. "Who else is to come?" she asked.

"Actually," Mr. Jonathon Browning said, "Doctor Hadley has agreed to join us. He is a distinguished physician in his field, and I thought it best to include him in case . . . well, it can't hurt to have a doctor included in the party."

"And you must invite Mr. Fausett as well." The words were out of my mouth before I realized my impertinence.

Claudia clapped her hands together again. "Oh yes! Do invite Mr. Fausett."

While Claudia smiled with enthusiasm, everyone else stared, and I turned red. "He is friends with Doctor Hadley, after all," I added in an effort to justify my request.

Mr. Jonathon Browning cleared his throat. "Of course. Fausett is welcome to join us."

"Although in his present state, I'm not sure that's the best idea," the elder Mr. Browning said.

"True," my father agreed.

Anger flared. Why did my passive Father suddenly have an opinion on the matter? Who was he to judge Mr. Fausett and his circumstances?

"I understand your hesitation, Father, but please remember that Mr. Fausett is responsible for procuring Doctor Hadley. We owe him a great deal," I said.

With narrowed eyes, Father responded, "Perhaps we do, but the Brownings owe him nothing."

The younger Mr. Browning raised his hand. "I see no harm in the idea. Mr. Fausett is welcome to join us."

I hoped Mr. Fausett would be agreeable to the notion. He could be relieved of worry over his finances, as all of his meals would be provided. The retreat would also provide an escape to the country, away from the gaming hells. I nodded my head and smiled at Mr. Jonathon Browning. His willingness to acknowledge the importance of my request and act accordingly was noble, a characteristic I considered vital in my future spouse. Indeed, the house party would be a welcome diversion.

CHAPTER 19

Mr. Devlin Fausett

I READ THE MISSIVE THREE times and still doubted the accuracy of the invitation. The idea that Mr. Browning would include me among the guests at Lily Glen, his family home in Yorkshire, was preposterous. Certainly Miss Ellsworth was behind the solicitation, which was both touching and humbling. Nonetheless, I smiled as I considered which of her many charms she used to coax her intended to agree to the idea.

Not many years ago, the invitation to a house party would have been a welcome reprieve. Life was simpler then. I would flirt, ride, and enjoy the food. Now everything had turned complicated. My future, my finances, my horrid habits—all seemed unmanageable, and I felt that I wandered about in a thick fog. Around Miss Ellsworth a light appeared through the clouds. Her reassurance, her confidence in me, allowed me to take a small step forward. It began with the invitation to sing and continued with the promise of a friend. Many a lonely night I'd been tempted to wander to the tables, convincing myself I could watch and not participate. But I recognized the lie for what it was, and I could not lie to Miss Ellsworth. The gift of her trust was too great.

My monthly stipend would be available on the morrow. I could give notice and quit my rooms in two weeks. Mother had written again and begged me to come visit. Perhaps I could pay Brumley a visit, then travel to Lily Glen, and afterwards arrange a visit with my mother.

I paced in my room, counting off the days and calculating the expenses in my mind. Then I wrote to Browning and accepted his invitation. Mother would not mind the delay if it meant I was associating with eligible young ladies. But she could not know that the one lady who caught my eye was the one I could not have.

CHAPTER 20

Miss Nora Ellsworth

RETURNING TO ELLSWORTH MEADOWS PROVED to be a balm for Claudia. After the oppressive skies of London, the call of birdsong and cloud-filled skies were a warm welcome home for the both of us. Father was well, but life was uncertain. The only thing I knew for sure was that one day, Mr. Trenton would be the master of Ellsworth Meadows, and that knowledge broke my heart.

After taking tea, Claudia took a turn with me through the rose garden. It was infinitely larger than our accommodations in Town, and after fifteen minutes of exercise, she was ready to rest. I returned my sister to the house and then continued my walk.

Our home was not lavish. But it was comfortable. Undeniably, Mr. Trenton was correct in his assessment that there were repairs that needed doing. Father did make repairs, only they were completed on his terms and usually not in a very timely manner. In a strange way, I understood his procrastination. How could one find joy in perfecting something that would soon be taken? So I was quite surprised when upon our return, Father immediately set to work. He hired one of his tenants to patch a leak in the roof. The servants were set to making repairs to the outer wall, and Father even insisted on a new coat of paint. I was intrigued by his sudden zeal to set things right.

One evening, after a quiet dinner with the family, we sat together in the drawing room. Mother worked on a sampler, and Claudia stared absently at the low-burning fire. Father sat in his favorite chair near the window, perusing his paper.

"I've been surprised at the improvements you have made to Ellsworth Meadows. Did you find you missed home so very much, Father?" He turned from the window, and despite the darkened corner of the room, I saw his face heighten in color.

"We are expecting visitors soon, Nora. We must make a good impression," Mother answered for him.

And suddenly, Father's motivation was clear. He would not bend to Mr. Trenton's selfish complaints. But to impress the Brownings, he would exceed expectations.

"Of course," I said softly. I turned towards my mother. "But you do realize their impending visit does not secure an agreement?"

"Oh, Nora!" Mother said. She rolled her eyes and pinched her lips in a condescending rebuke. "Your betrothal is imminent." She rose and walked to where I sat. Taking both of my hands in hers she said, "Don't worry, my dear. It may not happen on this visit. But I assure you, you will soon be engaged."

"Mother," I chided and pulled my hands from hers.

How she could be so bold as to claim knowledge of Mr. Browning's intentions was beyond me. It had been only a handful of weeks since I had been properly introduced to the man, and Mother itched to prepare my wedding trousseau.

Mother's faith in her plotting was both infuriating and amusing. To her the arrangement made perfect sense. The judiciousness of her theory proved sound enough to send her running to order a wedding gown. What Mother failed to take into consideration were the feelings of both Mr. Browning and myself. Convenience was not enough to secure happiness, as society had proven time and again. A very few number of visits together was hardly enough to consider us inseparable. Mr. Browning *was* pleasant and handsome and polite . . .

"Nora, are you certain Mr. Fausett will join us at Lily Glen?" my sister asked.

I shook myself from my reverie and turned towards Claudia, who sat tucked into a corner of the sofa. "I'm not certain," I admitted, and Claudia's smile faltered.

"Well, I hope he comes, since you and Mr. Browning will occupy each other's company. Perhaps I may play a piano duet with him," Claudia said.

"Come now," Mother said. "Enough talk of Mr. Fausett. We have plans to make."

"Plans?" I repeated.

"Yes," Mother said and leveled a stare at me. "The Brownings will arrive in three days and stay the night on their way to Yorkshire. We must make the most of their visit."

No wonder Father had immediately set to work on Ellsworth Meadows. He did not speak of it as Mother did, but he too obviously believed the arrangement with the Brownings to be secure.

"Shall we play cards, or maybe you can sing with Claudia?" Mother tapped her fingers together. "Or maybe we should host a dinner party and invite the neighbors; the Bastians might come, and the Hudsons."

"After spending the day in the carriage, the Brownings will not want to indulge our frivolous neighbors," Father said.

"Marianne Hudson is a flirt," Claudia added. "I don't want to spend the evening watching her flutter her lashes at Mr. Browning."

"Quite right." Mother rubbed her hands together as she considered her options. "We shall have a quiet night at home. But perhaps you can sing a little something, Nora."

"Perhaps," I agreed, hoping the subject would be forgotten.

Tuesday afternoon, the Brownings' carriage rolled to a stop in front of Ellsworth Meadows. The moment the step was lowered, Mrs. Browning swept across the drive to embrace Mother. From the way the women doted on each other, one would think this was their initial reunion after being separated for seventeen years. The elder Mr. Browning alighted and walked with the matrons into the house.

Mr. Jonathon Browning followed behind the carriage, astride a beautiful black horse that I recognized the moment I saw it. Mr. Browning dismounted with a happy smile, but I could not return the gesture. He handed the reins to the groom, and I stared after Raven as she was led away.

"How are the lovely Ellsworth sisters?" Mr. Browning asked as he offered a bow.

My face must have mirrored the emptiness I felt, because when Mr. Browning turned to me his eyes filled with apprehension. There was no avoiding the topic. "Why do you have Raven?" I asked, with an ache in my chest.

Mr. Browning looked to where the animal disappeared into the stable then turned back to me. "My horse?" he asked.

Fury swept through me. "Your horse!" I inhaled deeply and dug my fingernails into the palms of my hands.

Claudia looked between us, her lips closed.

"Raven's rightful owner is Mr. Fausett," I said.

Mr. Browning stood tall. His jaw clenched, and he removed his hat. "Mr. Fausett forfeited that right when he wagered the animal with a measly hand of cards. Raven belongs to me now."

My lungs constricted, and tears pricked my eyes. I knew Mr. Browning was not at fault for Mr. Fausett's error, but I had hoped Mr. Fausett might be reunited with his horse.

I bit back the retort on my tongue, curtsied quickly, and walked away as fast as I could manage. Once I rounded the house, I huffed and growled, stomping and pacing until my feet ached. Life could be so unfair.

Determined to clear my mind, I retrieved a set of shears and a basket from the gardener's shed. One gloved hand held the shears, and the wide basket balanced on my other arm. I snipped and pruned around the already-tidy garden.

"Miss Ellsworth." Mr. Jonathon Browning stood near.

I hung my head, embarrassed by my earlier behavior.

Mr. Browning walked closer. "I'm sorry for your friend's loss, but I did not come by the horse nefariously. Raven was actually a gift from my father."

I sighed and placed the shears in the basket. "I owe you an apology, sir. I should not have lashed out the way I did."

A smile spread wide across his face. "All is forgiven," he said. The light touched on his dark hair and tanned skin, and he looked extremely handsome in that moment. He stepped to the side and motioned to the path in front of him. "Would you care to walk back to the house with me?"

"Thank you, but I should complete my task," I said and raised the basket to show him the product of my efforts.

"Then perhaps I may keep you company?" he asked.

I watched him and attempted to decipher his purpose. "Wouldn't you rather rest after your journey?"

"I've been astride my horse for too long. It's rather refreshing to stretch my legs in your lovely garden," Mr. Browning said.

"Thank you. Ellsworth Meadows is not the most lavish of homes, but I believe it to be the perfect blend of comfort and nature," I said.

Mr. Browning visited with me for another thirty minutes. Once the wind began to pull at my skirts and rattle the trees, we decided to return to the house. The evening was filled with pleasant conversation. Mr. Browning entertained us with stories from his time in India. Claudia played a few pieces, and I agreed to sing one song.

Mother fairly gloated, assuming her machinations complete. I, however, remained unconvinced. I didn't want to analyze my heart or its spectrum of feelings. Mr. Browning was kind, attentive, and engaging, but I was not yet in love with him. And the concern that plagued me most was whether I ever could be.

The morning of the Brownings' departure, I wandered through the house pondering my feelings on the matter and happened upon Father and the elder Mr. Browning talking in the library. I turned unnoticed from the doorway and heard my father say, "What does your son have against my daughter?"

I slipped around the corner and pressed myself against the wall.

Mr. Browning answered, "Nothing, I assure you. He was quite taken with her."

"Then why the delay?"

"My man of business said it should only take a week or two. It should all be sorted soon."

"What is there to sort?" Father's voice growled in agitation. "We had an agreement. Either you honor it, or you do not."

For all of the joy Mother found in her reunion with Mrs. Browning, it seemed Father was not so enthusiastic with the woman's husband. Father was not a confrontational man, but the tone of his voice sent my heart racing. What was this agreement he referenced? Voices echoed down the hallway. I pulled away from the wall and pressed my hands to my stomach, willing my heartbeat to slow, and made my way to the drawing room.

The servants loaded the carriage, and Mother dabbed her eyes as she bid farewell to her dear friend. Mr. Browning climbed into the equipage with a grunt, and Father turned back towards the house. The coach lurched forward, and Mother released a strangled sob.

The younger Mr. Browning mounted Raven, and, with reins in hand, he offered a resigned smile. "'Til we meet again." He tipped his head and turned down the lane.

Mother waved her handkerchief after the disappearing carriage, and I walked forward. I laced my arm through Claudia's and squinted as I watched the Brownings disappear.

"Lily Glen promises to be a grand time indeed," Claudia said with a wistful sigh.

I squeezed her arm and hoped she was right.

CHAPTER 21

Mr. Devlin Fausett

Now that Miss Leah was officially Mrs. Brumley, she had become a permanent fixture at Riverton Park. Upon my arrival, the new Mrs. Brumley maintained that the title better fit her mother-in-law, and she insisted I call her Leah. The change took a little adjustment, but I acquiesced to her request and asked her to use my Christian name as well. Leah made Brumley happy, and that was welcome indeed.

I'd been a guest at Riverton Park for three days before Brumley's bride accosted me in the library. "Tell me again, Devlin, why did you not ride Raven?" she asked.

I placed the book I'd been reading in my lap. When Leah asked before, I'd made a shoddy excuse about leaving her in someone else's care. A partial truth but also a lie. She had been nothing but kind. So I resigned myself to the whole truth. "I unwisely used my horse as collateral in a bet."

Her eyes widened, and she placed a hand over her mouth. "You lost her?" Leah said and lowered herself into a nearby chair. "No wonder . . ."

I cocked my head and watched her. "No wonder what?" I asked.

Leah blinked and straightened in her seat. "Cousin Nora wrote to me."

At the mention of Miss Ellsworth, my pulse quickened.

Leah's hand shot forward. "Please, don't think she gossiped. In fact, she was very vague. But she did mention seeing you a few times and asked if Charles kept a regular correspondence with you." Leah's eyes turned sad. "She knows, doesn't she?"

I nodded.

"And is there more, Devlin? Of course, you don't need to tell me, but Charles and I are very fond of you. I hope if you're ever in need, you will consider us friends."

"And not let your deuced pride get in the way," Brumley said, stepping through the doorway.

"You're one to speak about pride," I said and settled back in my chair.

"And who knocked some sense into me?" Brumley asked, sitting beside his wife and pulling her hand into his.

"The last year has been rough," I said solemnly. "But I've mended my ways."

Brumley narrowed his eyes. Obviously he wanted further explanation, though he did not push me for it.

"Suffice it to say, my greatest loss was Raven. But I can assure you all my debts are soon to be settled, and your hospitality is greatly appreciated."

Leah smiled. "I'm glad to hear it. You know you are welcome anytime."

"Well . . ." Brumley hedged.

"Charles," Leah said and pulled on his hand. "I happen to know that my Cousin Nora is very fond of you as well. She speaks of you quite extensively in her letters."

"Is that so?" I asked casually, suppressing a grin. "And what did she write to you about her mother's chosen suitor, Mr. Browning?"

Leah's eyes danced, and she smiled wide. "Very little."

CHAPTER 22

Miss Nora Ellsworth

THE NEXT MORNING, COOPER INFORMED me that my sister was not feeling well. It seemed she felt the palpitations return to her heart, and only through Cooper's insistence did she remain in bed.

"I doubt she'll stay put all day, miss, but I did convince her to eat breakfast in her room," Cooper said.

"Thank you for telling me." I quickly dressed, and Cooper pinned up my hair. Then I went to Claudia.

She gave me a wan smile, but her coloring was rosy. For that I was grateful. "I understand you're feeling heart palpitations."

Claudia rolled her eyes. "I knew Cooper would tattle."

I smiled and sat beside Claudia on the bed. "She's only looking out for you."

Claudia pushed herself up on the pillows. "I agreed to breakfast in my room, but then I am determined to come downstairs."

My protest died on my lips. Claudia's expression confirmed her determination. "Very well. As long as you are sure," I said.

"I'm quite sure," Claudia said and lifted her chin a bit higher. "Come join me. There's plenty of food on the tray for us to share." Claudia shifted over on the bed, and we shared a filling breakfast.

Seeing Claudia's appetite, I no longer doubted her determination to get out of bed. I checked her pulse and found the rhythms were strong and steady.

"See," she said brightly, "it was just a passing trifle." She handed me her glass, and I returned it to the tray. "Please call Cooper for me, and I will see you downstairs shortly."

I walked to the bell pull and rang for Cooper. "I believe I'll go for a walk in the garden. The color will last only a week or two more, so I must enjoy it while I can."

When I returned from my walk, I found Claudia pacing near the front door. "Are you waiting for someone?" I asked.

"Oh, hello, Nora," Claudia said and shook her head. Her eyes flitted to the door before she brought her hands together in front of her. "The post should arrive any minute."

I could not hide my surprise. "The post?"

"Well, yes. I hoped there might be a letter from Doctor Hadley, if you must know," Claudia said. "I wrote to him to clarify some of the techniques he explained to calm my heart. In case I have any further trouble. Mother and Mrs. Hudson are in the drawing room. I'll come join you in a moment." Claudia offered a convincing smile.

I nodded mutely and wandered down the hall to say hello to our neighbor. Mrs. Hudson and Mother included me in their conversation, and Mrs. Hudson brazenly suggested that I would soon be spoken for. Mother cut me off in my attempt to correct the woman's assumption and let the charade continue.

Claudia arrived with letters in hand. She kept one for herself and asked Mitchell to deliver the remaining letters to Father. After Mrs. Hudson took her leave, Father joined us for luncheon. He read one of his letters then passed the missive to my mother. When they exchanged a worried glance, my curiosity piqued.

"What is it?" I asked.

Mother clutched a fist to her bosom, and my quest for information suddenly seemed frightening.

"We will be having company soon," Father said.

"Who? Who is coming?" Claudia asked.

"Mr. Trenton," Father revealed.

"Oh." Claudia's voice deflated.

"He is on his way through Northamptonshire—" Father began.

"And will no doubt come to chastise us. Remind us of our duty to our name, to his inheritance," Mother said haughtily, tossing the letter onto the table. "Always sticking his nose in things. That man should learn his place."

"Why can't you turn him away?" I asked. "The estate is entailed to him, but there is no reason he should assume ownership while you are alive and well."

"No, Nora. He cannot assume ownership yet, but he is fully aware of the details of the entailment. Mr. Trenton is not coming to check up on me . . ." Father shook his head and stared at his lap. His voice lowered. "No, no." His eyes met mine again. "He is coming to check on you, Nora."

"Me?" I asked.

"Mr. Ellsworth, no!" Mother said and shot to her feet. "You promised." She ran over and grabbed Father by the arm. Claudia and I sat in a shocked stupor as Mother tried to shake her will into my father. "You will ruin everything!" Mother wailed and finally collapsed onto Father's shoulder in tears.

Father stood and wrapped his arm around her trembling frame and held her close until her cries became muffled against his suit coat. "I'm sorry, my dear," he said softly into her hair. "But it's time we told the girls."

Father insisted Mother lie down and asked Claudia and me to meet him in the library. I sat on the sofa in front of the fireplace and stared at the portrait of my grandfather hanging over the mantel. Claudia restlessly paced behind me as if she thought she could outrun whatever news Father meant to share. I knew something dreadful was coming. I could only hope that if I sat still long enough, the storm would pass by without pulling me in among its turbulent winds.

"Claudia, come sit by Nora," Father instructed as he entered the room. Claudia joined me but fidgeted relentlessly. Father stood before us, his hands clasped behind his back. He looked at each of us in turn and then, after inhaling deeply, he raised his chin and said, "You are both aware that there is an entailment on the estate. However, I do not believe you are privy to the details of that contract."

I looked at Claudia, and we shook our heads.

"Your mother and I married young. I was not yet one and twenty, and your mother was only seventeen. Nora, you were born only a year later. After Claudia was carried to term, your mother experienced several unsuccessful pregnancies."

These were all details I knew and could not fathom how they related to the entail on Ellsworth Meadows.

"My father, your grandfather, watched your mother suffer through these losses, and eventually the doctor said she would not conceive again. My father could not accept that the estate would be entailed away to a distant relation, and he suggested we break the entailment."

My fingers latched on to Claudia's arm. She jumped at my gesture, and her eyes grew as wide as mine.

Father dropped his hands and turned to look at the picture above the mantel. He continued. "To alter the entailment, three living generations must agree on the new arrangement. My grandfather was still alive, but his health was rapidly deteriorating. My father wanted to act quickly to ensure it could be done. That way, you girls and your mother could inherit the property and never be left wanting."

"So you did it?" I asked on a whisper. "You altered the contract? We can remain at Ellsworth Meadows? It is not entailed?"

Father turned around and offered a defeated shrug. "That was our intent. However, my grandfather was a proud man and did not believe a woman capable of running the estate. He wanted assurance that the estate would be well looked after and required that the contract include a restriction." Father's dark eyes pierced mine. "In order for Ellsworth Meadows to pass to you . . . you must be married.

"Your husband would manage affairs, and the estate would remain in the family through the maternal line." Father sighed deeply and offered the obvious conclusion. "If you don't marry, then upon my death, the entail will fall to Mr. Trenton."

Claudia straightened in her seat. "Does it matter which one of us marries? Does it have to be Nora?" A small frown marred Claudia's pretty face.

Father's lips twisted, and he didn't answer for a moment. He looked between us then finally said, "Yes, the contract stipulates it must be the eldest child. It is similar to the rules of inheritance. The other condition is that you wed a gentleman."

The news fell upon me like droplets of freezing rain. At first the revelation was welcome—the entail was altered. The women of my family would be safe and protected. We could remain at Ellsworth Meadows. Cared for and nurtured—until it was revealed that my grandfather insisted on the condition of marriage. Men could be so arrogant, thinking only their sex had the ability to manage an estate. Now, everything rested on me. My mother's insistence on the arrangements with Mr. Browning became abundantly clear, and Father's *arrangements* with the elder Mr. Browning made sense as well.

"I heard you and Mr. Browning talking in the library." I forced my fisted hands to hold still in my lap. "Are you forcing his son to marry me?"

Claudia gasped and raised her fingers over her lips.

Father paraded in front of the mantel again. "I suppose it might look that way. You realize your mother and Mrs. Browning have been planning your nuptials since your infancy."

"That's not what I asked. Please, Father, tell me the truth."

"We do have an agreement of sorts—"

I jumped to my feet. "A marriage contract?" I stomped my foot.

"Calm down, Nora. It's nothing like that. In fact, it's nothing you need to concern yourself with."

"If it has to do with my future, my husband, and this ridiculous stipulation, then I have every right to concern myself with it," I said. "As you've just explained, retaining Ellsworth Meadows depends on it."

Father rubbed a hand over his face. "There is not a contract binding Browning to ask for your hand."

"Then why were you so upset with his father?"

"He convinced me to join him on an investment that went badly. You must have heard us discussing business." Father moved back to the mantel. "A union between you and Browning would benefit both of our families, but regardless, the decision lies entirely with Jonathon."

"And me," I said.

"Yes." Father's eyes narrowed. "But I hope you will consider the conditions I have explained. Your mother, your sister, and the estate all depend upon you now."

I walked to the open window. My mind spun with the new knowledge, confusion and details all mixing around in an ominous tempest. Mr. Browning and I did not have a marriage contract, and I had no way to determine his intent. And what if, upon further acquaintance, I did not want to become his wife? Our mothers could plot away to their heart's desire, but if Mr. Browning did not want to marry me, their conniving could not force his hand. I always knew I needed to marry, but I hoped to have a choice in the matter. Now everything felt forced and heavy. The revelation that I could save Ellsworth Meadows flipped my viewpoint. My need to marry had shifted from necessary to urgent. Not only did Mother and Claudia's futures depend on it, my happiness did as well.

Father insisted that Mr. Trenton not be turned away and that we treat him with civility. But that did not mean I had to mince words. I had avoided the man when he called on Father earlier in the day, but he had extracted an invitation to dinner. Father led most of the conversation, until the main course was served.

Mr. Trenton dug into his pork with gusto and flashed me a pompous smile. I spoke before my brain had processed the words. "So, Mr. Trenton, you have come to inquire after possible suitors?" I fixed my eyes on him and awaited an answer.

The man smiled wickedly and casually dabbed the corner of his mouth before answering. "Nonsense. I have come to inquire after your sister's health. When I last called in London, she had not yet recovered from that dreadful illness. I only wondered if her recovery was complete," he said.

"An inquiry that could be satisfied with a simple letter," I said with a false smile.

"But it is so much better to confirm for oneself." Mr. Trenton winked and took another bite.

"How long will you be in Rigdon?" Mother asked.

"I'm afraid I have business in Town I must attend to. I will be on my way tomorrow." Mr. Trenton motioned for the servant to dish him another helping of potatoes.

"Pity," I said.

After dinner, Mr. Trenton approached me as I sorted through various sheet music at the piano. "I understand you will be attending a house party at Lily Glen. No doubt, you hope to secure your arrangement with Mr. Browning."

My hands stilled.

"Dear Cousin," Mr. Trenton continued. "There's no reason your dowry needs to be settled on a pauper or a gambler simply to secure Ellsworth Meadows." My eyes shot to his, the lines on his face pulled into a nefarious grin. "You could marry me. You can satisfy the entail and be married to a gentleman you deserve. Your mother and your sister would always have a place with us."

"Mr. Trenton, are you proposing?" I asked on a whisper.

He placed his sweaty hand over mine. "We would make a handsome couple."

"Surely, you know I cannot accept you." I slipped my hand from his.

His face darkened. "You'll choose a man whose father ruined him or a man who prefers his cards to you, when I could give you everything you want? I could make you happy."

My mind churned in confusion. The references he made to Mr. Browning were unfounded, and his accusations of Mr. Fausett hit too close to their mark. Yet there was one truth I knew. "You, Mr. Trenton, will not make me happy."

He snorted and pulled back. "You are making a mistake, Cousin."

No matter the trepidation I felt, I knew the larger mistake would be accepting his hand.

Claudia scurried between her room and mine, comparing dresses and slippers, bonnets and eveningwear. She held a pale-blue day dress to her shoulders and lifted her foot to see if her dark-blue slippers would adequately match. I laughed as she hopped around on one foot and finally collapsed onto the floor.

"I think it will work," she said and jumped to her feet.

"Have you felt any more palpitations in your heart?" I asked, and her head jerked up suddenly.

Her eyes fixed on mine, and after a long moment she answered, "My health remains unchanged."

Such a curious response. I walked to the window and watched the billowing clouds transform into a multitude of shapes. "Are you still corresponding with Doctor Hadley?"

"I write weekly as he requested."

I inhaled deeply and spun around. "Claudia, I want to talk to you about the entail." She turned her eyes back to the dress in her hands. "I wish the responsibility to save Ellsworth Meadows did not fall to me."

She looked up through her lashes and asked, "Are you very much in love with Mr. Browning?"

"In love?" I laughed. "Oh, Claudia. What fairy tale have you concocted in your pretty little head?"

"Oh, never mind, Nora!" she snapped and turned away again.

I sighed and walked to where she stood, setting the dress aside and taking her hands in mine. She turned her head away from me and stared at the floor. "Claudia? I'm sorry. Please look at me."

She slowly turned her head, and my heart ached at the hurt she tried to hide.

I squeezed her hands. "Claudia, I did not mean to offend you, but you must know that I cannot declare myself in love with Mr. Browning. I've only seen the man half a dozen times." I smiled and squeezed her hands again. Her shoulders relaxed, and her stubbornness began to slip.

"You must have some idea if you like him," she said.

"I do like him. But it's a very large step to conclude that I am hopelessly in love just because I like the man," I said. "Besides, it seems highly unlikely that he's formed more of an opinion than I have. We simply need to spend more time together. The house party provides an ideal opportunity to do that."

"So you don't believe in love at first sight." Claudia pulled her hands away and turned her back to me. I was at a loss. Why was she so anxious for me to declare my undying devotion for Mr. Browning? Unless . . .

"Claudia, do you feel that you are very much in love?" Maybe she was certain of her feelings for someone while I had just declared romantic notions were an impossible fairy tale. No wonder she was upset with me.

Claudia glanced over her shoulder, and I caught a glimpse of color in her cheeks.

"Ah," I smiled. "See, there it is. You are in love."

"No, Nora, it's not . . . I mean, I can't be certain. Like you said, it's been such a short time." She stumbled around her words, while the crimson in her cheeks deepened.

"Oh, Claudia! Why did you not say so? You are beautiful and bold and idealistic, and if you are in love, then I'm happy for you." I stepped forward and pulled her into a tight embrace. I squeezed hard, hoping to convey my joy, but when I stepped back, Claudia was no longer glowing rosy and red. Instead, her face was slack and she looked as if she were about to cry. "Claudia?" I said and shook her by the shoulders. "Claudia, what's wrong?"

The color continued to fade from her cheeks, and she slowly shook her head. In barely a whisper she said, "He doesn't feel the same. I think his heart is elsewhere."

My brows pulled together in confusion. "What do you mean?" I asked. Then I watched as Claudia's eyes rolled back in her head and her body crumpled to the floor.

The apothecary stayed with Claudia over the course of the next day, and her pulse raced too many times for anyone to be convinced all was well. After Claudia's initial collapse, Father wrote directly to Doctor Hadley and sent the letter express. Doctor Hadley's reply was quite a shock. Claudia's assurance that her heart was well was far from the truth. Doctor Hadley had been informed of her continual episodes over the past weeks from Claudia herself. She had been forthright in her letters with him but purposefully neglected to mention her relapse to us. Father was furious and decreed that any future correspondence would be channeled through him.

Mother held a constant vigil at Claudia's side, and I dared not breach our previous topic of conversation again. I wondered if the conversation itself was the reason for Claudia's speeding heart. Could a simple discussion have caused her sudden swoon? Then I thought upon those final moments before her faint. She'd asked about my feelings for Mr. Browning and wondered about being in love. The hopeful innocence in her eyes as we talked about romance was not scripted, and I was certain she would confess her sentiments about some local lad she'd met in Rigdon. Instead, her eyes grew large right before she crumpled to the floor. Were the flutterings of her heart merely from her ailment, or was she harboring tender feelings for someone she should not? The topic would have to be addressed with great precaution. I wanted answers, but I also wanted my sister to be well.

Over the following days, Mother and I received the vicar's wife and Mrs. Hudson, in addition to several other families of our acquaintance.

Doctor Hadley surprised us all when he arrived on our doorstep the next week. "I detest leaving the care of my patients to others," he said to Father as

Mitchell took his things. "I'm sorry it took me so long to arrive. I planned to head to Lily Glen at the end of the month but decided to leave directly and had to set things in order." After holding my gaze, he nodded once then asked, "May I see Miss Claudia?"

"Certainly," Father said and led the procession to her room. Father's acceptance of the doctor had grown to respect. While he was unhappy to learn of Claudia's frequent episodes, Father did not consider Doctor Hadley to be at fault for the secrets she'd kept.

Claudia was no longer confined to her bed, but still she remained in her room. She sat at her writing desk, her hair in a long plait over her shoulder. Her eyes lit when Doctor Hadley entered the room. "Doctor Hadley! What brings you to Ellsworth Meadows?" The cheeriness in her voice had been absent for a long time.

"My patient, of course." The doctor took Claudia's hand and gave a quick bow. Holding on to her fingers, Doctor Hadley turned her wrist over and felt for her pulse. "Hmm," he mused. "Your rhythms appear to be steady now."

"Yes, I am feeling quite well. I'm sorry to have troubled you to come all this way," Claudia said, and then her eyes fluttered downward and her cheeks tinged pink.

"'Tis no trouble at all." Doctor Hadley smiled. He then grabbed the chair that Mother had used to sit near Claudia's bed. He moved it near the writing desk and sat down. "If you are feeling well enough, I would like to ask you a few questions."

"Certainly," Claudia said, and she repositioned herself to better face the man.

Father, Mother, and I stood and watched the interaction without a word. While it was strange to see Doctor Hadley sitting so casually across from Claudia, it was even more shocking to see Claudia so content. Her posture was relaxed, and she talked easily with him, recounting how she had felt over the past few days.

"In your letters, you described subtle changes—" Doctor Hadley began, and then Claudia leaned forward and raised her hand to cut him off.

"Those were just slight flutterings. Nothing too concerning, which is why I did not tell my family about them." She cast a furtive glance at Father and lowered her hand back to her lap.

Doctor Hadley's eyes skirted our way as well. He looked back at my sister. "But something more happened this time. Can you please share the circumstances surrounding your latest episode?"

Claudia blinked rapidly then settled her eyes on her twisting hands in her lap. "Well . . . I . . ." she hedged.

"Nora," Father finally spoke. "You were there."

I nodded and watched Claudia, uncertain how I should proceed.

"Speak up!" Mother chided.

"We were simply talking here in her room. I asked Claudia a question—"

"And suddenly my heartbeat was frantic and I collapsed," Claudia finished quickly. She shrugged it all off with a delicate smile.

Doctor Hadley narrowed his eyes and asked, "What were you discussing?"

Claudia answered, "I can hardly remember—dresses or some such. I'm sure it was nothing of consequence."

Doctor Hadley looked to me, and I nodded affirmation. "It was all very sudden," I added.

The doctor asked a few more questions and then retired to his room. Mother had insisted he stay at Ellsworth Meadows, rather than in Rigdon. Claudia did not appear that evening, but the following day she dressed for dinner.

"Do you know much about Lily Glen, Doctor Hadley?" Claudia asked while dessert was being served.

"I've heard it's a beautiful estate," he responded.

"Indeed," Mother agreed. "As I recall, the estate sits on a premier parcel of land in North Yorkshire," she said on a sigh. "I can't wait to see it again."

"Are you feeling well enough for your visit?" Doctor Hadley asked Claudia.

"I've used the techniques you suggested whenever I think I may be having an episode. They work well." She lowered her lashes. "So well, in fact, that I was able to hide my condition from my family." Claudia had the decency to look ashamed.

Her acknowledgment of her duplicity settled into the silence. Claudia knew better than to deceive us, yet she had. Her hands fell to her lap, and she did not look up again. Tears began to pool in her downcast eyes, and I wondered at the reason for her silence. Why would she not tell us?

Doctor Hadley studied my sister. He fidgeted in his chair until he suddenly raised his glass. "To Lily Glen."

CHAPTER 23

Mr. Devlin Fausett

Despite my refusal, Brumley insisted I take one of his mounts to Lily Glen.

"Stop being so stubborn," Brumley said. "I've no doubt you'll want a bruising ride on occasion. Besides, I'm not offering Mouse." We walked through the stall, and he pointed out options.

Arguing with Brumley was pointless, so I settled on a chestnut filly named Juno.

Leah pulled her shawl tighter around her shoulders. "Give Cousin Nora my love," she called as I mounted the horse.

"Better yet, give her your love," Brumley said with a vibrant chuckle.

I shook my head and turned north, hopeful that the two-day journey would help strengthen my resolve. Brumley and his wife made a persuasive argument, listing multiple reasons I should pursue Miss Ellsworth. But my scars ran deep, and while I recognized my feelings for Miss Ellsworth were beyond friendship, I didn't want to offer her a shell of a man, especially if she could find happiness with Mr. Browning.

I scheduled my arrival two days after the other guests. Lily Glen was an impressive estate. The south-facing entrance consisted of towering walls crested with gabled roofs. The multitude of windows formed a sort of geometric artwork on the façade, and the grounds appeared to be meticulously maintained.

A stable boy led Juno to the paddock, and Mrs. Browning welcomed me graciously. Brumley had paid to send my trunks ahead, so the housekeeper, Mrs. Norse, guided me to the prepared room.

"Dinner will be served in one hour," the woman said and then excused herself.

Regardless of his sentiments regarding my stay, Browning proved himself a cordial host. My accommodations were comfortable, far more so than my rooms in London, and the west-facing window offered a view of the stables. I watched the boy brush Juno down before he turned her out for the evening.

The water in the pitcher had turned cold, but I poured it into the wash bin and scrubbed the dust from my face. Leah had assured me of Miss Ellsworth's regard, but I knew the competition would not let her go without a fight. I pulled out my newest jacket and recognized the odds were not favorable. Nevertheless, I hoped gambling for Miss Ellsworth's affection would prove well worth the risk.

CHAPTER 24

Miss Nora Ellsworth

UPON OUR ARRIVAL TWO DAYS prior, we had an amiable reunion with the Brownings. Mrs. Browning could not wait a half hour before she declared that Mr. Browning had agreed to host a ball.

Mother clapped, her elation evident from her wide smile. "Oh, my dear Mrs. Browning! It shall be the talk of Yorkshire!"

Mother's jubilation seemed to be the general consensus. Even Mr. Jonathon Browning seemed pleased with the notion. He found me watching him and inclined his head with a noticeable twitch of his lips. The ball would be an ideal opportunity for him to declare himself. No wonder Mother was so enthralled with the idea. She'd probably planted the notion in Mrs. Browning's head to begin with.

Mrs. Browning turned to Mother. "Once Mr. Browning agreed to the event, I sent the invitations immediately."

"When is the ball to take place?" Mother asked.

"Friday next," Mrs. Browning said and placed a hand on Mother's arm. "I shall require your assistance, as we have so much to plan."

"Of course," Mother agreed and the two wandered off, leaving Mrs. Norse to show us to our rooms.

I took in all the details of the estate. The long, slender windows symmetrically spread throughout the wide expanse of the house gave the air of meticulous precision. The décor reflected the same exactness. Every piece of furniture and the various framed portraits were placed in perfect order, nothing askew. I wondered if the semblance was too ideal. What was life without a little disarray? Yet nothing about Lily Glen felt uncomfortable.

I knew Claudia should have told me about her dizzy spells, but I should have been a better sister and taken notice myself. So although the estate was large, I insisted we share a room.

Mrs. Browning planned nothing of extravagance the first few days, allowing Claudia to rest while we acquainted ourselves with the property. On the journey, Mother had explained that Lily Glen got its name due to the abundance of wild lilies on the estate. The gardens had been tamed near the house, but off the paved paths, the wild lilies grew in an assortment of colors and varieties. Mother also described a pond, hidden from view by a series of grassy knolls, which she claimed were impossible to navigate without an escort. I hoped to find this secret oasis and see for myself if it contained the hundreds of lily pads and colorful flowers Mother asserted, but by the third day I was no closer to discovering its location. I'd explored the gardens and wandered around the perimeter of the house but had not ventured far into the untamed hills.

When Mr. Browning and I returned from an afternoon stroll, his house-keeper informed him that Mr. Fausett had arrived. My heart jumped with the happy news. I'd missed my friend's smile.

I wore my light-green silk gown to dinner, and Cooper finished her ministrations as I pulled on my gloves. "Claudia, would you like explore a few more rooms before dinner is officially announced?"

"Go on ahead," she said and waved a hand at me. "I want Cooper to try a new twist I saw in *La Belle Assemblée*."

I'd already explored the west wing and the first floor. On the ground floor, I was familiar with the drawing room, the breakfast room, and the dining room, but there remained ample rooms to discover.

I wandered past the dining room and turned down a long hallway. The first door on the right opened into another parlor, where the furnishings were covered with sheets and the room smelled of dust. The Brownings had been away for so long it was impossible to air the house entirely. I closed the door and heard music coming from farther down the hallway.

The melody grew louder, and I found myself drawn to the sound. I peeked around the door to find a well-equipped music room. Mr. Fausett sat at the pianoforte lulling the keys into a heavenly tune. Behind Mr. Fausett, a door led out to the garden. A beautiful patterned mosaic of various shapes and hues of glass was inlaid in the door. In the last rays of sunshine, the colors glowed with a muted ambiance, and I could imagine the beautiful kaleidoscope they would create when in the direct path of the sun. I determined to return to admire the window on a bright afternoon.

While I regarded the intricate door, Mr. Fausett stopped playing. My attention returned to him, and he watched me intently.

Ignoring the flutterings in my stomach, I dropped into a curtsy. "Good evening, Mr. Fausett."

He stood slowly, stepped away from the piano, and bowed with precision. "And to you, Miss Ellsworth."

Mr. Fausett was very handsome in his dark-gray tailored jacket and high boots. I noticed how his jacket matched the shade of his eyes. And then I noticed his eyes remained on me, and I enjoyed the pulsing vibration I felt in the connection. We stood silent as the powerful pull increased between us.

"We should go to dinner," I said, pointing awkwardly towards the door.

Mr. Fausett grinned and, without a word, offered his arm.

"What was the song you were playing?" I asked as I slipped my arm through his.

Mr. Fausett led me down the long hallway. "It's an arrangement I made from a lullaby my mother used to sing."

"It was lovely," I said.

We neared the drawing room where the other guests gathered, and Mr. Fausett slowed. "Actually, you're quite lovely this evening," Mr. Fausett said. "Forgive me for not saying so earlier. Your appearance caught me off guard."

We'd stopped completely. Voices drifted from nearby, but my concentration was entirely on the man before me. His expression was soft yet solid at the same time, and I searched his eyes for some explanation of the tumult coursing through me.

Claudia laughed nearby, and I jumped back as she and Doctor Hadley walked into view. "Mr. Fausett." Claudia greeted him with happy eyes. "I'm so glad you've arrived. How was your journey?"

Mr. Fausett bowed to Claudia and greeted his friend. "Everything went well, thank you. I see you've recovered beautifully," Mr. Fausett said.

The happy confusion I felt iced over as I watched a pretty blush creep through Claudia's cheeks.

"Shall we join the others?" I asked hastily.

We entered the room, where Mrs. Browning introduced Mr. and Mrs. Thorne and their niece, Miss Wells, who had also arrived earlier in the day. She was a pretty creature, with soft brown hair and large doe-like eyes. Mr. Fausett stood near the wall and was barely spared a glance before dinner was announced. I entered on Mr. Jonathon Browning's arm and sat near him for the remainder of the meal. Mr. Fausett sat at the far end of the table, near Claudia, Miss Wells, and Doctor Hadley. I found it hard to concentrate on Mr. Browning's conversation as Claudia's laugh frequently filled the room.

After supper I feigned polite conversation and waited for the gentlemen to join us. When they finally arrived, Mr. Fausett was noticeably absent. Before I could ask about his whereabouts, Claudia did.

"I asked Jonathon about his new mount and Fausett excused himself," Father said and waved a dismissive hand. "He's probably worn out from a long day of traveling."

Mr. Jonathon Browning had the decency to offer an apologetic shrug. Mr. Fausett's loss was his doing, but the sting of his humiliation pricked something inside of me. I tried to put on a stoic face and reciprocate the false flattery and meaningless prattle oozing from Miss Wells's mouth. But after half an hour, I could stand it no more and despite Mother's threatening glare, I excused myself for the evening.

Mother surprised me the following morning when she appeared in the breakfast room. She fluttered her eyelashes as Mr. Jonathon Browning dished her a plate and then held her chair. Mother made quite a spectacle on her own, but then moments later Mrs. Browning bustled in with even more jubilance.

"I've thought of the perfect décor for the ball!" Mrs. Browning said.

Mother's eyes lit, and the women immediately left the breakfast room, ignoring their food and the rest of the party.

Mr. Browning watched his mother's exit with a smile. "May I offer you ladies a tour of the house today?" he asked.

"I'm sure my aunt would like to join us as well," Miss Wells said.

We agreed to meet in the foyer at ten thirty, and I decided to wander the gardens until the appointed time. I inhaled the welcome breeze, grateful to be outside, and pondered on the duty that fell to me. Breaking the entail had become my responsibility, and the obligation overwhelmed me.

My feet shuffled along the garden path until I sensed someone watching me. Beyond the garden wall, Mr. Fausett sat astride a light-brown horse marked with a bright-white blaze.

He touched his hand to his hat. "Miss Ellsworth," he said in greeting. "Are you enjoying the gardens?"

"Not really," I said.

The horse skittered beneath him, and he adjusted the reins between his hands.

"What is her name?" I asked, walking towards him.

"Juno," Mr. Fausett said. "Brumley loaned her to me. The new Mrs. Brumley asked me to pass on her greeting and well wishes."

"So they are settled at Riverton Park?" I asked.

Mr. Fausett dismounted and walked the horse near enough that I could reach out and pet Juno's muzzle.

"They are indeed settled and very content," Mr. Fausett said with a smile.

"I envy their situation, to be able to marry for love," I said. Then I shook my head. "I apologize, Mr. Fausett; I find I don't filter my thoughts when I'm around you."

He laughed lightly. "Society would have us compose ourselves at all times. However, I think we all need a confidant with whom we can speak freely."

"Is that what you are? My confidant?" I asked.

Mr. Fausett tensed and drew in a long breath. "I've been grateful for your friendship. In fact, I'm rather indebted to you. Your trust has been a guiding factor through a difficult time. If you'd like to consider me your confidant, I'd be honored." His gray eyes focused on me, charged with an emotion I couldn't decipher. "The truth is, Miss Ellsworth, I'm at your disposal. I'll be whatever you'd like me to be."

Sincerity lingered in his words that were both kind and serious. My pulse quickened, and my mind cycled through numerous responses. I considered him a friend. I wanted to help him, support him, but he was switching things around, making me feel friendship and inklings of something more. I didn't know the answer. What did I want Mr. Fausett to be?

I opened my mouth, hoping to diffuse the seriousness that had settled between us with some witty banter. But the thoughts formulating in my mind never reached my mouth.

"There you are," Claudia called, and I spun around to see her walking towards us. "We are gathered for our tour. Oh, hello, Mr. Fausett," she said and curtsied prettily. "Would you care to join us?" she asked.

"No, thank you." He bowed his head. "Ladies," he said, and in one fluid movement he mounted Juno and kicked her into a canter.

Claudia slipped my arm through hers, and we walked back towards the house. She leaned close. "Mr. Fausett looks especially fine this morning, wouldn't you say?" Claudia giggled. "Now, let's go see all that you are to be mistress of."

She squeezed my arm and skipped through the door. I knew I should feel the same enthusiasm, but for all the beauty that was Lily Glen, I felt little joy in the idea of becoming Mrs. Browning.

CHAPTER 25

Mr. Devlin Fausett

I'D COME TO LILY GLEN to get away from the temptations in Town. But I also accepted the invitation so I could be in the company of Miss Ellsworth. Brumley encouraged me to pursue more, but my priority had become Miss Ellsworth's happiness. If she entertained feelings for Mr. Jonathon Browning and wanted to pursue a match with him, I would not stand in the way. Yet, my observations yielded no indication of her feelings. The woman was impossible to read, and the jumble of sentiments roiling through my chest did not help matters.

The next day when I returned from exploring the nearby town of Lundsworth, the guests were enjoying luncheon in the warm afternoon sun. Mrs. Ellsworth chastised me for throwing off the numbers in croquet, as she'd been required to step in and partner with Miss Wells. Following my profuse apology, she waved me away.

"Mrs. Browning has planned an evening of music," Miss Claudia said. "She's invited some of her neighbors to perform, and, of course, Nora will sing. Mrs. Browning asked me to play, and I agreed, but I convinced her to have you play as well, Mr. Fausett."

I glanced at Mr. Jonathon Browning. His face remained impassive.

Miss Claudia continued. "Perhaps we could even play a duet?"

I wanted to excuse myself, but I'd just promised Mrs. Ellsworth I'd be more accommodating, and a duet with Miss Claudia was the perfect solution. "A duet sounds delightful," I said.

After eating and visiting a while longer, I escorted Miss Claudia to the music room, where selected a tune with a romping melody. After bumbling through a few times, we matched our rhythms, and the light, playful song actually sounded quite good.

Supper was served early so the entertainment could begin, and Miss Wells opened the evening with an extravagant selection from a well-known Italian opera. Her natural vibrato filled the room, and while she carried most of the song quite well, her voice pinched the final note in an ear-wrenching squeal.

I applauded from my seat in the corner of the room, grateful to move on to something more tranquil. Mrs. Lansing, one of the Brownings' neighbors, played a lovely sonata, and then Miss Claudia and I performed our duet. I fumbled the very first note, and although I recovered nicely, Miss Claudia snickered through the remainder of the piece. Her joviality was contagious, and when we hit the last chord in unison, we both laughed freely.

Doctor Hadley and Mrs. Lansing appreciated the humor, but the rest of the company sat stoic, offering only resigned applause. I assumed Miss Ellsworth would share in the levity, but when our eyes met, she looked away and asked Mrs. Browning if she was next to perform.

Miss Claudia and I relinquished our seats at the piano, and Mrs. Ellsworth came forward to accompany her daughter. I coveted any opportunity to hear Miss Ellsworth sing, but it became immediately clear that something was wrong. The words were clear, the volume ideal, but her voice lacked passion. I wondered where her heart wandered, for it was not in the music. Miss Ellsworth concluded and curtsied, but I could tell by the set of her face that the melody did not fill her. I clapped with extra enthusiasm, hoping to buoy her spirit through the steady thrumming of my hands.

"Beautiful, Miss Ellsworth," Mr. Jonathon Browning said.

Miss Claudia jumped to her feet. "Come, Mr. Fausett, let's play our duet again."

"Claudia!" Miss Ellsworth said, and immediately her eyes scanned the room. She stepped towards her sister. "You've already showcased your talents this evening. I'm sure Mr. Fausett is not inclined to play again."

Miss Claudia smiled and reached forward to grab Miss Ellsworth's hand. "But your song was so depressing. We can't end the evening on such a dour note."

Miss Ellsworth's mouth dropped open. She pulled her hand from her sister's, and her fingers curled into fists. "Claudia," she said with a pinched smile. "You are overstepping your bounds."

In an instant, Miss Claudia's face flushed crimson, and I stepped forward before she could unleash the storm brewing in her eyes. "I'm grateful we could laugh at my expense, but I think I need a bit more practice before we try again," I said. "I think I shall retire."

Miss Claudia finally turned her hardened gaze from her sister. "Then perhaps you will escort me to the east wing, Mr. Fausett," she said. I offered my arm, and when we stepped through the doorway, Miss Claudia spoke evenly so her words would not be missed. "My sister seems to believe she is already mistress here."

CHAPTER 26

Miss Nora Ellsworth

MY INSIDES TUMBLED. NEVER HAD my sister been so forceful with me. What had caused her sudden outburst? What had I done to deserve her patronization? I wasn't always patient with her over-jubilant perceptions, but I tried to be. I'd sat next to her bedside for weeks until she recovered from her illness, and for that she owed me. I straightened my shoulders, made my excuses, and marched after my sister.

Once Cooper had been dismissed for the evening, Claudia climbed quickly into bed and turned to face the wall. Determined to discuss her earlier outburst, I lifted the candle from the dressing table and carried it to the nightstand.

"Claudia?" I called to her back. "We need to talk." Silence hung heavy in the room. "Please?"

Right when I thought she would not respond, Claudia offered a heavy sigh. "Very well."

"Could you please turn around? It's much easier to speak to your face than your back," I said.

This time her breath came out as an indignant huff, but she flipped onto her opposite side and propped herself up on her elbow. "Better?" she asked sarcastically.

"Infinitely," I said and smiled at her show of defiance. I sat on the bed, facing her. "What upset you?"

"You did," she said.

"I gathered that much. Are you going to tell me why?"

Claudia pushed her lips together and moved them around as she contemplated. "You're always determined to outdo me." Her gaze quickly dropped to her blankets. "You have no claim on Mr. Fausett," she said.

It was as if a cold bucket of water had been dumped over my head. "What are you talking about?"

Claudia pushed herself up and leaned against the headboard. "You manipulate all of his time. Mr. Fausett is thoughtful enough to acknowledge me, which is more than I can say for your Mr. Browning. Yet, when Mr. Fausett is around, you engage all of his attention. He'll share things in your presence that he would never tell me otherwise, even when I pose the exact same question. It's hardly fair, Nora. You're promised to Mr. Browning and should not pursue Mr. Fausett. I get one of them. You have to share." She crossed her arms and tucked her chin to her chest with a pretty little pout. Claudia's dramatics had never before crossed over to jealousy.

"Don't be ridiculous. I'm not pursuing Mr. Fausett," I said.

Claudia leveled me with a stare, and her hands dropped to her lap. "Isn't he at Lily Glen at your request?"

With a scoff, my voice rose. "Mr. Fausett is a friend whom I thought could use a holiday and so mentioned he might be included in the invitation. I only wish to survive Mother's presumptions and Father's interference and fulfill my duty to break the entail. All while ensuring that you have the chance to attend the ball and don't end up back in the sickroom."

Claudia rolled her eyes. "Doctor Hadley's advice is sound. I now know how to calm my heart once it begins its rapid pulse. But that is not the issue here."

"Then what is the issue, Claudia? I'm trying to understand the riddle coming from your mouth. Do you think I should not try to marry? It's my duty to break the entail! To save Ellsworth Meadows! What would you have me do?"

She pulled her legs from the blankets and scooted forward until her knees touched mine. Kneeling before me, she grabbed both of my hands. I resisted shaking free of her hold. I had a feeling that she was about to share something very important. "Nora, I want you to be happy, but I want to be happy too."

"Then go. Go find your happiness," I said.

Suddenly, Claudia fiercely squeezed my fingers. My eyes froze on hers, my emotions teetering on a ledge, waiting for Claudia to share the secret that flashed behind her innocent eyes. Her face fell, and she looked as if she might cry. "Nora, I want to be happy. But I'm afraid that if I pursue my happiness, then you will lose yours."

"What do you mean?" I shook her arms and willed her to finish her thought.

Her face paled, and I turned her hand over to check her pulse. When I lay my fingers across her wrist, she abruptly pulled her hand from mine and huffed. Claudia looked into my eyes. "Do you remember what we were discussing when I last fainted? I asked you about being in love." Claudia's eyes widened, and she shook her head. "I'm in love with Mr. Fausett, and I think you are too."

For the second time in a matter of hours, Claudia rendered me speechless. My chest tightened, my breathing halted, and I pressed my eyes closed. In the blackness behind my eyelids, I tried to collect my thoughts, but there was no understanding to be found. I opened my eyes and stood up from the bed.

"Nora?" Claudia called from behind me. "Don't hate me."

I spun around. "Hate?" I repeated and tried to shake the daze from my mind. "I could never hate you. I'm only . . . confused," I said softly.

"I didn't mean for it to happen." Claudia scrambled across the bed and came to stand next to me. "It's just that he's been so kind. He always asks after my health, he brought me flowers, he ensures I'm well, and when he looks at me I can't help but feel . . . happy." Claudia touched my arm. "Please don't be angry."

Mr. Fausett's kindness affected me in much the same way, and I could not decipher my jumbled feelings. "I'm not angry, Claudia. I just need some time." I grabbed the candle from the nightstand and a blanket from the foot of the bed, and then I walked out of the room.

My confusion was not anger, for I truly was not vexed with my sister. I was vexed with myself. Because of my selfishness, Claudia had been neglected. Mother was too busy to notice, and with her interference and assumptions about Mr. Browning, she may have not really cared. The worst part was that Mr. Fausett witnessed all of it. He had swooped in numerous times to save Claudia. He made sure she was acknowledged at the ball, procured Doctor Hadley, regularly followed up to ask after her progress, and included her in conversation when she would otherwise have been ignored. All the times I should have interfered, he watched me do nothing and instead rescued Claudia himself. No wonder she considered herself in love with her knight in shining armor.

My stomach roiled and turned. I harbored guilt for my neglect of my sister, but none of the particulars bothered me. The unease churning through me boiled down to one question. Did Mr. Fausett return her regard?

I wandered around the house, recalling every interaction between Claudia and Mr. Fausett in an effort to determine if he harbored feelings for my sister.

It was too late and my mind was too muddled to settle on anything with certainty. My wanderings led me to the music room. The moonshine through the colorful glass door could not compare to the vibrant reflection of the sun, but the pattern cast across the floor was beautiful in an entirely different way. I fell into a chair and watched the muted colors crawl across the space until my eyes fell closed and I slept.

I woke in the early hours of dawn and immediately recalled my deliberation from the night before. I could not dismiss my sister's sentiments, because I had seen Mr. Fausett's administrations. But neither could I dismiss the flutterings in my heart that erupted with a simple touch or glance from that same man. The fault could not be his. Mr. Fausett was kind and attentive, he made me feel special, and therein lay the problem. He made Claudia feel special, too.

I determined to think on it while searching for the lily pond. I quietly slipped into my room and gathered my boots and my coat without disturbing Claudia. I could change out of my nightdress later. The morning was young, and I would find the pond and return before anyone could question my absence.

I crested one ridge, then another, taking time at the top of each one to assess my surroundings and note the direction of the house. The sunrays began to chase the dew from the grass, and once the warmth reached the lilies they opened wide.

Atop the summit of the fourth knoll, I noticed a glint of reflection farther east. I'd found it! I surveyed my surroundings once again, determined not to get lost, and memorized the path I'd taken from the house. Then looking towards the pond, I found a large cluster of rocks that would serve as a landmark to my location. I would walk to the rocks, and from there it would be an easy distance to the pond. I skipped with anticipation down the hill. Slowing at the bottom to catch my breath, I shook my head at my childlike levity. If only life's difficulties could be solved with a hearty run or an energetic skip.

My stomach rumbled, and I realized my quick trip had become something akin to a quest. From the small hollow between the hills, I could not find the rocks I was destined for, so I began to climb again.

Finally, after trudging up and down three more crests, I found the rocky tor. I walked around the outcropping, hoping for a glimpse of the pond, a reflection, another landmark to guide me—there was nothing. Nothing but more hills, more grass, and more lilies. I frantically circled the rocks one more time, searching for a view of the house, but only wild, grassy mounds could be seen.

I was lost.

Clenching my fists, I growled at my stupidity. Why could I not have asked to be shown the pond? My stubborn need for independence had led to my predicament. I was not afraid—simply hungry, embarrassed, and still flustered over my conversation with Claudia.

One option presented itself. I slowly walked around the rocks again, found a suitable route, and began to climb. My feet slipped only once, and triumph washed over me as I climbed atop the highest point. I stood like a king surveying his land. Unfortunately, my view did not reveal the location of the house, but I did see the pond, nestled in a basin nearby. The slopes of the hills rolled gently down and appeared to melt beneath the water.

"Naturally," I mumbled aloud and then wondered if I should continue to the pond or attempt to return to the house. Hunger rumbled through my stomach, and I realized that if I continued my journey to the pond, I still did not know how to return to the estate. I circled the top of the rock again, desperate to recognize something familiar that might lead me back to Lily Glen.

The sound of horse hooves pulled my attention to the horizon. I shielded my eyes and beckoned the rider. I shouted, but when he took no notice of my cries, I became frantic and flapped both hands above my head. The rider turned and moved his mount in my direction. He rode with confidence, his posture precise. It was Mr. Fausett.

CHAPTER 27

Mr. Devlin Fausett

"Miss Ellsworth?" I called and pulled Juno to a stop. "Might I ask how you came to be up there?" My lips pinched into a smile, and I tilted my head, awaiting her answer.

Miss Ellsworth's golden hair radiated in the sunlight. She crossed her arms, and despite the distance between us, I noticed the blush filling her cheeks. "I got lost and hoped the added elevation might help me find my way back."

"I see," I said, swinging off my horse and evaluating the tor of rocks. "And might there be some way I can help you get down?"

Miss Ellsworth huffed. "I can manage. If you would please turn around." She twirled her finger.

I couldn't suppress the smile that pulled on my lips. "Of course." I turned my back and stroked Juno's muzzle. "I, uh . . . noticed you were in your nightdress. Are you certain you can navigate your descent?"

Miss Ellsworth stood roughly thirty feet above the ground. A fall could prove fatal, and my chest constricted with the realization.

Suddenly, she squealed. I tossed Juno's reins over her mane and spun towards the rocks. "Miss Ellsworth?"

"I . . . I'm fine," she answered, but the quiver in her voice said otherwise.

After confirming she was stable, I again averted my eyes. "Do you really expect me to stand here when I could be of assistance?"

I heard her shift, and she squealed again.

"Blast," I said. "I insist you let me help before you fall and dash your beautiful head to pieces."

"There's no reason to raise your voice, Mr. Fausett," she said with a tremble in her words.

I sighed and walked to the side where her fingers gripped the rock. "It's much easier to scramble up than down," I said.

She yelped again.

"I'm going to talk you down, all right?" I didn't wait for a response. "Move your right foot a little lower left."

Miss Ellsworth's calves began to shake, and she pressed herself into the rock. As she searched for the place I indicated, I shifted my stance to better assess the situation.

"I don't doubt your instruction, sir, but I fully doubt my ability to carry it out," she said on a shaky breath. She shifted again and called down, "I can't do it."

"Come, Miss Ellsworth, you've faced a London ballroom and utilized your fan to bloody a man's nose. You can most certainly handle this."

"But I . . . I can't see the next step," she said.

"It's just below you, to the left," I repeated.

She remained frozen in place.

"Nora. Listen to me," I said. "I swear, I will lead you to safety."

Miss Ellsworth took a deep breath, and something shifted. She nodded her head slightly. "What do you want me to do?"

CHAPTER 28

Miss Nora Ellsworth

MR. FAUSETT NO LONGER CALLED up or shouted instructions. The timbre of his voice vibrated smooth and rich, like the cascading embrace of a warm fire.

"Do you trust me?" he asked.

I lowered my chin and saw him intently watching me. When our eyes connected, I nodded.

"Good," he said with a smile. "Now, slide your right foot along the rock, diagonally. There is another foothold, just below."

I inhaled then let out a shaky breath and willed my leg to relax and move to the place Mr. Fausett indicated. Right when I questioned his instruction, my toes came to rest on a sturdy ledge.

"There's a good girl," he said. "Now lower your right hand to the crack by your shoulder." I easily found the crevice he referred to and complied.

Mr. Fausett stood far enough back that he could not see my indecency, but hanging with my arms and legs splayed across the rock face, I felt exposed and vulnerable. Thankfully, he said nothing about my appearance and continued to offer instruction from below. Slowly, I descended. The ground drew closer, and my nerves began to abate.

Mr. Fausett's voice remained calm. "You're doing brilliantly, Miss Ellsworth. Only about ten feet more. Now bring your right foot straight down."

As irrational as it was, I missed him calling me Nora. Perhaps it made me feel less foolish for landing in this predicament. I moved my right foot as Mr. Fausett directed and immediately spied another foothold. I stretched my left foot to the place, rested my toes, and applied my weight just as Mr. Fausett yelled for me to stop.

It was too late. The ledge crumbled away beneath my boot. My fingers could not compensate for the weight of my body, and I fell backwards with a scream.

The wind emptied from my lungs and my arms flailed wildly, searching for something solid but finding only air. My muscles tensed, waiting for the impact of the ground, but in the next moment I found myself in the very sturdy arms of a very handsome man.

My heart beat riotously, and it felt as though my lungs had forgotten how to function. As I struggled to find a breath, my eyes drifted to Mr. Fausett's face.

He chuckled and, after a long silent moment, said, "That was a much quicker way to get it done, I suppose."

"I apologize," I said then scrambled from his arms, pulled my nightdress straight, and stood awkwardly, fiddling with the end of my braid. Mr. Fausett quickly looked me over, and his lips pulled to one side. "I was up early this morning," I offered, hoping to explain my state of undress.

"There's never a dull moment with you," Mr. Fausett said.

My eyes found his again, and I immediately understood Claudia's attraction to the man. He was a specimen of perfection, on the outside at least. He'd trusted in me enough to confide the demons that haunted him. What would happen if I extended the same trust and told him the pressure I felt at breaking the entail?

"Thank you for your assistance," I said.

"Oh, I assure you, Miss Ellsworth, the pleasure was all mine," he said with a grin.

"Mr. Fausett, are you flirting with me?" I asked around the fluttering in my chest.

"Maybe a little." He grinned again and walked to where Juno stood nibbling the grass. He pulled her reins from her neck and held them in one hand. "Would you like me to stop?" he asked.

"I . . . I don't know." My voice dropped away.

Mr. Fausett stood holding his horse, his eyes fixed solely on me. I considered the thrumming in my heart and thought that perhaps Claudia was correct. Perhaps I did feel some *tendresse* for Mr. Fausett, but I was not naïve enough to think he felt the same towards me. He considered us friends. But as we stood there assessing one another, the pull between us seemed too strong to deny. Surely this was more than friendship.

"Are you enjoying your time at Lily Glen?" he asked.

I blinked and cleared my mind. "Um, yes . . ." I managed to answer around the lump in my throat.

A sad smile played at the corners of his mouth. "Your mother must be pleased," he said.

"Excuse me?" I asked.

"Forgive me, I don't mean to pry. But your mother's made it clear that she intends for you to make a match with Browning." Mr. Fausett shrugged. "I thought perhaps my flirting would bother you, as I'm not your intended."

I sucked in a quick breath. Mother had spoken openly about Mr. Browning. I suppose I should have realized Mr. Fausett understood her implications. "A match with Mr. Browning would make my mother happy, yes."

"And your father?"

"I don't assume he cares much. As long as I marry," I said.

Mr. Fausett's eyes narrowed. "Surely he wants you to be happy."

I heaved another sigh. "Do you mind if we sit?" I turned and walked to a nearby boulder. I took a seat, and Mr. Fausett stood beside me. "Are you prepared to be shocked?" I asked with a light laugh.

Mr. Fausett's grip on the reins tightened.

"Oh, it's not all that, I assure you," I said. "You see, Father only wants me to marry to break the entail on Ellsworth Meadows."

"Break the entail?" Mr. Fausett asked. "Can it be done?"

I explained to him the legalities and the additional provisions Grandfather had contrived. "Mother always insisted on the match, but once Father told me the details of the entail, I better understood why. I can save our home."

"So she would resign you to an arranged marriage?" Mr. Fausett asked.

"I believe her intentions were pure, and she believed Mr. Browning and I might fall in love," I confessed.

"Have you?" he asked softly.

My pulse quickened once again.

"Forgive me," he said. "It's not my place."

"Mr. Fausett." I stood and pressed my fingers into my fisted hands. "I don't mind sharing. We've conversed on a number of subjects, and . . . I find it easy to talk with you. It helps me sort everything out." I looked at the sky then back into his charcoal eyes. "Mr. Browning is kind enough, and we get on well. But I do not wish to be married to a man simply because he feels it is his duty."

Mr. Fausett's eyes narrowed. "You do realize the irony of that statement? Members of society often marry for no other reason than duty. It is the exact situation you've found yourself in."

"Yes, others do. But that's not what I want." Somehow, standing in the open country, wrapped only in my coat and nightdress, I felt bold. Perhaps my blood was still racing from my fall, or maybe I was done playing games, but once the words came to my mind, I asked them without hesitation. "What do you want, sir?"

He took a step closer, and my breathing stopped altogether. He lifted my chin until I looked into his eyes. Then, almost reverently, he said, "Marrying you should not be considered a duty, Miss Ellsworth, but rather a great honor."

If Mr. Browning asked for my hand, I would be obliged to accept the offer. However, I desperately, selfishly, wanted more. "I've been given a duty to fulfill. I don't have the luxury of love," I said on a whisper.

"Everyone deserves to be loved, Miss Ellsworth," he said. "Perhaps you can serve both: duty and love." He moved his finger from my chin and clasped a strand of rogue hair that had escaped my braid. My heart sped, and I was convinced that he knew the havoc his touch and words evoked.

"Perhaps," I repeated on a breathless whisper.

Too soon, he dropped his hand and stepped back. The soft breeze pulled at my hair, replacing the heat from his touch.

"We should get you back to the house before someone starts to worry," Mr. Fausett said.

He walked Juno to where I stood then looped the reins back over her neck. "May I?" he asked.

I inhaled quickly and nodded. Mr. Fausett's touch was like a branding iron as he laid his hands on my waist and lifted me up to the saddle. I sat sideways in the forward-facing saddle and adjusted to a semi-comfortable position. Before I realized, Mr. Fausett swung up behind me, straddling the horse. He reached around me to hold the reins, and I felt his breath near my ear. My body went rigid. He clicked, and the horse walked forward. I slipped in my awkward position, and immediately Mr. Fausett dropped one hand off the reins and wrapped his arm around my waist.

"Are you all right?" he asked.

I could only nod. 'Twas true I was safe and physically unharmed, but my emotions were an entirely different matter.

"You have a very healthy constitution to have walked so far without breaking your fast." His fingers shifted on my waist. "What brought you out so early this morning?"

"I couldn't sleep anymore," I said. "I thought a walk might clear my head."

I heard the humor in his voice. "So you pulled on your boots and just began to walk? You do realize that if Juno and I hadn't been out riding . . ." He leaned forward, the heat from his body pressed closer, and he petted the horse's neck.

"My mother told me there was a lily pond among the hills. I hoped to find it," I said softly.

"Next time maybe you'll ask for directions?" Mr. Fausett's head tilted forward, and he caught my eye.

I glanced at him quickly and said, "Perhaps." Then I dropped my eyes to Juno's mane. "Thank you for . . ." I paused and took a calming breath. "Rescuing me." What was happening? My heartbeat sped and my mind felt jumbled and happy, and I could not seem to form a coherent thought. I never lost my senses. I was the reasonable one, but in that moment I was beyond baffled.

"As your rescuer, do I get to claim a reward?" Mr. Fausett said softly near my ear.

My breath froze inside my lungs.

"Will you dance with me at the ball?" Mr. Fausett's hand shifted again on my waist as he awaited my response.

I recalled how it felt to dance with him. His confidence had lured me into a blissful trance as he swept me around the room. Now I had the opportunity to return to his arms and feel that bliss again. Knowing I would evoke my sister's anger, my mother's displeasure, and my absolute delight, I answered with a simple "Yes."

CHAPTER 29

Mr. Devlin Fausett

While I wanted to ask Miss Ellsworth for the first dance, the last dance, and every dance in between, I knew better. Surely, she would lead out the first dance with Browning, but she'd agreed to a dance. The prospects of the ball were greatly improving.

Mrs. Leah Brumley had made me promise to write and keep her informed of every entertainment at Lily Glen. She seemed convinced that my correspondence would be full of romantic notions about her cousin. The notions were there, but it was nothing I could write about because there was no reciprocation of my feelings. So I wrote about the beauty of the estate with a trivial update to include everyone's good health and the upcoming ball.

The following morning, Juno and I rode into town to post the letter. I could have asked Browning to frank it for me, but my pride would not allow it. Sleeping in his home and eating his food was driving me mad enough.

I asked about the post and was directed to the local inn, The Drawbridge. I left Juno at the stables and walked into the establishment. The open room was less than half-full, and, upon my entrance, the few patrons scattered among the tables eyed me up and down. I couldn't resist the challenge their attention provided, and, straightening to my full height, I raised my brows and met their stares directly. After a few grumblings, the majority of heads turned away, and I walked to the bar.

A tall man with sandy-colored hair handed a sloshing mug to a customer farther down the bar. I assumed he was the proprietor. When he moved towards me, he limped, favoring his right leg. "What can I get ya?" he asked.

I pulled the letter from my jacket. "I hoped to post this."

He told me the price and said, "Where you from?"

"Essex originally," I said.

"Hmm," he said and looked at the address on the letter. Then he shook his head. "Staying out at Lily Glen, I assume."

"Why would you assume that?" I asked.

He gave a gruff laugh. "Name's Bernard. I've lived here my entire life. Lundsworth didn't used to be so dismal. First Payton Place burned then the Brownings left Lily Glen. Them genteel families are all the same, too much money to care about their tenants or the men who rely on the work to feed their families." I handed him an extra coin with my payment. "Not that they're all bad," he said, eyeing my money and taking the coin with a disgruntled snicker. "Haven't seen gentlemen like you around for years. Now two in one day."

"Two?" I asked. "Someone else from Lily Glen?" I thought I'd been the first to arise this morning.

"Nah, some gent arrived late last night. Took a room and said he'd be staying for a week or so," he said.

"Did he have business in the area?" I asked. I'd scheduled the remainder of my payments to Higgins, but he'd been tracking and threatening me for so long, I couldn't dismiss my unease.

"How am I supposed to know?" The man huffed but a grin split his rough cheeks.

I slipped another coin from my pocket and placed it on the high table between us. "Perhaps you could check the register?"

With a sly twist of his lips, the man covered the coin with his hand and walked into another room. I waited, ignoring the stares upon my back until the innkeeper limped back. His eyes scanned the room and then he leaned close. "Smith's the name. Wrote he's here for business."

Higgins liked to handle his business himself and would have no need for an alibi. "Thank you." I flipped him another coin and took a step back from the table.

"Maybe them Brownings losing their fortune ain't so bad for the rest of us," Bernard said and raised the coin in front of him.

"What do you mean?" I asked.

The man looked down his nose at me, but I'd given him more than enough incentive to answer my question. I stared him down until he blinked and turned away.

"They may have thought they could outrun the gossip. News takes a while, but it gets here eventually." He pulled a rag from his pocket and began wiping down the bar.

"And . . ." I prompted.

Bernard shrugged. "Heard the Brownings lost it all. Got swindled by some bloke who ran off to them new American colonies. Family only came back 'cause they had to."

I watched the man; his eyes flickered between me and his work. There was no reason for Bernard to lie, but if he spoke the truth, why did Browning pose as a rich entrepreneur come to claim his bride? Did Miss Ellsworth know Browning well enough to know his circumstances?

I tipped the stable hand, a young, black-haired, dirty boy, and turned Juno east, suddenly anxious to get back to Lily Glen. Browning had arranged for a day of hunting. Doctor Hadley decried the sport and happily agreed to remain behind with the ladies. The outing with the gentlemen would grant me an opportunity find out more about Jonathon Browning and his circumstances.

Juno had proven a good horse, and I was indebted to Brumley for her use, but seeing Browning astride Raven pricked my pride as well as my conscience. I'd suppressed my itching for the tables, mainly for the benefit of Miss Ellsworth. I wanted to rightfully earn her esteem, but the impulsive craving to sit in on a hand still tortured me. Watching Raven move into a trot at Browning's command nettled the natural inclination to find a solution through wagers and bets. The aching longing burst through me. I wanted my horse, and with equal adamancy, I didn't want Browning to have her.

Juno turned in a circle, eager to join the party. The moment I touched my heels to her flanks she took off like a lightning bolt. My justification may have been childish, because I knew I could not get Raven back, but I needed to prove to myself, to Browning, and maybe even to Miss Ellsworth, that I was a man to be reckoned with. If cards were no longer an option, then the wager was here and now, and while Browning may not have verbally agreed to the stakes, he realized there was a game afoot.

I closed the distance between us and passed his left side. Browning leaned into Raven, and she took the clue, immediately matching Juno's stride. We left the older men behind, no longer riding for the pleasure of the hunt, but to claim some unspoken prize.

The horses huffed beside one another, their coats gleaming with sweat. The absurdity of my brash move hit me at once. Browning and I had not discussed a reward, let alone agreed to a race, and we'd set no boundaries, but none of that mattered. We rode. Hard.

Through the hills, the horses seemed determined to keep pressing onward. There was not a set path, but their bodies moved together in formation. Juno would pull ahead before Raven would hasten into the lead. We rounded another hill and dropped into a basin with a beautiful lake. It became the unspoken finale.

My thighs pressed into Juno, begging her for more, for one final push. She answered, but she could not best Raven. In the final yards before the waters' edge, Raven pulled half a length ahead. Browning smiled in triumph, and the horses veered in opposite directions.

I reined Juno in, both of us breathing quick and heavy, and I walked her in a large circle to cool her off. Browning walked Raven along the water's edge, and only once my breaths had calmed did I turn to meet him.

I had difficulty accepting a loss at the tables, but I knew I'd been beaten. "You're impressive in the saddle, Browning. You gave me quite a run."

Browning smirked. "You've a good seat yourself. It's remarkable how she responds to you seeing as she's not your own." Browning reached forward and gave Raven a hearty rub. "We're still getting acquainted, but I'm impressed with this beast." He sat back up. "Thank you for the challenge, Fausett." Browning touched his hand to his hat and turned when the other riders appeared at the top of the ridge.

Indignation pooled in my gut. Browning remained on Raven's back while I rode a borrowed horse. Raven belonged to him, he'd reasserted his claim, and there was nothing I could do about it.

CHAPTER 30

Miss Nora Ellsworth

AFTER THE GENTLEMEN'S DEPARTURE, I went in search of Claudia. We had not discussed her confession of feelings for Mr. Fausett. Rather, she had been avoiding me altogether.

A song floated down the hallway, and I recognized it as one of Claudia's favorite melodies. I listened at the doorway until she finished the piece, and then I knocked and pushed the door open.

Claudia stared at me but said nothing.

We locked eyes, and I took a breath before asking, "May we talk for a moment?"

Claudia stood. "What more is there to discuss? I heard you did a commendable job of guaranteeing Mr. Fausett as your knight in shining armor." So she had heard about my disastrous attempt to find the pond.

"That wasn't intentional." Claudia rolled her eyes. I walked to her side and wrapped my fingers around her clenched fist. "Come here." She let me lead her to the couch, and we sat together. "I wanted to tell you that if you are sure of your feelings for Mr. Fausett . . ." My throat felt dry, and I licked my lips. "I will not stand in your way."

Claudia raised her eyes to mine and then narrowed them in doubt. I shrugged and faked a smile. Claudia unclenched her hand and grasped my fingers in her own. "Are you sure, Nora?"

"I want you to be happy, Claudia. And if Mr. Fausett will do that, then you deserve each other."

Before I registered her movement, Claudia had thrown her arms around my neck. "Oh, thank you, Nora! He will make me happy, I am sure of it."

My heart felt suddenly hollow, and I took a deep breath to try to fill the void with assurance that I was doing the right thing. The chasm only opened wider. I briefly returned Claudia's embrace, afraid she would feel my rapid pulse. I sat straight and quickly changed the conversation to the ideal weather.

Early in the afternoon, I sat with Mrs. Browning and Mother as they continued preparations for the ball. We conferred on menus, décor, and the set of music. My heart warmed as I remembered Mr. Fausett's request for a dance.

"The tea tray should arrive soon," Mrs. Browning said. "Do you think Miss Claudia would like to join us?"

"Would you happen to know where she is?" I asked.

"Only a moment ago she was in the music room with the doctor," Mrs. Browning said. "I'm so grateful his ministrations have brought her smile back. I was so worried for the dear girl."

I offered my agreement and left to find my sister.

The music from the piano stopped, replaced by Claudia's tinkling laugh. I, too, felt relief at her recovered health, but when I recalled her confession of feelings for Mr. Fausett, my insides scrunched into a tight knot. Conversation would not reverse her dreamy notions, but I hoped reason would help her understand why I had accepted his request for a dance.

I walked into the room to find Claudia sharing the piano bench with Doctor Hadley. He was leaning close and pointing at the music spread above the keys.

"Excuse me," I said aloud and turned to leave. Doctor Hadley sat next to Claudia the way I had numerous times, but somehow this scene was different, intimate.

"Miss Ellsworth," Doctor Hadley called with a cheery voice. "Come in, come in." He rose from his place on the bench and inclined his head. "Please, join us. I'm afraid music has never been a talent of mine. Miss Claudia was teaching me some basic piano technique."

"I don't mean to disrupt your lesson," I said. Claudia harrumphed.

"Oh, we were finished." Doctor Hadley moved clumsily around the piano. At the door, he bowed awkwardly to each of us. "Ladies," he said then turned and made an abrupt exit.

"Thank you for interrupting my pleasant morning." Claudia sighed dramatically before thrashing out a robust composition.

I frowned as Claudia pounded out the march-like cadence, but she didn't take notice. With a clenched jaw, I focused on the beauty of the variegated glass and raised my voice to speak above the cacophony. "I've only come at Mrs. Browning's request. She wondered if you might like to join us for tea."

"I would like that very much." Claudia halted her song and stood. She began gathering her papers from the piano.

I walked to where the mosaic window reflected on the floor and stared at the colors. "You had a lengthy conversation with Mr. Fausett after dinner last night."

"Yes, he was very kind."

I traced the reflection of the blue tile with the toe of my slipper. "What did you discuss?"

"Music." A moment passed. "Are you coming, Nora?"

When I lifted my head, Claudia stood in the doorway, her music papers pressed against her heart. I stepped away from the rainbow reflection and walked to where she stood. "Be sure this is what you want, Claudia, and don't let the gentleman think you are leading him on if you are not truly interested," I said.

"Doctor Hadley would never think that," Claudia responded quickly.

My head tilted to the side, and I evaluated my sister. "Doctor Hadley?"

Claudia blushed. "Or Mr. Fausett." She quickly moved down the hallway.

"Claudia?" I considered her fumbled words and hurried to catch her. She walked as if her skirt was on fire. "Claudia?" I called again. "Wait for just a moment!"

Claudia stopped then. She did not turn to face me. Her papers fluttered to the ground, and I quickly moved to stand in front of her.

"Claudia?"

Her face paled, and she raised a hand to her chest, just over her heart.

"Help!" I shouted.

Claudia's knees buckled, and she fell towards me.

"I've got her." Doctor Hadley appeared beside me. With surprising grace, he wrapped one arm around her shoulders and scooped up her legs with his other arm. He carried Claudia to a nearby sitting room. After he gently laid her on the brocade couch, Doctor Hadley knelt beside her. He pressed his fingers to her neck, and his lips moved in a slow count to ten.

Mother, Mrs. Browning, and several servants joined us in the room.

"Oh, my dear girl!" Mother cried.

"Shhh," I said and placed my hand on her arm to stop her progression towards the couch. We all stood and watched as Claudia's eyes slowly opened.

"There you are, my dear," Doctor Hadley said on a whisper. He smiled at my sister and brushed a piece of hair from her face. "Feeling better?"

Claudia blinked at Doctor Hadley a few times, and then a smile touched her lips. "Yes," she said, her voice as soft as a whisper.

Mrs. Browning leaned over to Mother and me. "It looks like she is in capable hands. Let's let them be." Mrs. Browning led Mother from the room, and the servants dutifully followed.

I remained for only a moment more, watching the pair exchange a few words. Perhaps Claudia had found her own dashing knight.

CHAPTER 31

Mr. Devlin Fausett

BROWNING AND I RODE TO meet the other gentlemen—Mr. Browning, Mr. Wells, and two neighbors he'd invited to join us. Mr. Ellsworth was noticeably absent. He'd been saddled and ready when we left the house, but Mr. Browning explained that Ellsworth had a sudden upset stomach and returned to the house to rest.

The next few hours passed with minimal conversation. I discovered no more about Browning's financial situation. I shot well, but the game was sparse and the party decided to call an early end to the hunt. We returned to the house, and I tended Juno myself, while the stable hands unsaddled and brushed the other horses. She'd earned an extra bucket of oats for her efforts, and I wanted to reward her personally. I secured Juno in her stall and walked to where Raven stood eating her fresh hay.

"Valiant effort out there, my friend," I said. She turned from her meal, and when I extended my hand, she pressed her forehead against my palm. "I'm sorry." Raven pushed forward and applied more pressure. After standing still a moment, she tossed her head and turned back to her hay. I hoped it meant I was forgiven. I returned to the house to bathe and dress for dinner.

The company gathered in the drawing room, and upon my entrance, I immediately spied Miss Ellsworth. Her blue gown brightened her eyes, and she looked beautiful. Irresistible.

"Mr. Fausett." Miss Claudia must have approached without my notice. I regretfully pulled my eyes from her sister and gave her my attention. "How was your sport?" she asked.

"Bah!" the elder Mr. Browning called from nearby. "You can't call what those two did today sport."

Miss Claudia looked confused. "Of course it's sport," Browning said. "Horseracing is considered a gentleman's pastime."

"Oh. There was a race?" Miss Claudia's face brightened, and she clapped her hands together. "And who won?" she asked.

Browning smirked from across the room and nodded for me to answer.

"It was all very unofficial," I said. "No wagers. Only for good fun." I chanced a glance at Miss Ellsworth. Her smile grew, and my heart clenched. "Browning bested me in the end."

Browning shrugged one shoulder. "You made a formidable opponent."

Hadley entered the room, and Miss Ellsworth's eyes shifted to him. "How's my father?" she asked.

Hadley didn't turn to completely face her, but instead he nodded sideways at her inquisition and looked at Miss Claudia. "He's no better, I'm afraid," Hadley said, and Miss Claudia raised a hand to cover her mouth. "Something he's eaten has upset his digestion. I've asked Mrs. Norse to instruct Cook to prepare a mild tea to settle his stomach."

"I'm sure a good night's rest will be just the thing," Mrs. Ellsworth said. "Mr. Ellsworth has always had a hearty constitution, and he wouldn't want us to spoil our evening worrying over him." Her free smile validated the truth she felt in her brash dismissal.

Hadley's jaw clenched, but I seemed to be the only one who noticed.

CHAPTER 32

Miss Nora Ellsworth

THE DAY OF THE BALL arrived. Ignoring Mother's request to stay away, I insisted on seeing my father. He'd been sick for six days, despite Doctor Hadley's efforts. Father's illness brought melancholy to the entire party. Mr. Thorne suggested postponing the ball, but Mother and Mrs. Browning wouldn't hear of it.

Doctor Hadley admitted his concern over Father. Vomiting and stomach pains usually subsided within two days' time, but Father showed no improvement. The hours I spent standing vigil over Claudia served as a reminder of the precious gift of life. I would never forgive myself if something happened to my father and I had not visited his bedside because Mother feared I might get sick and miss a frivolous ball.

Father's continued illness punctuated the need to break the entail. Mother did not address it directly. Instead, she dropped tiny hints and insinuations about a match with Mr. Browning, and as the days progressed, her comments referenced the need for a quick engagement. Her quiet whispers and implications only stoked my nerves and caused further confusion within.

As I neared Father's room, voices sounded from inside. At the door, I paused and listened. Father's voice was easily recognizable. "Your father and I have an agreement. Let me die knowing all has been rectified," he said.

My hand covered my mouth. How could Father talk of dying? He sounded so sorrowful; certainly, whomever he spoke to would not deny him his wish. But then I remembered the conversation I'd overheard at Ellsworth Meadows. What was the agreement of which Father spoke?

I sucked in a breath as I recognized the second voice as Mr. Jonathon Browning's. "Surely, you would not wish me to force this upon your daughter."

"Nora has a good head on her shoulders. She'll make you a good wife." Father's voice drifted off to silence.

Mr. Browning spoke again. "I would really like to hear her opinion on the matter. No one should be forced into marriage."

Father's voice was softer, but I detected his derision as he drawled out, "Is that what this is about? Don't like your old man telling you what to do?" He began to laugh, but the noise shifted as he moaned in pain. "Blast!" He groaned again. "Post the banns, and do your duty," Father spat. "Marry Nora and save both our families."

After a moment Mr. Browning spoke again. "Fine, but don't pretend you're not the one pulling the strings."

I did not want to hear any more. I'd always assumed our mothers pushed for the match, but it seemed as though our fathers played their roles well and with much more anonymity.

My emotions undulated between frustration and anger. I considered postponing my visit, but Mother insisted we begin our toilette immediately after tea, so my time was limited. If I wanted to visit Father before the ball, it had to be now. I knocked on the door and did not wait before entering his room.

"Hello, Father. Mr. Browning," I said without pretense.

Mr. Browning's eyes widened, and he quickly looked me over.

"Nora, you should not be here," Father said. He clutched his middle as he spoke.

I waved off his comment. "I wanted to see you." His eyes softened, and I knew he appreciated the effort I'd made to come to him.

"I promised Doctor Hadley I would not stay long," I said.

Father began to raise his hand, but the effort proved to be too much and it dropped again to his side. I sat near the edge of his bed and took his hand in mine.

"Nora," Father said, as his eyelids grew heavy.

"Perhaps we should let him sleep," Mr. Browning said.

Father groaned again, and his grip tightened on my hand as he repeated my name.

"Shh," I hushed him.

"No!" he said, the sudden volume startling both Mr. Browning and myself. "You must listen . . ." His voice strained with his effort to speak.

"Father?" I asked.

His eyes shot open, and he pegged me with an intense stare. His fingers tightened again, and he said, "I'm sick, Nora. Very sick. Break the entail. Once the banns are posted, Trenton has no claim. It's all I have left, my dear. Please."

A chill washed over me, and I dared not turn around to face Mr. Browning. Father's plea pierced my heart. He spoke as though this was the end, and while

I knew he was sick, I never considered Father would not rise from his bed. I wanted to fulfill his wish, his dying wish. Could it really be his last request?

A lump formed in my throat.

I felt Mr. Browning's presence. He stepped up beside me and quietly said, "We should let him sleep."

I nodded mutely, rose from the bed, and followed Mr. Browning out the door. But once I reached the hallway, my feet would not move. Father's grim prediction, along with his request, cycled again through my mind. He was asking so much, so soon.

"Miss Ellsworth? Are you all right?" Mr. Browning asked.

I looked up at him, and before I could process my thoughts, words began tumbling from my mouth. "I heard you," I said. Mr. Browning's jaw tensed. "You obviously know the specifics about the entail on Ellsworth Meadows. You said I should have a choice, and for that, I thank you." Mr. Browning's eyes narrowed as he listened. "But you should have a choice too. My father requested that I break the entail, and while I must maintain faith he will recover . . ." I paused a moment to steady my voice, then with a deep breath I raised my chin and continued. "He believes otherwise. But realize his request falls to me. I release you from any agreement between our fathers or mothers or any other party who would forcefully bind us together. You have no obligation to me."

Mr. Browning's hands fell to his side. His chin angled sideways, and a muscle tensed in his jaw. He moved towards me. "Miss Ellsworth . . ."

"No." I stepped away and raised my hand. "Please, say no more. I've been a pawn in this game long enough. I will honor my father's request on my terms." I ignored his exasperated sigh and walked away.

CHAPTER 33

Mr. Devlin Fausett

THE ANTICIPATION OF DANCING WITH Miss Ellsworth burst through my entire being. We'd danced before. It was thoroughly enjoyable. Permeating. Addictive. Perhaps that was why I couldn't wait to take her in my arms again.

However, the ball was hours away, and I hoped a ride in the fresh air would deviate my thoughts. After exploring the hills, I led Juno to the pond, which was better classified as a small lake. The weather was perfect, and the sight of the floating flowers atop the vibrant-blue water brought tranquility.

Even in my younger years, I could not back down from a challenge, which explained my fixation with winning at the tables. But despite my stubborn nature, I didn't consider myself brave. A brave man would have the strength to walk away from a bet. A brave man would know when to quit and have the poise to do so. A brave man would not be afraid to share his feelings with a lovely woman. My confidence was growing, but I had yet to consider myself brave.

Looking out over the scene, a new desire took root in my heart. The natural beauty before me was not grand. It was intricate in a simple, peaceful way. I wanted that peace, the serenity that came with recognition of the things that were truly important. The things that made me feel more than the thrill of a bet, more than a claim to victory. I wanted substance, the budding fibers of joy that were found in a smile or a word of praise from one particular woman. I said a silent prayer for strength. For courage. For bravery.

Juno loped back towards the tamed gardens around the estate. We slowed to a walk as we passed the servants' entrance, where a young lad slid out the door. He only glanced at me briefly before turning his eyes to the ground and scampering away, but I recognized him as the dirty stable boy from the inn, and I wondered what errand brought him out to Lily Glen.

I turned Juno to walk parallel to the outer garden wall, and after passing a flowering cherry tree, I spied Miss Ellsworth pacing the meticulous grounds. I watched her without revealing myself. Her hands hung at her side, her fingers opening and closing as she turned to cover the path she'd recently walked. Back and forth she turned, her face contorting with her thoughts in what appeared to be a vain struggle to find peace.

Juno snorted, and Miss Ellsworth's attention turned to me. The opportunity to be brave had arrived. "May I join you?" I asked.

Miss Ellsworth offered a single nod.

I kicked Juno forward and whistled for a stable boy to come tend her. After passing off the reins, I entered the garden and found Miss Ellsworth exactly where I'd left her.

"Is everything all right?" I asked.

"Yes." She hung her head. "No."

My heart sped. "Your father?"

"There is no change," she said.

"There's something more bothering you . . ."

"If Father passes, and I'm not married, it's too late. Why did they only tell me about the conditions of the entail a few weeks ago? If I'd known, maybe I could have . . ." A small cry escaped, and she pressed the back of her hand to her mouth. "Father was healthy only days ago. I don't understand it."

I reached forward, wanting only to pull her into my arms and hold her, anything to bring a small measure of comfort. But there was a line between being brave and being improper. My fingers fell back to my side.

"Can I be of assistance?" I asked.

Moisture pulled at her eyes as she turned to look at me. "Doctor Hadley says there's nothing more to be done. What if something happens and I've yet to break the entail?" Miss Ellsworth sniffed, and I offered my handkerchief.

"I'm sorry," I said, but the words felt hollow and cowardly. "Perhaps . . ."

"Miss Ellsworth." Browning's voice rang over the flowerbeds, and he appeared instantaneously in front of us. "Your mother is asking for you." Browning looked every bit the scorned lover, and I cursed myself for allowing the moment to slip away.

Miss Ellsworth dropped into a shallow curtsy. "Please excuse me," she said, and we both watched her go.

When she disappeared from sight, Browning turned to me. "Tonight I plan to ask Miss Ellsworth to be my wife."

My face remained impassive, but my heart felt as if it were clamped in a vice. "If you don't mind, I'll save my congratulations until it's official," I said.

Browning smirked, and without another word, he turned and walked away.

I looked heavenward, soaking in strength from the radiant sun. The time to stop being a coward had come. My happiness depended on it. Tonight I would offer a solution to Miss Ellsworth's dilemma. Tonight she would receive not one proposal, but two.

CHAPTER 34

Miss Nora Ellsworth

The modiste Mrs. Browning procured did not disappoint. My dress was exquisite. Cream-colored chiffon lay ethereally over a straight matching muslin skirt. The bodice fit comfortably around my torso, and when I walked in the flowing gown, I felt like an angel skimming lightly over the floor. I insisted Cooper complete her ministrations to Claudia before helping me, and when my turn came, I chose an elegant, simple hairstyle. Feeling beautiful, I left my room determined to catch the eye of a possible suitor.

I was uncertain what to expect from Mr. Browning since I'd released him from his obligations. While I needed to marry out of duty, he did not. According to Mother's recurring updates, Mr. Browning's wealth far surpassed the benefit that would come from my generous dowry or the entail. Perhaps I would meet a gentleman in need of my money, my home. My stomach tightened at the thought of being wed to a fortune hunter; however, it seemed the only viable solution.

I descended the stairs to find the household in a bustle. The first guests were expected any moment, and Mrs. Browning was in a fret because her husband had not yet appeared and therefore could not greet those arriving.

Mrs. Browning called to her son, waving at him frantically. "Jonathon! Come. Come. Please come stand in place of your father."

Mr. Browning walked to the place his mother indicated, and before I realized her intentions, Mrs. Browning wrapped my arm in hers and deposited me on her son's left side. "This is, after all, in your honor. A celebration of your visit and things to come," she said with a wink.

The tedious task exhausted me after only a half hour. My mind weighed too heavy to dole out hollow greetings and false salutations. The majority of the guests had come to see Lily Glen, to celebrate the return of the Brownings, to claim an acquaintance, no matter how shallow.

Mr. Browning leaned near. "Are you all right?" he asked, but my gratitude that he'd noticed my discomfiture dissolved with his next words. "We'll of course dance the first dance, but there is no need to be nervous."

I opened my mouth to explain, but Mr. Fausett inserted himself into the line and saved me the trouble. "Excuse me," he said to the guests he'd misplaced. My eyes shifted to Mr. Fausett, and the air in my lungs hitched. Amidst the greetings and chatter, Mr. Fausett stood regal, focusing solely on me. His eyes reminded me of dark-gray velvet, and I could scarce take in the rest of his appearance because his gaze held me spellbound. "Miss Ellsworth, Doctor Hadley's just come from your father. He hoped to speak with you."

My stomach dropped, and I stepped out of line and took Mr. Fausett's proffered arm. "Your father's condition is unchanged, Miss Ellsworth," he whispered as we left the press of the crowd.

"Then why . . . ?"

"You looked upset," Mr. Fausett said and took a few more steps. "Given our earlier conversation, I figured you might appreciate a reprieve."

Mr. Fausett was far too observant.

I whispered my gratitude, and we walked to the music room, where he released my arm and remained standing in the threshold. I walked to where the colors poured across the floor and stopped when the kaleidoscope transferred from the ground onto the hem of my skirt.

"You look especially beautiful, Miss Ellsworth," Mr. Fausett's warm voice called from the doorway. His head tilted and his eyes swept over my head. Then he smiled and walked towards me until he stood only a foot away. "However did you manage to capture the sunrays and weave them through your hair?"

His warm breath stirred the curls near my ear, and a ripple of heat flowed through me. I pressed my eyes closed in a vain effort to ground myself.

I opened them again and blinked a few times to free myself from the trance that was Mr. Fausett. "We should see if the dancing has begun," I said.

Mr. Fausett's eyes never left my face, and the pounding in my chest intensified. I stood torn between wanting to remain in that space forever and wanting to break free from this enchantment I could not understand. The lucidity in my mind ebbed and flowed with each breath, and when I felt I would burst, my feet propelled me to the door.

I didn't turn around to see if Mr. Fausett followed. I felt him there. The moment before I stepped back into the clamber of guests, he called my name.

I stopped, and he moved near me. "No matter what happens, I hope I may still have the honor of dancing with you this evening," he said. "I think I may have a solution to your dilemma."

My eyes flicked to his for only a second, but the intensity I saw in his gaze burned through my entire being. I could only blink and nod, but when his face split into a smile, I knew he knew my answer was again—yes.

CHAPTER 35

Mr. Devlin Fausett

THE ANTICIPATION FOR MY DANCE with Miss Ellsworth built then crumbled with frustration as each song seemed longer than the last. I'd asked her to partner with me for the cotillion, which would be danced later in the evening. There were more ladies than gentlemen, a situation that occurred all too often, so I tried to compose myself and dance a few numbers for the benefit of my hosts.

I danced the minuet with Miss Wells and asked Miss Claudia to dance the quadrille. She regaled me with questions and stories; however, she knew me well enough to recognize my hollow smile. "Mr. Fausett, whatever is the matter?" she asked when we finished the set.

"What do you mean?" I feigned.

Her pretty little face pushed into a pout. "You don't fool me, you know. Everyone else is excited to be at the ball. Don't you see all the smiles? Can't you feel the enthusiasm of the evening?"

I knew exactly what she referenced. The guests laughed and twirled, diverted by the enticement of a dance. But my pulse pressed like the tide, waiting to break free. It was a restless sort of energy building like a waxing moon. The moon depended on the reflection of the sun but my resolution depended on more, so much more.

"You've been walking around forlorn all evening," Miss Claudia said and playfully touched my arm.

"I apologize, Miss Claudia," I said. "I admit my mind is elsewhere this evening."

She ducked her chin and smiled at me through her lashes. "Am I not a diverting enough partner?" she asked.

I couldn't contain my smile. "Miss Claudia, is there something in your eye?"

Her face fell, and she promptly straightened her stance. She huffed her dis-pleasure, and I couldn't control the laugh bubbling in my chest. Once we reached her mother, I lifted Miss Claudia's hand and gave her fingers a gentle squeeze.

"Now run along and enjoy the festivities," I said.

Her jaw dropped farther, and I laughed again while I walked away. My dance with her sister was next, and I needed to find Miss Ellsworth.

I extended my neck and searched the room for a golden-haired beauty. I spied Miss Ellsworth visiting with two gentlemen across the room. I quickened my pace, maneuvering through the crowd, anxious to catch a glimpse of her again.

My grin erupted with the joy bounding through my chest. I planned to dance with Miss Ellsworth and afterwards suggest our alliance. I didn't know if her feelings mirrored mine, but I was certain she felt at least a vague fondness for me. She'd been a voice of reason, a friend, a confidant, and a believer in my goodness. I hoped to offer her a solution to her dilemma. I hoped it was enough, that I was enough.

Emerging in the place I saw her last, I discovered the gentlemen who'd been vying for her attention, but Miss Ellsworth no longer stood there. I straightened and searched for her again. Where had she gone? I'd patiently awaited this moment all day, and my frantic heart pled for resolution. But Miss Ellsworth was nowhere to be found.

I turned back to the gentleman I'd last seen her with. "Do you know where I might find Miss Ellsworth?" I asked.

The man snickered. "If you hope to claim her for a dance, get in line."

No matter the anxiety flowing through my veins, these men were not my enemy. I inhaled a breath then released it. "She'd promised her hand for this set," I said.

The taller man looked at his companion. "Do you want to break it to him, or should I?"

My heart clenched and turned like a rock tumbling down a hillside. "Go on," I said.

"It seems Miss Ellsworth was already spoken for," the man said with a shrug. My eyes narrowed, and he expounded. "Your dancing partner was collected by our beloved host." He gave me a conciliatory pat on the back.

"Browning," I said. The tightening in my chest moved to my jaw.

"He said they needed a moment and told us to be prepared for an announce-ment. Sorry, chap," the man replied.

I walked away with my head held high and trudged through the crowd while attempting to sort through my trampled emotions. Browning said he would propose tonight—was that his announcement?

I laughed aloud at my stupidity. To think Miss Ellsworth would consider my offer, to assume she would be interested in courting, in deepening the friendship that had grown between us. Somewhere along the way, I'd thought there had been a promise of something more, a spark of a deeper connection. She deserved better. I'd always known, and it was obvious now that she agreed; although she should have explained herself rather than abandoning her promise of a dance. She had given her word, the one thing I counted on from her, and, in the end, it hadn't been enough. I hadn't been enough. Miss Ellsworth's promise to me was forgotten, and with it, so was I.

My emotions undulated between self-pity and blame. My rank as a gentleman matched Miss Ellsworth's standing in society. Holbrook, though humble, provided a steady income. But due to my weakness, I fell short. A few nights at the tables offset the rest of my life's worth.

I'd changed. At her bidding, with her promise of friendship, I'd changed. Yet I still fell short. She'd walked away. It was time I did the same.

CHAPTER 36

Miss Nora Ellsworth

MISS WELLS INTRODUCED ME TO Mr. Montgomery and Mr. Chase. While both gentlemen were kind in their attentions, I couldn't focus entirely on the conversation. I knew my dance with Mr. Fausett was next, and my stomach quivered in happy anticipation; however, before I realized what had happened, Mr. Browning had approached and asked if he might speak to me.

We stepped aside as the applause from the previous set died away, and the musicians began the first notes of the cotillion.

"Excuse me, Mr. Browning, I believe my mother is sitting on the opposite side of the room," I said.

He smiled and put his free hand on my arm. "I shall only take a moment, Miss Ellsworth," he said. "But I hoped to speak with you alone."

Mr. Browning grasped my elbow and led me out the doors and through the open hallway. My heart immediately began to speed, but not in a pleasant, exciting kind of way. "Surely we can talk here," I said. "I wouldn't want Mother to worry when she can't find me."

Mr. Browning's feet kept moving forward. "I've spoken to your mother and your father regarding my intentions."

As Mr. Browning led me towards the library, the sounds of the music muted, and the anticipation of my dance with Mr. Fausett warped into frustration with Mr. Browning for denying me the opportunity. At the doorway of the room, I stopped my feet completely.

"We have privacy here. You certainly wouldn't want to cause whisperings of scandal among your guests." I pulled my arm from his, clasped my hands, and turned to look him in the eye.

Mr. Browning's mouth pushed up into a narrow grin. "Miss Ellsworth, surely you know my intent. As your parents have condoned our match, any claim of impropriety would be hollow. Come," he said and wrapped his fingers around my wrist, pulling me into the room with him.

I gasped at his boorish behavior. We spun into the library, and he swiftly closed the door behind us. Mr. Browning's eyes narrowed for only a moment before he opened them wide and resumed a feigned lightheartedness.

"Mr. Browning! I demand you release me at once," I said.

A deep chuckle resonated his response. "You are not a hostage, my dear."

I flinched at the endearment.

"I mean you no harm," he said and held his hands up in surrender. "I only wish to talk."

"Conversation could have been had in the hall or the ballroom or anywhere where you do not stand between me and an exit," I said, the thrumming in my heart becoming more unpleasant with each beat.

"Miss Ellsworth, you know our arrangement has been destined from your birth. Let's fulfill the wishes of our families and announce our engagement tonight." Mr. Browning took a step towards me, and my chest restricted in frantic confusion.

"Are you proposing?" I asked.

Mr. Browning smiled at my shaky voice. "Indeed, I am," he said and took another step.

I looked over his handsome face. "And you *want* to wed?"

"Of course," he said with a laugh.

"But why?" Suddenly, the answer to the question became very important.

"I've already told you"—Mr. Browning's mouth still held a smile, but his eyes narrowed—"ours is a match that is mutually beneficial. It would ensure happiness and harmony in both of our families."

"Mutually beneficial?" I repeated. "I assume you refer to my dowry?" There was no need for him to answer. "Is that what would bring happiness to your family?"

"It certainly won't bring sorrow," he said.

"What of your vast wealth from India?" I asked.

Mr. Browning's jaw tightened. "You know better than to believe everything you hear. Not every plantation reaps success."

"So you are proposing marriage for the sake of my money? This is the agreement our fathers made?" My head felt light, and I raised a hand to my forehead. Everything became clear. "You get my dowry, and the entail is broken."

"As I said, our union would bring happiness to both of our families."

"What about happiness for us?" I asked.

"Indeed, we would be happy. Most content." Mr. Browning closed the final feet between us and took my hand in his.

His thumb stroked over the back of my hand. The touch he intended to be pleasant only stirred more bewilderment. My conscience focused on the words, the emotion, or the lack thereof, and my chest constricted, pinching my heart with the painful realization that he'd mentioned nothing of love.

"What about—" My words were cut short as Mr. Browning moved his hands to my shoulders and leaned over to press his lips to mine.

My mind whirled with the sensation of his kiss and the disappointment that it left me with nothing more than a jumble of confusion and a desire to wash my mouth.

He pulled his head back and looked at me with a smile spread across his lips. "Shall we announce our betrothal?" he asked.

Mr. Browning held my gaze, and for all of his beauty, his attentions, and expectations, I wanted to say yes. But for my heart, my happiness, I wanted to say no. For the benefit of my family and the prospect of a clear mind, I settled for neither.

"Do we have to announce it tonight?" I asked.

Mr. Browning cocked his head to the side. "'Tis the perfect occasion." His hands trailed down my arms, and he took my hand again. "We can share our happy news with our guests." He began to walk towards the door.

I stopped and pulled my hand free. "I'd like to think about it."

Mr. Browning's smile slipped. "What?"

I spoke quickly. "Please, I don't need the fanfare or the congratulations of the guests. But I do want to be confident in my decision. May I let you know in the morning?"

Mr. Browning watched me for a very long time. He didn't blink, and I wondered if he even took a breath. The air weighed of uncertainty and accusation.

"I . . . I would just like a little time," I said again.

"You realize you do not have the luxury of time? Your father . . ."

I lifted my chin. "Yes, thank you. But I must be sure."

"Very well," Mr. Browning said and stepped aside from the door. "But in the end, the decision may already be made."

Without a second glance, I left the library and rushed back to the ball, but when the music reached my ears, I recognized the song had changed. Disappointment clenched my chest, and my breaths became short and difficult.

Once I reached the ballroom, I quickly circled the perimeter. Mother called excitedly from her seat near Mrs. Browning, but I waved her away. Mr.

Fausett was nowhere to be seen. I'd promised him my hand. I'd promised him a dance. For him, and for myself, I wanted to keep my promise.

My lips matched the trembling in my heart, and I knew tears would soon follow. I rushed from the room, trying to outrun my tears, wondering how to make things right. It was a race I could not win, because there was no solution.

I entered the music room and snuffed the lit candles. The dying fire provided a small amount of light, and I craved the dark solitude. The darkness hid my problems, shrouding them in shadows. Light only illuminated the burden that fell to me: saving Ellsworth Meadows, marriage, the dependency of my family and pleadings of my father, all compounded on top of me like a rockfall. And no matter how deeply I breathed, the giant boulders crumpled my lungs, and I hurt. Every breath hurt.

I sat on the piano bench and wept.

Once my breathing slowed and the tears stopped falling, I looked around the room. Without the moonlight, the splash of colors turned dull and gray, and the dismal aura of the vacant reflection reminded me of Mr. Browning's proposal.

I pushed up from the piano stool and my arm slipped, bumping several keys and making a rather pitiful sound. However, something in the cacophony of the discordant ring jarred my senses. A hum rose through my lungs, and my fingers trailed lightly over the keys, never pressing firmly enough to hear the notes, yet searching for the melody that was fighting to escape. My hand moved in rhythm to the song bubbling inside, first dancing around middle C, then moving an octave higher. It was a song that wanted to be found, a verse or a memory striving to be rekindled. I hummed louder, conceding bits and pieces of the tune, until I fully recognized the song, and I thought my heart would stop altogether. The memory of Mr. Fausett's voice was embedded in my soul.

> *By Venus, Mother of Desire,*
> *Your eyes have set me on fire.*
> *There's magic in your touch,*
> *There's magic in your touch.*

I hummed aloud.

> *My eyes! dear Sir, a-well-a-day,*
> *Tears must have wash'd their power away:*
> *Indeed you say too much,*
> *Indeed you say too much.*

The sentiment of the song hit me with full force. How could I ever settle for a loveless marriage, when I'd felt the emotion with profound clarity?

The stained-glass mosaic was bland in the dark. There was no inspiration, no beauty, no purpose for the tinted glass. I needed color, and I needed love. Yet Mr. Browning's reminder of Father's dismal condition sliced through my needs with a cold steel blade. The decision might not be mine to make.

I returned to the ball and searched again for Mr. Fausett, without success. Claudia stood near Mother, and when I approached, she took my hands and eagerly pulled me aside.

"Oh, Nora, where have you been? You've missed all the excitement," she said. "I'm so grateful I didn't retire early. I almost did, you know, when Mr. Fausett so rudely dismissed me. But then Doctor Hadley discovered me and insisted I return to the ball."

I raised my hands to massage my temples. "Claudia, I don't know what you're talking about."

Claudia huffed. "Well, Mr. Fausett dismissed me entirely. I was so upset I went to the music room to sort it all out. I had decided to retire, when Doctor Hadley entered. He saw I was upset and worried that I might have an episode. He wanted to call for you, but I would not let him, so he insisted I rest on the couch until I calmed myself."

I leaned towards my sister. "Did your heart falter? Did you feel faint?"

"No," Claudia said. Her head tilted sideways, and she shook her head. "I was merely upset at Mr. Fausett's dismissal. He . . . he . . . treated me like a little girl." She sighed and continued. "Doctor Hadley remained with me until he was certain I was not in danger. I wanted to retire, but he insisted we should dance." Claudia smiled mischievously, and I closed my gaping jaw.

"Did you tell Doctor Hadley about your expectations?" I asked.

Claudia shrugged and had the decency to look away. "Doctor Hadley asked what had upset me. It wasn't unlike other questions he's posed about my health, so I saw no harm in sharing."

"Except that Doctor Hadley is Mr. Fausett's friend. What if you offended him?" I asked.

"I doubt it," Claudia said. "Doctor Hadley seemed quite upset with Mr. Fausett. Besides, it was his idea, after all, to return to the dance in order to make Mr. Fausett jealous." A blush pulsed through Claudia's cheeks.

We sat in silence for a long minute while I reviewed the information Claudia shared. The good doctor frequently sought out Claudia, with the pretense of his responsibilities as her physician. He also indulged her odd requests, and when he looked at her, his eyes filled with tenderness.

I finally said, "Doctor Hadley is a good man."

"Yes, he is," Claudia answered quickly, and I began to wonder if he was in fact the perfect man for my sister.

"What of Mr. Fausett?" I asked, and my heart pinched at the mention of his name.

Claudia rolled her eyes and waved a dismissive hand. "Oh, he left over an hour ago."

"Left?" I asked, squeezing her hands tighter.

"Yes."

"Are you sure?"

Claudia crossed her arms and pouted. "Of course I'm sure. Doctor Hadley and I were both looking for him, to make him jealous, you remember. When we couldn't find Mr. Fausett, Doctor Hadley suggested we take a walk outside, and that's when we saw Mr. Fausett slip out the back door," Claudia said.

"Was he alone?"

"Quite. He'd even changed out of his formal coat and swapped his slippers for boots," Claudia said.

"He left?"

"That's what I've been telling you. It wasn't more than ten minutes later we saw him riding off somewhere," Claudia said with a shrug, and then she began to swing our hands back and forth.

The throbbing in my head increased. If Mr. Browning hadn't pulled me away, would Mr. Fausett have found me for the promised dance, or did he leave prior to the set? I turned the possibilities over in my head and realized that I trusted Mr. Fausett. I had no doubt he had searched me out for the dance.

Claudia released my hands, and I hung my head in shame. Mr. Fausett's request to dance served not exactly as a trial, but a sort of test. He needed to know that I would be there, that I would keep my word. I'd failed. When our friendship was tested, I'd let him down. Now he was gone, and I desperately wanted to make things right, but the questions remained: where did Mr. Fausett go, and was I the one to drive him away?

CHAPTER 37

Mr. Devlin Fausett

I SAT AT A TABLE at The Drawbridge, leaned back in my chair, and held my eyes steady. If I had any hope of winning, I had to force the other three men to fold. The worthless cards in my hand would get me nowhere.

My bluff would not be good enough to redeem my wager, and I would return home empty-handed. But no, I couldn't go home—rather, I would return to Lily Glen more broken than when I'd left. The round passed to me, and my stomach churned. I was weak and broken, and no matter how much I wanted to walk away, the pull to stay was stronger. Sitting at the table, I could pretend to forget Miss Ellsworth's slight. I could pretend to ignore the sting of jealousy as I watched her dance in the arms of another man. My bruised ego was nothing compared to my shattered heart.

"You in or not?" asked the unshaven man sitting across the table.

I reached forward and fingered the few shillings scattered in front of me. The door to the inn opened, and the room quieted in an instant. I turned to see Miss Ellsworth step through the doorway, followed by one of the footmen from Lily Glen. She still wore her formal gown, and she resembled a furious siren, fearsome and captivating. She searched the room, and when her eyes landed on me, there was a momentary flicker of joy before tension crackled in the air and she blew across the room like a tempest. The other gentlemen had the wherewithal to stand, but I dared not move.

"Mr. Fausett," she said with her hands clenched at her side. Her blue eyes were dark with fury. "What are you doing here?"

A chasm opened in my chest. I cleared my throat and motioned to the table. "I needed a diversion."

The real diversion I needed stood before me. She'd come to find me. Miss Ellsworth left the ball, the guests, and Browning and searched me out.

I slowly stood and said, "I came to find you for our dance, but you were gone."

Her hand flew across my face.

Through trembling lips she said, "Don't you dare blame me for this." She pointed a single finger at the table, spread with cards and coins. "You left. You brought yourself here, and you sat down at this table. This has nothing to do with me and everything to do with you."

She was both right . . . and wrong.

"Why did you come?" I asked.

Tears pooled in her eyes. "Because I thought . . . I hoped . . . you'd changed."

The emptiness inside funneled out through my limbs. "I'm afraid I'm the coward I always was," I said.

"No." Miss Ellsworth shook her head and reached her hand up to touch my stinging cheek. "You are so much more."

Her gentle touch, her words, pierced my heart. I placed my hand over hers and closed my fingers.

"If you two don't mind, I came to play poker, and there's a bet on the table," the man said and sat back down in his spindle-backed chair.

Our joined hands lowered to the space between us, and Miss Ellsworth squeezed gently before letting go. "Will you leave this now and escort me back?" she asked.

My chest lightened, lifting like the steam of a breath on a frigid morning. "It would be my pleasure."

I tossed my cards on the table. "Fold," I said and scooped the shillings into my hand. Then I offered my arm to Miss Ellsworth and escorted her from the inn.

I handed Miss Ellsworth into the carriage and then headed back to the barn to retrieve Juno. An unfamiliar stable boy yawned as he handed over the reins. I secured Juno to the back of the carriage and instructed the footman not to drive too quickly. I opened the carriage door and a movement caught my eye. The lad I'd seen exiting Lily Glen more than a week ago scuttled out of the inn.

"Mr. Fausett, is Juno settled?" Miss Ellsworth called.

I turned and stepped into the equipage. "Yes, thank you," I said and sat across from Miss Ellsworth. I looked out the window, but the boy had disappeared into the shadows.

The carriage lurched forward, and the movement jarred my words free. "Miss Ellsworth, I am ashamed that you knew where to find me tonight. I hope you can forgive my weakness."

"Actually, I cannot." Disappointment drifted through the darkened space between us. I hung my head. "We are friends, Mr. Fausett, and I believe in you. If I let you off this time, you will assume you are forgiven, and it will make it easier for you to falter again. I don't want you to falter. Therefore, I cannot forgive you."

Her diatribe brought a smile to my lips. "So you will punish a man for his weakness?"

"You asked me to help you," she said. "That's what I'm attempting to do."

"By withholding your forgiveness?" I asked.

"Don't worry, sir. I'm sure you can earn it eventually."

"Really?" I leaned back in my seat. "How shall I go about it?"

"You must differentiate between those weaknesses that are good and those which aren't," Miss Ellsworth said. Her tone was serious, and given the darkness, I could not decipher if she was teasing.

"Is any weakness truly acceptable?" I asked.

"Certainly weakness is a natural consequence of our nature," she said. "We can't all be stalwart all the time. But there are weaknesses which strengthen and weaknesses that, well . . . weaken."

"Are you certain?" I asked. "By definition, a weakness is always a flaw."

"But how do you use that flaw? One of my weaknesses is singing—"

"Hardly," I said and cut her off with a chuckle.

"Truly, 'tis. When I was little, I sang all the time. I'd spend hours in the nursery humming some made-up tune or singing a familiar lullaby. It drove my parents mad. They never had silence when I was around. They would scold me and try to get me to refrain, but no matter how much I tried, I could not. However, Mr. Ambly, my vocal teacher, told me that my constant singing allowed my voice to develop. Of course, I don't sing all the time now. I save it for the appropriate situation, but as you can see, I turned my weakness into something more."

"Hmm. I'm afraid there's no positive recourse for my addiction." I wished I could overcome my preference for the tables by humming a childhood tune.

"Why did you go? Tonight?" Miss Ellsworth's voice turned serious. "Why did you leave?"

I rubbed a hand over my face. "I . . ." I blew out a breath. "I was upset. I resorted to what I knew."

"Why were you upset?" she asked.

"I'd rather not say," I said.

"Please." Miss Ellsworth shifted, and a moment later, her hand lay on my arm. "We are friends. I'd like to know."

Warmth burned beneath her hand. The contact was minimal, but the emotions it evoked made me want to tell her all. I settled for a summarized excuse. "Suffice it to say, jealousy is another weakness of mine. I'm afraid it got the best of me. I . . . I was very much looking forward to dancing with you."

"Oh," Miss Ellsworth breathed. "As was I." She shifted, and I missed the contact the moment she lifted her hand away. "Perhaps, Mr. Fausett, your disappointment this evening could transform a weakness into something more."

How I wished I could look into her eyes. Her suggestion flipped something inside of me. "What course do you recommend?" I asked.

"You could ask me again . . . to dance." She finished the sentence with a whisper, but I heard every word as clearly as if she'd shouted.

We pulled up to Lily Glen, and I quickly jumped down to assist Miss Ellsworth. Music, laughter, and conversation spilled from the open windows. Without a word, I pulled Miss Ellsworth's arm through my own and led her towards the door.

As we climbed the front steps, I leaned near and asked, "Would you do me the honor of dancing with me?"

Miss Ellsworth turned her head and offered a radiant smile. "I would like that very much."

The butler stood sentinel at the door, and I didn't miss his look of censure at my casual attire. I looked cautiously at Miss Ellsworth. "I'll change and return shortly," I said.

"Nonsense." She immediately tightened her hold on my arm, and led me towards the music. "It's late, and the dancing will end soon. If you wish to completely transform your weakness to a strength, it's best not put off. Besides, you look rather dashing in your gray coat."

I couldn't help the grin that erupted. "Very well," I said, and we stepped through the entrance to the ballroom. I lifted her hand from my sleeve and bowed. "Miss Ellsworth, may I have this dance?"

CHAPTER 38

Miss Nora Ellsworth

THE UNRESTRAINED PLEASURE ON MR. Fausett's face would have made me swoon, if I were that sort of girl. The dancing lasted for another hour, and with the exception of the required dance figures, Mr. Fausett did not let me go. Various guests whispered and cast looks of derision at Mr. Fausett's informal attire, but it all wafted by like a prickling breeze and only made me burrow further into the comfortable cloak of Mr. Fausett's attentions.

Every glance, every smile, every touch from Mr. Fausett was like an intimate caress. Mother blanched when she saw us, but Claudia seemed to recognize the legitimacy of the connection, for she offered a sweet smile of reassurance. Perhaps she recognized some of the same emotions she had felt throughout the evening. It seemed her feelings had shifted towards the doctor she once considered only a friend.

I felt Mr. Fausett's eyes on me again and considered how it felt both peculiar and right to know that feelings of friendship had shifted into something more. To love someone based on a developed friendship seemed the best sort of companionship possible.

While I did not know Mr. Fausett's intentions for certain, every time he glanced at me, there was an acknowledgment of something more. The tender way he held my hand, the lingering feeling of his touch, and his insistence on remaining by my side all lent support to my own growing affections.

As the evening ended and the guests departed, Mr. Fausett walked me to the top of the stairway and bid me good night. When he turned to walk away, I called to him. He turned back around. His hands clasped behind his back, and his charcoal eyes sharpened their focus. "Thank you for a lovely evening. I . . . I think you redeemed yourself completely."

"Am I forgiven, then?" he asked.

I lifted one shoulder. "I'll think about it."

His lips twitched into a smile, and he nodded once again before he turned and walked away.

CHAPTER 39

Mr. Devlin Fausett

I SLEPT CONTENTEDLY FOR THE first time in a long while and awoke early, eager to ask Mr. Ellsworth for his daughter's hand. Doctor Hadley stepped out of Mr. Ellsworth's chamber just as I approached. We exchanged a greeting, and I asked after Miss Ellsworth's father.

Hadley shook his head. "I'm at a loss. His stomach clenches and tightens. It's very painful. I've prescribed the most basic tincture and an extremely bland diet, but nothing seems to help."

"Is there another doctor you could consult?" I asked.

"The nearest doctor is in Flynn, nearly a two-hour ride away. I've sent an express detailing every symptom and complaint. Hopefully I'll hear back by day's end." Hadley shrugged. "I'm afraid there's not much more I can do."

I put my hand on his shoulder. "I count it a blessing you're here. Certainly Ellsworth is better off in your care than he otherwise would have been. No matter what happens."

"I only hope Miss Claudia will concur with you," Hadley said. I moved my hand away and watched my friend shrug in defeat. His eyes met mine briefly before looking away. "Miss Claudia seems to have unwavering faith when it comes to my medical skills. She's confident I can heal her father. I would do anything to make it so, but I'm afraid this is out of my hands."

"You really think this is the end?" I asked.

Hadley nodded. "If he can't keep down any nourishment . . ."

"How long?" I asked.

"Three days. Maybe less."

I started at the grim assessment and ran a hand across my forehead. Through the door, I heard Mr. Ellsworth wail in pain.

"Can I speak with him?" I asked.

"You can try," Hadley said. "He keeps mumbling about settling a debt. Making things right." Hadley huffed in discouragement. "I've no idea how to help the man. I've tried everything I know."

"I know that, my friend. Miss Claudia does as well." For some reason the assurance felt important to offer.

I clapped Hadley one more time across the back and then pushed open the door to Mr. Ellsworth's room. If I was going to pursue a courtship with the man's daughter, I hoped to get his blessing.

When I stepped through the door, he moaned again. His face contorted in a pained scowl, sweat banded his forehead, and he growled at me. The room smelled of moisture and rancid food. I swallowed past the bile rising in my throat.

"Mr. Ellsworth," I said, and he growled again, weaker this time. "I'm sorry for intruding, and I'm sorry for your"—I waved my hand towards the bed— "discomfort."

Ellsworth gave a caustic chuckle. "What do you want?" he asked.

Now was the time to be brave. I took a step forward. "I want to marry your daughter," I said. "I've become quite fond of Miss Ellsworth, and I'm interested in pursuing a match."

Mr. Ellsworth's eyes pinched closed, and he held his breath, finally releasing it and inhaling again quickly. It took a moment for his features to smooth. "Heard about the entail, did you?" he asked between spurts of breath.

"No . . . I mean, yes. Your daughter told me the details of the entail on your estate, but that's not why—"

"Ha!" he exclaimed forcefully then bent forward. He reached for a bowl from the side of the bed and vomited.

My stomach clenched in time with his retching, and I raised a hand to cover my mouth. When the heaving subsided, Ellsworth grabbed a nearby towel and wiped at his chin. He set it aside, leaned back into his pillows and pointed a single finger at me.

"I know about you, Fausett. Played around after school, didn't want to take responsibility . . ." He groaned again, and I stood still until he quieted and continued. "Bitter at the old man, then lost big at the tables."

I ground my teeth together in an effort to control my emotions—and my stomach.

"Trenton told me all about you," he said and closed his eyes again. "Besides, Nora's already spoken for," he said quietly.

I wanted to ask about Trenton's insinuations. Why did my past concern him? But I focused on my goal—courting Miss Ellsworth.

"No doubt by Browning," I said, shifting my stance. "So you approve of their match?"

"I do," he said without opening his eyes. "He may need her money too, but their union would make Nora's mother happy."

"So that's it?" I asked. "You'd dismiss *my* request to make Miss Ellsworth happy? What about your daughter? What about what she wants? Has she no say in her future spouse?" Mr. Ellsworth didn't respond, so I continued. "And what do you mean Browning needs her money? What about his vast fortune in India?" I couldn't contain the sarcasm in my voice. Mr. Ellsworth heaved a mirthless chuckle. "Shouldn't Browning marry your daughter for something more than her dowry?" I asked.

With a great amount of effort, Mr. Ellsworth opened his eyes again. "India? You mean the fortune his father squandered away on some ridiculous investment?" He laughed once again then lifted one hand off the bed before letting it fall back down to the blankets. "It's all been in place for so long, it hardly matters. Browning will suit. As long as he hurries up with it. If I die before he can post the banns, 'tis all for naught."

Ellsworth's information, along with his disregard for his daughter's happiness, pierced my soul. Each breath burned raw with a determination to set things right. Miss Ellsworth did not deserve a contemptible marriage. She deserved to love and be loved, and the thought of her father settling for anything less charred like scalding lava.

"Have you asked Miss Ellsworth what she wants?" I asked. Mr. Ellsworth turned to evaluate me. "If your only concern is preserving your estate for your wife and daughters, perhaps Miss Ellsworth might have a say in the matter."

"What are you playing at?" he asked.

"I love your daughter, sir. I'm doing my best to forsake the tables, and she motivates me every day to be a better man. Let her decide whom she will marry." I stood taller as I spoke, the words buoying me up.

"As I said, it hardly matters. Nora needs to wed. Either she can make her choice, or I'll make it for her," Ellsworth said. He waved his hand at the teacup and half-eaten biscuit sitting on his bedside table. "Now, take that away and leave me be."

It wasn't exactly a blessing, but it wasn't a refusal. I wanted Miss Ellsworth to be happy. I wanted her to have a choice. And I hoped her choice would be me.

I picked up the plate and cup and headed for the kitchen, anxious to find a quiet moment to speak with Miss Ellsworth about my conversation with her father. I hoped to confess my shortcomings along with my growing affection.

Some moments I was sure she knew of my feelings; moments when the air felt both thin and heavy at the same time. When words or entire conversations seemed to pass without a single utterance.

In the kitchen, a young woman with a soiled apron chopped potatoes. Another girl pushed and pulled a pile of dough while one of the footmen I recognized moved a boiling pot from the stove to a nearby table.

Cook saw me, and when I held out the dishes, she took them and offered her thanks. I escaped through the propped-open door, grateful for the welcome breeze stirring the air.

"Excuse me, sir." I turned to see a young girl standing with a sprig of rosemary. "Are you looking for Marcus?" she asked, brushing a strand of hair from her eyes.

"Marcus?" I asked.

She nodded. "The yellow-haired boy always came before, but since the man came yesterday lookin' for him, I thought maybe you was too." She looked down at her apron. "Mama's sick today, so Marcus stayed home to help."

The girl was adorable but obviously vulnerable as well. "How long has your mother been sick?" I asked.

"Two days." She broke off the end of the rosemary twig and popped a sprig in her mouth. "Marcus took her some of the healing herbs they've been givin' to Mr. Ellsworth, but if they ain't doin' him no good, I don't think they're gonna help Mama." Moisture pooled in her eyes, and I knelt down and offered her my handkerchief. "Thank you, sir," she said and then sniffled. "You're much nicer than that man yesterday."

"What did the man want?" I asked.

Her little shoulders lifted and fell. "Marcus said he wasn't supposed to tell, but I heard the man yellin', so I sneaked into the garden and listened."

"What did you hear?" I asked.

"The man was angry that Mr. Ellsworth was still sick. He told Marcus that the tea had to be made from the special herbs and promised it'd make him better. That's why Marcus took some to Mama. He thought they'd help her too."

"Did they?" I asked.

"Not yet. She's still vomiting," the girl said and wiped her nose before she remembered the rosemary in her hand. Her eyes grew wide. "I best get this inside if I want supper tonight."

She held the handkerchief out to me. "Keep it," I said.

Her thumb rubbed over the linen. "Sir?"

"I insist," I said and stood.

She dipped a quick curtsy and ran inside.

Hadley took his role as doctor seriously, and although he could come across as brash and blunt, I didn't think he would yell at a young boy. The girl probably mistook Hadley's rough manners for anger. He thought he was going to lose a patient and there was nothing more he could do. I decided to seek Hadley out to tell him he'd frightened the poor girl.

The door of the small sitting room sat ajar, and I silently peered inside to see Hadley sitting beside Miss Claudia. He held her fingers in his, and neither of them noticed my presence. Hadley whispered soft words to Miss Claudia while he tenderly caressed her hand. I backed into the hallway, happily resigned to speak to Hadley at a later time about a boy named Marcus and the doctor's sudden regard for Miss Claudia Ellsworth.

CHAPTER 40

Miss Nora Ellsworth

WHY? WHY DID GRANDFATHER HAVE to insist on the stipulation of marriage? Why did Father not tell me sooner? Why was I born the eldest daughter? And why did my stomach churn every time I considered Mr. Browning's loveless proposal?

Pacing the music room brought little comfort. I turned and marched towards the door to the garden, but Mr. Browning's voice halted my exit.

"Miss Ellsworth," he called.

I turned around.

"May I have a moment?" He walked forward until he stood only two feet away. Mr. Browning put his hand on my elbow and led me to the couch. "I understand your father's condition has not improved," he said and sat beside me.

I shook my head. Words stuck with an ache in my chest.

Mr. Browning shifted his shoulders and moved to catch my attention. "I'm sorry for your difficulties. I truly am. Have you given any more thought to our conversation last night?"

My eyes pressed closed. Of course I had thought of his proposal, and while I wished I could shut it out and put it far from my mind, I knew I could not.

"Time is limited," he said, and while his voice was soft, the reminder stung.

I opened my eyes but could not find the energy to feign another smile. "Mr. Browning, I do appreciate your offer. However . . ." There was too much turmoil churning within me to sit still. I quickly stood, and Mr. Browning's blue eyes shifted to resemble a turbulent storm. "I cannot accept your hand."

"Truly?" he asked with a callous chuckle.

I fisted my hands and looked him in the eyes. "I'm sorry."

"That's it? You're sorry?" He stood. "Your mother has been conniving for years, and now that everything she's worked for is possible, all you have to offer is, you're sorry?"

"You know I had no part in our parents' arrangements," I insisted as my chest rose and fell.

"Nor did I," Mr. Browning thundered. "Yet I stand here and offer you the perfect solution. I offer to bind our families together, to see our parents' wishes honored. I offer you stability and comfort, a home for your sister and mother, and you would refuse me? For what?"

My hands trembled, but I held my chin high. "My mother meddled in affairs and decisions that were not hers to make. And for that I apologize, but I owe you nothing, sir."

"You are prepared to lose your home?"

"Yes," I said.

"And turn your mother and sister out into the street?" Mr. Browning's eyes narrowed, but I held his gaze. He slinked forward slowly. "I did not think you were so selfish, Miss Ellsworth."

His words hit their mark. Tears gathered in my eyes, but I refused to look away from him. "You would deny your father's dying wish?" His voice rose as he continued his advance. "If he passes and we are not engaged . . ." Mr. Browning's words died away as he raised his hand and reached for my cheek.

I turned my head away from his touch, and the tears fell.

"I am a prideful man, madam. Your father could pass, even this very hour. If you refuse me and walk away now, I cannot help you," Mr. Browning said. His voice sliced the breaths between us like a cold blade. "This is your last chance."

My fingers throbbed from clenching them so tight, but my conversation with Mr. Browning only served to strengthen my resolve. "I cannot marry you," I said.

Mr. Browning stepped close. My body tensed as he whispered in my ear, "Then I pray your father will rest in peace knowing you defied his final wish." Mr. Browning grunted in disgust and stormed from the room.

His parting words collided violently in my heart, and I collapsed onto the couch and sobbed.

CHAPTER 41

Mr. Devlin Fausett

I DETERMINED TO FIND MISS Ellsworth and ask for her hand. I walked towards the south drawing room but stopped when I heard elevated voices coming from farther down the hall.

I recognized Mr. Browning's demanding voice but could not decipher his specific words. The noise suddenly ceased. The quiet pulsated outwards, more disturbing than the commotion, and I decided to investigate.

I'd nearly reached the door of the music room when Browning came barreling out with fire in his eyes. He pulled to a stop when he saw me, and his lips twisted in disgust.

"That infuriating woman is all yours, Fausett. Good riddance," he said before he stormed away.

I watched him for only a moment before pushing the door of the room wide. The sight of Miss Ellsworth's trembling shoulders, coupled with her sobs, nearly undid me.

I rushed to the sofa and knelt beside her. "Are you all right? What has he done?" I asked.

She dropped her hands from her face, and her red-rimmed eyes turned towards me. Miss Ellsworth tried to be strong; she tried to stop the flow of tears, but she could not. She only shook her head.

Part of me wanted to track down Browning and demand answers for Miss Ellsworth's distressed state, but the larger part of me wanted to wrap her in my arms and assure her that all would be well. If I discovered Browning had misused her or injured her in some way, he would suffer—immensely.

I reached for my handkerchief only to remember that it was gone. "I'm sorry I can't offer you a handkerchief. You've really terrible timing, as I bequeathed it to a little girl not more than thirty minutes ago," I said.

Miss Ellsworth laughed a bit through her tears, but her sorrow still hung heavy, and my hands hung useless at my side.

A sobering thought hit. "Has your father . . ." I began.

Her head shook. "No," she said and sniffled. "'Tis not that."

Miss Ellsworth wiped at her nose with the back of her hand and valiantly tried to convince me she was well.

"Allow me," I said, and I pulled my shirtsleeve over my wrist and leaned forward to clear the tears from her cheeks.

Miss Ellsworth wrapped her fingers around my arm. "You'll soil your shirt."

I continued my ministrations with a small smile. "A soiled shirt is a small price to pay for a friend."

"Truly?" she asked.

"Truly," I replied and couldn't hide my confusion when tears began to fall again. "Why more tears, my dear?"

"You, Mr. Fausett, are the best of men," she said.

There was nothing to do then but pull her close. It was highly improper for her head to be buried against my chest. My arms rested lightly across her back while I questioned the legitimacy of her claim that I was a good man. But she needed comfort, and I could not refuse her.

Once her tears subsided, she pulled back, sniffling some more. "Oh dear," she said, wiping the lapel of my jacket. "I'm afraid I've ruined your coat now, as well."

"Don't concern yourself with that, Miss Ellsworth," I said and grabbed her hand in mine. "Did Browning . . . did he hurt you?"

Her eyes softened. "No. He did nothing untoward," she said and shook her head.

"Then why the tears?" I asked.

"His actions were sound, as were his accusations." A sad smile filled her face. I instinctively tensed, and Miss Ellsworth squeezed my hand in hers. "There's no need to call him out, I assure you. He was simply angry with me for rejecting him."

"Oh," I said. I released her hand. "I heard raised voices and grew concerned. I apologize if I interfered."

"As I said, the best of men," Miss Ellsworth said, and with a heaving breath, she looked at her hands in her lap.

I wanted to proclaim my intentions to her then and there. I wanted to tell her how she fascinated me, how she improved me, and how I longed for our friendship to become something more. But Miss Ellsworth was sad, and I was not sure if my pronouncement would make her happy, and all I wanted in that moment was to make her happy. To see her smile a true, unfettered smile. So I spoke a truth I knew.

"If I am a good man, Miss Ellsworth, I owe it all to you. Surely, you know that."

Her eyes moved from her lap to meet my gaze. She breathed, and her lips parted as if she meant to speak, but then she said nothing.

"I'll leave you with your thoughts." I stood and after a quick bow turned towards the door.

"Mr. Fausett," Miss Ellsworth cried out. I turned around. She slowly stood, her hands hung at her side. "Father may pass soon," she said.

Her words floated through the air and hit my heart with precision. "I know," I said.

"And if he passes before I am married, Ellsworth Meadows is lost," she said.

"I know," I said again.

"And if our home is gone, my mother and my sister and myself . . . we've nowhere to go," she said with a shaky voice, her hands fisted at her sides.

"Do you think a friend would leave you to the streets? Do you think a friend would allow you to come to harm?" I asked.

Her head shook and with a whisper, she said, "No."

"And do you consider me your friend?" I asked.

"Yes," she said on the breath of a cry.

"Then I hope you will trust that all will be made right," I said.

Miss Ellsworth's fingers straightened at her side. "I will," she said.

I smiled and left to find Hadley.

I found the doctor pacing in the study on the second floor. "You've done all you can," I said as I stepped through the door.

He pinched his thumb and middle finger on his temples. "There has to be something more. Something I'm missing."

"How's Miss Claudia?" I asked.

His eyebrows rose in question. "She's well. Why do you ask?"

"You're fond of her," I said.

He looked at me sideways, evaluating, waiting, wondering if I'd say more. I didn't.

"Quite," he answered.

"Good," I said.

He sighed heavily. "Not if I can't save her father."

We were back at it again.

"Miss Claudia's injury was easy to diagnose. There was an obvious change in behavior. The symptoms were measurable." Hadley began pacing again. "I can work with that. But Ellsworth's case has given me nothing. He contracts a sudden violent stomach pain. The vomiting is to be expected, but why did the discomfort start to begin with?" He growled, planted both hands on his hips, and looked at me. "Since I don't know the source of the pain, the only thing I can do is limit his diet, which only makes him weaker."

"About that," I said. "Next time you speak with Marcus, you may want to apologize for frightening his sister. Your boorish behavior rattled the poor girl."

Hadley narrowed his eyes. "Marcus?"

"The lad in the kitchen. The one you gave the herbs to," I said.

Hadley's brow knit in confusion. "Fausett, I don't know what you're talking about."

Unease crept in with my next words. "The little girl in the kitchen told me a man gave her brother a selection of herbs to make Ellsworth's tea. She said the gentleman promised that if Ellsworth drank the tea, he would feel better. I assumed it was you who had spoken with the boy." Hadley shook his head. "Who else could it be?" I asked, though my gut already told me the answer. "Blast!" The unease I'd felt ignited. "The boy was so convinced, he took some home to his sick mother, but the girl said she was vomiting also."

"I gave Mrs. Norse the list of ingredients for Ellsworth's tea. I've not set foot near the kitchens," Hadley said.

We looked at each other, and in unspoken formation, we rushed from the study down to the kitchens. At our abrupt entrance, the bustle in the room ceased.

"Has Marcus arrived?" I asked.

Cook stepped forward. "His mum's still sick. Ain't seen him today."

"His sister?" I asked.

Cook looked over her shoulder. "Miriam," she called. "Step forward."

I shifted to see the girl, Miriam, peeking out from behind a large bag of flour. I stepped to where she could see me clearly then stopped and squatted low. "Do you remember me, Miriam?" I asked.

Her wide eyes looked over my face, and she nodded slowly. I waved towards Doctor Hadley. "This is my friend, Doctor Hadley. We want to ask you a few questions. Would that be all right?"

Miriam blinked but did not answer.

"Doctor Hadley's a very good doctor. He might be able to help your mother feel better. Would you like that?" I asked.

This time Miriam nodded. She waited a moment then stepped out from her hiding place.

"Is Doctor Hadley the man you saw talking to Marcus?" I asked.

Miriam turned her gaze to Hadley and squinted her eyes at him. Then she shook her head.

"No?" I asked. "Are you sure, Miriam? This is very important."

"The other man wasn't nice," she said softly. "Your friend looks nice."

I glanced back at Hadley. His face was tight, but he held his tongue.

"Can you tell me about the other man? The mean one?" I asked and held my hand out towards her. "Did he have dark hair? Was he tall?"

Miriam looked at my hand and came forward to take it. "His hair was like Peter's," she said and pointed to a brown-haired boy standing in the doorway. "And he wasn't as tall as you."

It wasn't a lot to go on. "Is there anything else you can remember, Miriam?" I asked.

"I told Marcus that he shouldn't take the mean man's money, but he said we could buy a few chickens and have fresh eggs," she said.

I gave Miriam's small hand a gentle squeeze and looked at Cook. "Please show us the herbs you've been using for Mr. Ellsworth's tea," I said.

The middle-aged woman pressed her lips into a tight line and wiped her hands on her apron. She walked to the stove, reached for a cloth bag behind the teakettle, and then handed it to the doctor.

Hadley sniffed the contents then dumped some into his hand and sniffed again. "Where did you get this?" he asked.

"Mrs. Norse brought a list. Said to gather the herbs for a tea and that I was to make it every three hours for Mr. Ellsworth," Cook said in between quickened breaths. She wrung her hands in front of her. "Marcus is in charge of bundling the herbs."

Hadley sifted through the jumble of herbs in his palm. "What's this red . . . is it a berry?" He mushed the offending berry with his finger and touched it to the tip of his tongue. He immediately spat and wiped his sleeve across his mouth. "This is holly! And you've been boiling the tea with this?" Hadley shook the half-full bag at Cook, and her lips began to tremble. "How could you not recognize a holly berry?"

"Hadley," I said. "Let her be. She's not responsible for this." I turned to the boy they'd called Peter. "Will you please find Mrs. Norse? Then return and take Miriam home to fetch her brother and bring them both back here. Tell the children's mother not to drink any more of the tea."

"Yes, sir," the lad said and bowed before hurrying from the room.

I knelt back down. "Miriam, will you wait here with Cook until Peter comes back to take you home?" The sweet girl nodded. I stood and released her hand. "When everyone arrives, please send them to the west drawing room. Something's not right, and we need to figure out what's going on." Cook nodded. "Come on, Hadley," I said, and with the tea bag in hand, he followed me from the room.

CHAPTER 42

Miss Nora Ellsworth

THE SUMMONS FROM THE HOUSEMAID to meet Doctor Hadley in the west drawing room made my stomach plummet to my toes. When I didn't follow her, she claimed there was an urgent matter, and it took an entire minute before my feet shifted forward.

The pilgrimage to the assigned room was both too long and too short. The maid curtsied at the door, and I walked in to find the room full, anxious gazes fixed on me. "Is it Father?" I asked.

"No." Claudia stepped forward and took my hands in hers. "I mean, in a way it is . . ."

"What do you mean?"

"Miss Ellsworth, your father's condition is stable," Mr. Fausett said. "Doctor Hadley believes he has a chance at a full recovery."

"If his heart holds strong," Doctor Hadley said, marching the length of the room and back again. He spun around, and with his hand on his chin, he tapped a finger against his lips. "And hopefully, there will be no lasting damage on his stomach and intestines." He began his trek again. "I'd like to consult a colleague who specializes in this area."

I looked at Mother. She lay sprawled on the sofa, and Mrs. Browning sat nearby fanning her.

"I don't understand," I confessed.

"Hadley believes someone has been poisoning your father," the elder Mr. Browning said from across the room.

"What?" I asked, looking around the room and feeling suddenly lightheaded.

"Come sit down," Mr. Fausett said and led me to a chair.

Claudia walked beside me, and when I sat, she grabbed my hand and squeezed. "It's really the most horrid thing, Nora," she said. "Can you imagine someone wanting to hurt our dear father?"

Confusion nested in my head, and I tried to shake it free.

"Doctor Hadley discovered holly berries in your father's tea," Mr. Fausett said. Mother wailed her grief from her place on the sofa. Mr. Fausett glanced at my mother and then turned back to me. "He believes the berries are the cause of your father's stomach pains. Mrs. Norse is with him now, trying to coax him to drink water to flush the poison from his body."

My head felt heavy, like it was filled with mud. "How? Why?" Words refused to form on my tongue.

"Mrs. Norse was given a list of ingredients for the tea. She gave the list to Cook, who claims to have gathered them exactly," Mr. Fausett said.

"We've no reason to doubt Mrs. Norse," Mrs. Browning said defensively.

"I agree," Doctor Hadley said. "That's why I sent her to assist Mr. Ellsworth, even now."

"We believe someone else swapped the herbs, replacing them with a mixture containing the poisonous berries," Mr. Fausett said.

"Who would do such a thing?" Mrs. Browning asked, and Mother wailed something about her poor husband.

Mr. Fausett's eyes darkened. He looked first at Doctor Hadley, then at the elder Mr. Browning.

"Excuse me," one of the servants said from the door. "The boy is here."

"Send him in," Mr. Browning said.

A thin, boy with a freckled nose and wiry brown hair stepped into the room. The poor child was visibly shaking. He looked around the room, and when his eyes met mine, he stiffened. I smiled, hoping to calm his nerves.

"Are you Marcus?" Mr. Fausett asked, and the boy turned to him and nodded his head slowly. "Do you know what this is?" Mr. Fausett lifted a fabric sack from the desk and walked it over to the boy.

"Think long and hard on your answer, boy," the elder Mr. Browning warned. "If I find out you've lied, you'll get a lashing you won't soon forget."

Mr. Fausett took a deep breath. "Do you recognize the bag?" he asked. Marcus nodded again.

"Where did you get it?" Mr. Fausett asked.

Marcus stood silent, tension pulling at his brow.

"Speak up, boy!" the elder Mr. Browning bellowed from across the room.

Mr. Fausett reached forward and put a hand on the child's shoulder.

"Marcus, I need to know if you swapped the herbs Cook gathered . . . for these." He held the bag up again. "You see, these are poisonous."

The boy's eyes widened, and he looked directly at Mr. Fausett. "Poison?" he asked.

Mr. Fausett nodded. "Yes, it was made with holly berries."

Marcus looked down at his feet, his head shaking in small quick movements. "But he said they would help . . ." The child began to breathe quickly, and his eyes darted back to Mr. Fausett's. "Mama," he said.

Mr. Fausett squeezed his shoulder. "Miriam told me you gave some to your mother. Did Peter tell her to stop drinking the tea?" he asked.

Marcus nodded. "Yes, sir."

"Then she should recover in a day or two. But now, we must find who is responsible. You must tell me everything you know about the herbs. Who gave them to you? What did he promise you? Money?" Mr. Fausett asked.

The boy flinched at the mention of money.

"I'm not going to lie, Marcus. Swapping the herbs was deceitful, and Mrs. Norse has every reason to dismiss both you and your sister," Mr. Fausett said as moisture pooled in Marcus's eyes.

"Dismiss him?" the elder Mr. Browning snorted. "Whip him proper and send him to a workhouse is more like it. Tainting my household, abusing my trust. That boy needs to be taught a lesson."

The boy deserved a scolding, but I couldn't stand watching the lad get reprimanded for something that wasn't entirely his fault. I moved from the couch to where Marcus stood and knelt down in front of him. "Marcus, I'm Nora. Whoever did this made my father very sick. He could have died. I know you didn't know that or else you wouldn't have given the tea to him or to your mother. Am I right?"

Marcus nodded, and a few tears spilled from his eyes. He wiped them away with his dirty sleeve.

"Doctor Hadley can visit your mother and make sure she will be all right, but do you think you can help us? If you can tell us who is responsible, perhaps Mrs. Norse can give you a letter of recommendation for a new position. We need to stop this man from hurting anyone else," I said and tried to smile. "What do you say? Can you tell us everything you remember?"

Marcus sniffed and tried to blink his eyes dry. "He asked about you, miss, the man did."

Mr. Fausett pulled his hand away from the boy's shoulder. He tensed beside me and asked, "What did he want to know?"

"Same thing as the boy that came earlier. He asked if there was going to be a wedding. He wanted to know if Miss Ellsworth was getting married." Marcus sniffed again. "I told him I didn't know nothin', didn't even know who you were, as I'm always b'low stairs." A smile touched the boy's lips. He looked back at his shoes. "He told me he'd pay me an extra shilling if I could find out anything. Told me to look for the pretty lady with golden hair." He looked at me again, his cheeks rosy red. "It's you he meant. I knew right when I walked in the room. You're the pretty one he asked about."

I steeled myself with a breath then asked, "Do you know the man's name?"

Marcus shook his head. "He told me he was family, and that you'd had a fallin' out, but he only wanted to help." He dropped his eyes to the floor. "I never meant to hurt no one."

"I know you didn't," I said and lifted his chin with my finger. "Thank you, Marcus, for telling the truth." I stood up. "Doctor Hadley, if you feel Father is stable, would you be willing to go with Marcus and examine his mother?"

Hadley looked at me, then Mr. Fausett. "We'll find him," Mr. Fausett said. "You should take a footman and go check on the woman."

"May I come with you?" Claudia asked.

Doctor Hadley agreed, and Claudia walked over to Marcus. She took his hand and sweetly asked him to take them to his mother. I stood and watched as Claudia walked to the door.

"Wait a minute!" the elder Mr. Browning boomed from his position near the fireplace. "That traitorous boy can't just walk away."

"Father, let the boy be. Go on," Mr. Jonathon Browning said and motioned for the trio to leave.

Mr. Browning's eyes filled with anger. "How dare you defy me! That scamp deserves a beating, and you want to let him walk away?"

"This isn't his fault," Mr. Jonathon Browning said forcefully. "If the imminent union of Miss Ellsworth and myself hadn't been paraded about, Mr. Trenton wouldn't have become desperate."

"Trenton?" his father asked.

Mother wailed again from her place on the couch. Mr. Jonathon Browning rolled his eyes and said, "Isn't it obvious? He's the one who gave the boy the herbs."

I gasped and raised my hand to my mouth.

"Are you certain?" Mrs. Browning asked as Mother grasped her hand.

"Who stands to gain if Mr. Ellsworth dies?" Mr. Fausett asked.

"Mr. Trenton," I whispered. My free hand wrapped around my stomach, and in the next moment Mr. Fausett stood beside me, leading me to a chair. "Would he really do such a thing?"

"He knew you were coming to Lily Glen for the purpose of securing the engagement," Mr. Fausett said. Mother gasped, and Mr. Fausett took a stealing breath. "It wasn't exactly a secret. Trenton knew he would lose his claim on the entail. His desperation pushed him over the edge."

Mr. Jonathon Browning stepped forward. "He must be staying at The Drawbridge. What do you say, Fausett? Do you fancy a ride into town?"

"Definitely," Mr. Fausett said, and the two men stormed from the room.

CHAPTER 43

Mr. Devlin Fausett

BROWNING AND I HEADED TO the stables and quickly saddled our horses. The ambiguous Mr. Smith had to be Trenton. We rode hard, any jealousy between us suppressed by the anger stewing from Trenton's treachery.

We arrived at the inn, quickly tossed the reins of the horses to a lad in the stables, and told him to leave the horses saddled. "How do you suggest we go about this?" I asked Browning.

Browning scoffed. "Trenton's a slight of a man. He's no match for one of us, let alone the both of us. We'll confront him and hold him here until the constable arrives."

He strode purposefully into the inn and looked over the patrons while I called for the proprietor.

Bernard grinned when he saw me. "You're fixin' to become a regular." He limped to where I stood at the bar.

"You lied to me, and I don't like to be lied to," I said, and his smile fell away.

"I don't know what you're talking about," Bernard said as he began to absently scrub at an invisible spot on the long counter.

"You told me Mr. Smith arrived last week," I said, and his strokes with his rag slowed.

"That's what the gent wrote. Who am I to question him?" he asked without looking at me.

I slapped a hand down on the counter. "His name wasn't Smith, was it?" I asked.

Bernard lifted one shoulder and glanced at me quickly before looking away again. "You know how it is," he said.

I lunged across the counter and grabbed his collar. Bernard's face fell slack, and his eyes bulged wide. "No, I don't know how it is. Why don't you tell me? And perhaps this time you'll tell me the truth."

Bernard gulped. "Trenton. His name's Trenton."

Browning walked up beside me. "Where's Trenton now?"

Bernard's head quickly shook back and forth. My hand twisted tighter around his shirt, and he turned his head to the side as if he thought I would strike him. "Where is he?" I ground through my teeth.

Bernard whimpered.

"The gent left," someone called from down the bar.

"When?" Browning asked.

"This morning, I think," the stranger said.

I turned back to the proprietor. "Is that right? Is he gone?"

Bernard's lips trembled, but nothing came out. He nodded in short frantic movements.

"Where did he go?" I asked.

Bernard only whimpered some more.

"Where?" I shouted.

"I . . . I . . . I don't know," Bernard said and raised his hands in surrender. "He paid his bill and left before eatin' anything."

I pulled Bernard halfway across the counter. Leaning close I whispered, "You'd better be telling me the truth this time."

"Yes, sir. Yes. I am. I swear." His words tumbled out in pathetic snippets.

I shook Bernard one more time before untwisting my hand from the tangle of his shirt and shoving him back behind the counter.

"What do you think?" Browning asked. "Maybe he left because he thought the job was done."

"I doubt it," I said and planted my hands on my hips. A boy carried a stack of wood to the large stone fireplace, and I recognized him as the blond-haired boy I'd seen on my previous visit to the The Drawbridge. Miriam had described a similar boy asking after Miss Ellsworth. "Hey," I called to him. His eyes met mine, and he dumped the load from his arms and bolted to the door. "Stop there," I called to the boy, but he made his escape before I could cut off his exit.

I ran after him with Browning close behind. Once outside the inn, I saw him round the corner towards the stables.

"I'll cut around back and block his escape," Browning said from behind me, but I knew the boy wasn't trying to circle the building.

I sprinted to the stables. Sure enough, Raven stood untied between the stalls, and the lad stood atop a ladder ready to jump on the horse. He leapt and landed with his arms and legs splayed across Raven's back. Before he could right himself, I grabbed the reins and settled the startled mare.

The boy tried to kick Raven forward, but he didn't know the familiarity I shared with the animal. With her reins in my hand, she would only move on my command.

"Where are you going?" I asked the lad.

The boy seemed to realize the horse would not provide his escape, and he swung his leg over, trying to slide off the opposite side. I easily maneuvered Raven sideways and caught the boy's arm.

"Answer me!" I said.

The boy struggled for a moment. He was strong for his age, but my fingers easily wrapped around his small bicep.

"Why are you running away?" I asked.

Finally, his shaking stilled. "Let me be," he said sullenly.

"Only after you answer my questions. Where are you going?" I repeated.

The boy shrugged.

"How about this," I said. "I'll let you go if you tell me where Trenton is."

The boy's eyes widened with fear.

"You know, don't you?" I asked. "Did you know Trenton tried to kill a friend of mine? I'm afraid he may try again." The color drained from the boy's face, and his frightened eyes rose to mine. "I have to stop him."

With a meek nod, the boy said, "He left this morning. Headed east. Said something about making sure the job was done."

My heart plummeted. I pushed the boy away and swung onto Raven's back.

"I didn't know . . ." the lad called, but I didn't hear the remainder of his words, because all I could do was pray I reached Lily Glen in time.

CHAPTER 44

Miss Nora Ellsworth

DESPITE THE CALM MASK I donned for my mother, my frantic heartbeat refused to settle. Mr. Trenton had tried to poison my father, not merely to injure him, but to kill him!

I wandered the long halls of Lily Glen hoping to outpace the insanity of the revelation, but escape proved impossible. My chest ached and my lungs labored to draw each and every breath. I raised a hand to my chest, anxious to release some invisible latch that might allow me to inhale freely, but the pain would not subside.

My footfalls became more frantic, and I rushed through the music room, ignoring the illuminated glass, anxious to be outside the confines of the house. I pushed through the door and ran into the manicured garden, gulping down the fresh air.

Tears fell slowly, and my breaths settled into a somewhat steady pattern, yet the pain would not leave. The cruel hand of reality had seized my heart, and its clutching claws refused to let go.

Mr. Trenton was behind it all. Mr. Trenton, who always appeared unflustered. Mr. Trenton, whose tedious lectures on decorum tested my patience. Mr. Trenton, who had proposed a loveless marriage in order to get his hands on Ellsworth Meadows. And while he surely despised me as much as I despised him, I couldn't fathom the reality of what he had done.

Father would be fine. Doctor Hadley confirmed his recovery, and I rejoiced in the knowledge. However, with the assurance of Father's recuperation, he was no longer the one I feared losing.

Mr. Fausett, at this very moment, could be confronting Mr. Trenton. Knowing Mr. Trenton to be capable of murder, I feared the outcome of a confrontation with the man. Of course, I didn't want Mr. Browning to get hurt either, but the gripping vice now clenching my heart acknowledged my fear for Mr. Fausett stemmed from feelings deeper than friendship.

I swiped a fist across my cheeks wishing I could clear my head as easily as I could clear the tears.

"Dear Cousin, whatever has upset you?" Mr. Trenton stepped out of the shadows of an ivy-covered trellis.

His voice cracked through the silence of the garden, splitting my heart into tiny fissures. Ice trickled into each vein as he walked towards me. I stepped backwards slowly, scanning for something, anything I could use to defend myself.

"How's your father?" he asked with a smirk smeared across his lips.

I couldn't answer.

"I understand he'll recover . . . this time." Mr. Trenton continued to move forward. He broke a twig off a bush then snapped it in two before tossing it aside. "It would be a pity if he fell ill again or some other *accident* robbed him of his life."

I whimpered. "What do you want? Why can't you leave us alone?"

"I thought I'd made my terms clear. I told you before what I want, and you refused. You could have prevented all of this from happening, Nora." Mr. Trenton spread his arms wide. "No one need get hurt."

I shook my head while my feet continued to move backwards. I kept my eyes on Mr. Trenton and stumbled before catching myself.

His eyes drew together, and he extended his hand. "Come with me to Gretna Green, and I can personally ensure your father's wellbeing. Once we are married, I give you my word that your mother and sister will always have a place with us."

"Your word is of little value, sir," I said with a trembling voice.

Mr. Trenton halted his advance. I glanced around again. I could now see the mosaic door leading to the music room, but Mr. Trenton would easily catch me before I escaped.

With a sneer, he tilted his head to the side and extended his hand. "What do you say, Cousin?"

I shifted my feet behind me, moving only inches at a time. I decided to run and hoped Mr. Trenton wouldn't pursue me. My head shook while I continued to step backwards, wanting to put as much distance between us as necessary before I bolted for the door. "I could never marry you," I said.

Mr. Trenton frowned, but quickly smiled again. He tsk'd. "We would make a handsome couple, Nora."

"On the outside, perhaps," I said. "But if I married you, I would die a little every day. Being your wife would kill me slowly; like the tea you gave Father, it would poison me from the inside out."

Mr. Trenton's smile dropped away, darkness filled his features, and I knew I needed to run. Fast.

CHAPTER 45

Mr. Devlin Fausett

RAVEN GALLOPED HARD, AND I pushed her harder. I approached Lily Glen from the west, angling for the front of the house, but as I neared the entrance, I heard a scream.

I pressed my knees into Raven's side, and she responded immediately, cutting right and then rounding the west side of the estate. Raven veered towards the gardens, circling just beyond the outer wall. When I heard a second scream, I slowed the horse and straightened my spine.

"Release me!"

I recognized the voice as Miss Ellsworth's. Panic gripped my lungs as I searched frantically for her.

"You've made your choice, Cousin. It didn't have to be like this."

I spotted them then. Trenton stood with one arm wrapped around Miss Ellsworth, pinning her arms down while he held her body against his. With his other hand, he attempted to smother her screams, but she tossed her head away and cried out again.

I kicked Raven, and she bolted forward, leaping over the half-wall circling the garden. Trenton turned at the commotion. I dismounted and charged towards him, prepared to pummel him senseless. Trenton positioned Miss Ellsworth between us, using her body as a shield to keep me from reaching him. Fire flowed through my veins and churned in my chest. I closed the distance quickly, and when I was only a foot away, Trenton released his hold on Miss Ellsworth and shoved her towards me.

Her arms flailed as she collided against my body. I stumbled backwards a few steps to prevent us from tumbling to the ground in a heap. My arms wrapped around Miss Ellsworth's frame, and I paused my furious advance in order to be sure she remained unharmed.

"Are you all right?" I asked.

She trembled against me and on a shaky breath said, "Yes."

I moved my hands to her shoulders and leaned down to look into her eyes. I meant to confirm her wellbeing, to verify that Trenton did no more than frighten her, but when our eyes met, my entire person filled with an intense burning, and the words left in my mouth were not ones I could utter. The love I felt for the woman in my arms far surpassed any rush from the tables. Any elation I'd felt before paled in comparison to the emotion now flooding through my soul.

"Stand aside, Fausett." Trenton's voice broke my reverie. "Miss Ellsworth will be coming with me."

I looked over her head and saw Trenton standing with a pistol aimed at us. If he fired now, Miss Ellsworth would be hit, though I doubted she was his intended target. Instinct took over, and I shifted sideways to pull Miss Ellsworth behind me.

She looked at Trenton and cried out, "No, he'll shoot you." I stepped forward to block Miss Ellsworth from Trenton's view as she pressed and struggled against my arm, trying to step up beside me.

I glanced at her quickly before looking back at Trenton. "Please, Miss Ellsworth, let me be brave," I said.

She gasped on a sob and stopped fighting me. Her arm still gripped mine, but once I was certain she stood behind me, I turned back to the threat at hand. "Miss Ellsworth is not going anywhere." If only I could create a diversion for her to run away to safety.

"Ha!" Trenton cackled and waved the gun through the air. "You think you can stop me?"

"I have every intention of stopping you," I said. Miss Ellsworth's fingers tightened further.

Trenton's eyes narrowed, and he steadied the gun in his hand. "You will not stand in my way. Not you! Not that trollop! Not her father!" His mouth turned down and he sneered. "I will do whatever is necessary. Ellsworth Meadows will be mine."

A gunshot echoed through the air, and Miss Ellsworth cried out. I sucked in a breath as searing pain ripped through my side. A second shot rang out. Through blurred vision, I saw Trenton fall to the ground, and his pistol clattered onto the cobblestone beside him. I doubled over, unable to breathe. Warm, fiery agony spread through my body and made my head swim. My legs buckled, and I fell to my knees.

"Devlin!" Miss Ellsworth cried out. Her voice rang both loud and welcome.

Blackness crept into my head. Miss Ellsworth put her hand on my back. I tried to blink and focus on her voice and push away the perpetual pain. She needed to run! She needed to leave! If only I could tell her.

The sound of a weapon cocking made me suck in a breath. I braced my hands on the ground and turned my head to see Hadley leveling a shotgun at Trenton.

Hadley moved forward, steady and sure. "One move Trenton, and you're a dead man," he said.

Relief coursed through me until another shot sounded. I gasped for air and watched Hadley kick Trenton's pistol away. Trenton moaned when Hadley rolled him onto his back. Blood saturated both of his thighs. The doctor lifted each of Trenton's hands and adjusted them to press against the man's wounds.

"Keep pressure there," Hadley told him, but Trenton didn't listen. He pulled a bloodied hand away, and after one look, he passed out.

Hadley lowered his weapon and scoffed. "Weak!" He turned from Trenton and walked over to me. "Come on, now," Hadley said, and he rolled me sideways until I sat on the pathway.

Hadley pulled back my jacket and tugged my shirt free. Miss Ellsworth gasped, and I looked down to see the mangled, bloody skin on my stomach. My body reacted to the raw, angry wound, and I vomited on the cobblestone.

"Fetch Mrs. Norse, some clean rags, and a couple of men to help me carry him to the house," Hadley told Miss Ellsworth.

My head felt light and detached as I watched Miss Ellsworth disappear. My mind became muddled, and all I could remember was that she needed to be safe. I *needed* her to be safe, and Trenton refused to let her go.

"Trenton!" I called, grabbing Hadley's arm. He shifted, and something pressed into my stomach. I cried out in pain.

"I took care of him," Hadley said.

"Shot him?" I asked, trying to recapture an image on the tip of my memory.

"Yes," Hadley said, still holding his hand against my wound.

I closed my eyes and concentrated, forcing each word to leave my mouth. "You don't hunt?" I opened my eyes again, wincing against the pain.

"I don't hunt. But I *can* shoot," Hadley said and smiled.

Then blackness surged in, surrounding me completely. "Keep Nora safe," I told Hadley right before I passed out.

CHAPTER 46

Miss Nora Ellsworth

I RAN INTO THE HOUSE screaming for help. A maid first appeared, with startled eyes, followed shortly after by a footman and Mrs. Norse.

"Mr. Fausett's been shot," I said and shook my finger towards the back of the house. "We need linens and . . . and . . . men to carry him, and Mrs. Norse you must come."

The housekeeper nodded, issued orders to both servants, and then asked me to lead the way.

When we returned to the garden, Claudia stood next to Doctor Hadley and helped him remove his coat while he continued to apply pressure to Mr. Fausett's wound. Mr. Fausett was no longer conscious.

"Is he all right?" I asked, flinching at the sight of Mr. Fausett's blood-saturated shirt.

"There you are," Doctor Hadley said, looking up at Mrs. Norse and me.

"Some cloths and a few men should arrive shortly," the housekeeper said.

"Very good. Miss Claudia, will you go to my room and fetch my bag? We will meet you in the . . . ?" Doctor Hadley looked to Mrs. Norse for an answer.

"The south drawing room," the woman said.

Claudia agreed and disappeared, and I turned to Doctor Hadley again. "Will he be all right?" I asked through my tears.

Doctor Hadley's eyes narrowed. "Worried are you?"

"Of course I'm worried!" I threw my fists down to my sides. "He was shot trying to save me."

"Hmm . . . Fortunately, my aim is better than Trenton's. He shot wide, missing the vital organs. I won't know until I retrieve the bullet, of course, but from what I can tell it should come out easily enough. As long as we can keep infection away, he should be fine," Doctor Hadley said. He looked up as the servants approached.

I watched Mr. Fausett and exhaled a long breath in unison with the rise and fall of his chest. Doctor Hadley instructed Mrs. Norse to fold one of the cloth strips, and then he pressed it against the wound.

He looked up at the two footmen. "Are there just the two of you?" When they nodded, he looked towards me. "Miss Ellsworth, I hate to impose, but we need to get Fausett inside, and I'm afraid I'll need to help carry him. Would you be willing to hold this firm while we move him? It's imperative we try to staunch the bleeding."

Doctor Hadley watched as my eyes shifted to his blood-covered hands. "Come, Miss Ellsworth." He nodded his head. "We need to move him quickly."

I looked at Mr. Fausett's face, peaceful in sleep, and stepped forward, determined to be brave for my friend who'd stood so bravely for me. Doctor Hadley told me where to place my hands and repeated the necessity of constant pressure. He sent Mrs. Norse to prepare the room and asked the maid to bring several kettles of hot water.

It took all three men to lift Mr. Fausett's limp body. Before we made it to the door, Mr. Jonathon Browning appeared. He looked over the scene, and before he could ask a single question, Doctor Hadley instructed him to restrain Mr. Trenton, who remained passed out on the pathway, and send someone to fetch the constable.

Mrs. Norse had worked efficiently, and by the time we arrived, the excess furniture had been moved against the walls, and a large pile of linens waited on a side table. Mr. Fausett moaned as the men set him on a long table that had been covered with a sheet. I kept my position while Doctor Hadley scrubbed his hands and removed his instruments from the bag Claudia brought him.

"Thank you," Doctor Hadley told me. "You may remove the compress." I looked at Doctor Hadley but did not move my hands. He seemed to understand my question. "I must get the bullet out. I'll be sure to let you know."

"Is there anything I can do for him?" I asked.

"I suspect you've done it already," Doctor Hadley said. He offered a small smile then motioned for me to step away.

I removed the soiled linen and dropped it into a bowl Mrs. Norse held. Claudia stepped behind me and put her hands on my shoulders. "Come, Nora. Let's get you a change of clothes and speak with Father."

I looked at my blood-stained dress and nodded, allowing Claudia to turn me towards the door and praying that Doctor Hadley would be able to work yet another miracle.

With the darkness of night, uncertainty crawled into my heart. I paced the hallway and kept a constant eye on the door of the sitting room. Numerous servants entered and left without offering any word of Mr. Fausett's diagnosis.

The constable sat with both the elder and younger Mr. Brownings in a room nearby, content to eat and chat and relax until he could talk with Doctor Hadley and, hopefully, Mr. Fausett. I'd given my report to the man, and they'd invited me to wait with them, but my fear would not allow me the peace to sit and offer pretend smiles.

Claudia assisted Doctor Hadley, and Miss Wells remained with me. She sat in a nearby chair for a long while. I appreciated her presence and her silence. When she looked up and offered me a weak smile, I asked that she go update Father and ensure my mother was well. Miss Wells asked if I would be all right. After convincing her I would be fine, she left with a promise to return. However, my words were a lie. How could I be fine, complacent, content, while Mr. Fausett fought for his life in the next room? I had confidence in Doctor Hadley's abilities, yet I also recognized the fragility of health, of existence.

The door opened once again, and Doctor Hadley emerged. He didn't notice me and turned to walk down the hall to where the constable waited.

"Doctor Hadley," I cried out and hurried after him. "How is he?"

Doctor Hadley's tired eyes met mine. "The bullet was imbedded deeper than I first expected. It took a long while to extract it and sew him up."

My hands clenched open and closed. "But you removed it? He's going to recover?"

Doctor Hadley rubbed a hand over his face. "Yes, I got the bullet, and for now, Fausett is well. I won't lie to you, Miss Ellsworth. He lost a lot of blood. He's weak, and there's always a chance of infection."

"What are you saying?" I asked as my stomach turned in on itself.

"Devlin will need a lot of support over the next few days and weeks. I believe he can pull through this, but a bit of prayer might do him some good as well," Doctor Hadley said.

"I'll do whatever I can," I said.

"I believe you," he responded. He stared at me a moment more before his eyes opened a little wider and the corner of his mouth turned up. "I've given him laudanum to help dull the pain, and he's asking for you."

"He is?" I asked. My heart jumped.

"I need to meet with the constable, but you should go in." Doctor Hadley turned down the hallway but called back over his shoulder, "Keep your visit brief. He needs his rest."

I hurried to the door, anxious to step through and see Mr. Fausett. I stilled my hands and walked in to find that he'd been moved from the table to a nearby sofa. He wore a loose shirt and was covered in sheets. His dark hair was disheveled, and his eyes were closed. His chest slowly rose and fell, and I realized I'd matched my breaths to his.

Claudia stepped beside me. Her sleeves were stained with blood, and her eyes were tired, but she radiated beauty. "He's a strong man, Nora. He'll be just fine." I nodded and blinked back my tears. "I'm going to go clean up," she said. "But I'll be back shortly."

Claudia left while Mrs. Norse continued to clear away the remnants of the surgery. She held a bundle of soiled rags and bedding, her hair fell around her face, her exhaustion evident. "Would you mind sitting with him while I dispose of these?" Mrs. Norse asked, indicating the linens in her arms.

"Not at all," I said. "I can stay for a while. You should get some rest."

Mrs. Norse offered a feigned smile. "I'll perhaps get a bite to eat, but I won't be gone long."

She left the room, and I turned back to Mr. Fausett. As I watched him, a strange pull began inside of me. My heart yearned and ached and throbbed all at the same time. I walked near the couch where Mr. Fausett lay, feeling a desperate need to be near him, to comfort him, to touch him, although I knew such a thing would be highly improper. Yet, my gratitude for his wellbeing, his heroic actions, was more than I could bear, and I wanted somehow to convey my overflowing emotions to him. I wanted to let him know, to communicate the sentiments churning through my soul.

I walked up beside Mr. Fausett, and before I could change my mind, I placed my hand on his face, leaned over, and placed a single kiss on his cheek. Mr. Fausett deserved nothing less. My fingers traced his jaw, running over the shadow of stubble. I stepped back and found a chair where I could sit and wait for him to wake up.

CHAPTER 47

Mr. Devlin Fausett

MY DREAMS WERE RIDDLED WITH conflict. Fear clutched my breast, and pain burned so thoroughly throughout my body I wanted to awaken, but I couldn't. Right when I wanted to succumb to the piercing ache, I opened my mouth to cry out and the image of Miss Ellsworth appeared. Her presence calmed me. Soothed me. Assured me that no matter the difficulty, I could triumph because she believed in me.

I realized the images in my mind were not reality, but I couldn't bring myself to the realm of wakefulness. Quiet slipped in around me, and I began to feel peace combined with another sensation. Then I snapped awake. My eyes remained closed, but I could feel the quiet, hear the relief, and smell the sweet scent of her. It was tangible long before her skin touched mine; her hand on one cheek before she placed a kiss on the other. It was a reality I would die a thousand times to experience over and over again. I wanted to open my eyes, to place my hand over her own, to not let her pull away as her fingers trailed down my cheek, but I didn't want to disrupt the tranquility. She remained close; I didn't need to open my eyes to confirm she was there. I could feel it.

My slumber may have lasted for hours, days, or weeks. I didn't know. But when I woke, I opened my eyes to the image of an angel. Miss Ellsworth sat in a nearby chair, embroidering while she sang. The tune was far from a lullaby, but it rang of truth. It was a song for us to share.

Miss Ellsworth's eyes focused on her needlework, and she sang, *"By Venus, Mother of Desire, your eyes have set me on fire. There's magic in your touch. There's magic in your touch."*

She hummed the next few bars unaware of my eyes on her, and although my throat burned raw, I croaked out the next refrain. "*My eyes! Dear miss, a-well-a-day, tears must have wash'd their power away.*"

Miss Ellsworth tossed her work aside and stood. "Oh! Devlin!" Her hands covered her mouth, and her eyes darted around the room. "You're awake." She took a single step towards me.

"Yes," I said and chuckled, which caused excruciating pain to roll through my stomach. I moaned and moved my hand to my midsection.

Miss Ellsworth held out a hand. "Don't exert yourself."

She stood close, looking more beautiful than I remembered.

"I should call for Doctor Hadley," she said. "He'll want to see you." She turned towards the door.

"Wait!" I cried out with a sudden surge of energy. "Please wait," I said through ragged breath. I raised my hand briefly before letting it fall back to the bedside. "Will you first tell me what happened?"

"You don't remember?" Her eyes softened as she walked slowly back towards me.

I shook my head. "Bits and pieces, but not all of it." My words were raspy, and I coughed then groaned as more pain shot through my stomach.

Miss Ellsworth moved to a table and poured a glass of water. She held it forward then pulled back.

"I can manage," I said and accepted the drink. After a long swallow, I sighed. "Thank you."

Miss Ellsworth retook the glass, shifting it between her hands. "Do you recall being shot?"

"By Trenton?" I asked, and she nodded. "Yes, I remember that part."

"His plan was to kidnap me and force me into marriage. I tried to run, but his grip was so tight"—her voice shook—"and I couldn't get free."

My jaw clenched as the scene replayed in my mind.

"Until you arrived," Miss Ellsworth said and blinked back the moisture in her eyes. She set the glass aside and moved to a chair sitting very near my makeshift bed. "When you refused to step aside, you were shot. Doctor Hadley then shot Mr. Trenton in the leg." She grimaced. "Both legs actually." Her hands twisted in front of her. "The constable was summoned, and Mr. Trenton is now locked up and awaiting trial."

"Were you harmed?" I asked. Miss Ellsworth looked well, resplendent in fact, but after the gunshot, my memories grew fuzzy.

A beautiful shade of red blossomed on Miss Ellsworth's cheeks. "I am quite well." Her voice grew quiet. "Thanks to you, Mr. Fausett. You were very brave." Her compliment touched my heart, and words hovered just out of reach.

Mrs. Norse walked into the room. "Oh, he is finally awake. Have you summoned Doctor Hadley?" she asked Miss Ellsworth.

Without shifting her eyes from mine, Miss Ellsworth shook her head. "Not yet."

Mrs. Norse cleared her throat. "Well then. I'll go find him." She stepped out of the room, leaving the door ajar.

"Miss Ellsworth," I said, extending my hand to her. She pressed her lips together and blinked several times before she accepted my invitation. She slid her tiny fingers into mine. "If I was brave, it was only for you." She shook her head, but I continued. "It's true. You make me brave, with your strength and your goodness. I'm a better man because you expect me to be." Miss Ellsworth blinked again and looked down at our hands. I dug my elbow into the sofa determined to sit upright. Pain shot through my abdomen, and I clenched my teeth to keep from crying out, but I refused to address her lying on my back.

"Mr. Fausett, you mustn't move!" Miss Ellsworth leaned forward and extended her free hand, as if she would force me to lie back down on the couch.

But my determination prevailed, and I finally sat upright, breathing heavily from the effort. After a few calming breaths, I said, "I think we're beyond surnames. Please call me Devlin."

Another blush stole through Miss Ellsworth's cheeks.

"Nora," I whispered. "Nora, look at me." Her blush remained, but her hands stilled and when her eyes met mine, warmth permeated my entire soul. "Will you call me Devlin?"

Her head nodded before she offered a verbal reply. "I will."

"And may I call you Nora?"

"Yes," she answered on a whisper. "I would like that."

CHAPTER 48

Miss Nora Ellsworth

"But . . ." Mother stuttered, glancing quickly at my father before she returned her eyes to mine, "but, what does Jonathon think?"

"Believe me, Mother. He is quite at peace with the idea," I said.

"How could that be? How can you so easily dismiss our arrangements?" Mother asked.

"Because they were your arrangements, Mother. Not mine. And not Mr. Browning's. In fact, he's confided that his heart belongs to another, a Miss McMann, whom he met in India. He hopes to return shortly and claim her hand." In the aftermath of the ordeal with Mr. Trenton, Mr. Browning and I had engaged in several civil conversations. He forgave me for refusing him and confessed his proposal had nothing to do with his heart.

I handed Father a glass of water. He'd sworn he would never drink tea again. I didn't blame him. I sat beside my mother on the sofa. She held her cup like a statue, the shock of my revelation settling over her. "He loves someone else?" she asked.

"Well, he could hardly love me," I said and laughed. "We've only been acquainted for a short amount of time. His interests lie only in my dowry and inheritance. Or rather, that's where his father's interests lie."

Father grunted.

"Surely the two of you would have suited," Mother said and lifted her chin.

I reached over and placed my hand on her arm. "Perhaps we would have, but I don't care for Mr. Browning the way I should care for my husband."

Tears gathered in my mother's eyes. She lowered her teacup and stared at the contents swirling within. Then she finally said, "I hope you know I only wanted you to be happy." Father coughed into his hand. Mother's head jerked up, and she scoffed. "Fine! I also wanted to break the entail, and perhaps I did push too hard. But my intentions were pure."

My fingers tightened around her arm. "I know. We are blessed that Father's health is restored. There will be other gentlemen that will suit."

Mother harrumphed. "We'll see."

Father stood from his chair and teetered a little before steadying himself. I hurried to his side. After I slipped my arm through his, he looked down at me and smiled.

"Now that Fausett's awake, I need to give him my appreciation. If he hadn't shown up . . ." Father swallowed hard. "Well . . ." He patted my hand.

"Father, there is something we can do to show our gratitude."

"Oh?" Father asked.

"Perhaps we could ask Mr. Browning about purchasing a particular black horse."

CHAPTER 49

Mr. Devlin Fausett

MR. ELLSWORTH VISITED MY SICKROOM and expressed his appreciation for confronting Trenton. The compliment settled uncomfortably, because protecting Miss Ellsworth was my natural inclination. But I could see the love Ellsworth had for his daughter as well as the sincere gratitude in his eyes.

"I would do it again," I said without pretense. Despite the emasculating circumstances of being only partially dressed and confined to bed, I asked the question that had been burning in my heart since I had awoken. "Mr. Ellsworth, I already told you how I feel about your daughter. May I have your blessing to marry her?"

Ellsworth worked his jaw for a moment before he responded. "You don't need my permission."

"Sir?" I asked.

"You were right before, Fausett. Nora should be the one to decide her future. The restrictions of the entail remain, but I want her to be happy. Whomever *she* chooses will have my blessing."

The room seemed suddenly lighter. "Understood, sir. I too desire only her happiness."

"Well, then. I understand you'll be returning to Riverton Park?" he asked.

"Yes. Once Hadley clears me to travel."

"We'll be passing through Derbyshire and have room in our coach." I raised my eyebrows, and Ellsworth shrugged. "It's the least I can do."

I nodded, and he quit the room.

The pain radiating through my body served as a constant reminder of my feelings for Miss Ellsworth. It was a pain I would suffer again and again to ensure her safety. While I refused to wait another day to ask Nora to marry me, I also refused to do it while lying on my back.

With exerted effort, I forced myself to sit up on the sofa and wiped the sweat from my forehead just before she slipped through the door. The moment our eyes met, she straightened and thrust both hands behind her back.

"What are you hiding?" I asked.

Her cheeks instantly flushed. "You weren't supposed to see that."

"But I did," I said, grinning at her adorable expression.

She walked to the chair she'd occupied on previous visits. "You also aren't supposed to be sitting up." Her attempt at chastisement fell short as her lips twitched and her eyes danced.

"Come." I held my right hand towards her. "Let me see what you've brought."

"Very well." Nora's closed hand hid the item until she dropped it into my open palm. It was my grandfather's pocket watch. "Are you pleased?" she asked.

The fullness in my heart robbed my lungs of oxygen. A full minute passed before I could speak again. "How did you come by this?"

"Doctor Hadley gave it to me and asked that I return it to you." Nora sat on the edge of the chair. "Although, he would not tell me why."

I turned the timepiece over in my hands, too choked with emotion to respond.

"Doctor Hadley has asked Father's permission to court Claudia," Nora said and clasped her hands near her heart. "It wasn't a surprise really. Claudia helped tend to Marcus's mother and then remained to assist Doctor Hadley while he worked"—Nora swallowed and blinked rapidly—"while he worked to remove the bullet from your stomach." She shook her head and pushed her lips into a smile. "Claudia's been asking constant questions about medicine and Doctor Hadley's research. She's even procured several books on healing herbs. It seems Doctor Hadley has grounded Claudia in a way nothing else could."

"They will make each other happy," I said.

"Yes, they will," Nora agreed. Then with a tilt of her head, she asked, "Why *did* Doctor Hadley have your watch?"

My heart burst as I looked at the woman before me. "Because Claudia is important to you, and you're important to me."

"But it belonged to your grandfather—"

I leaned forward and pressed a finger to her lips. "Shhh, let me finish." Nora's blue eyes widened. "I would do anything for you, my dear. Sell an heirloom or take a bullet. When I learned that Trenton was heading to Lily Glen, my only thought was for your safety. And then to see him restraining you . . ." My chest ached with the memory. "Instinct took over. My heart took over. You know it's been yours for a very long time."

Nora's breath caught as I took her hands in my own.

"I love you, Nora, and I want to spend every day of my life with you. I know I'm not wealthy or prominent, but I promise to protect you, and I promise to make you proud. Would you do me the honor of becoming my wife?"

Tears gathered in her eyes. "I think I fell in love with you the moment we sang our first duet," Nora said. She lifted my hands to her lips and brushed a kiss across the backs of my knuckles. My heart pounded in my chest. "Yes, I will marry you," she said.

Peace and a joy I could not articulate surged through my soul. I pulled Nora closer and cradled her face as I pressed my lips to hers. Sweet. Sensual. Perfection.

After two long weeks, Hadley cleared me to travel. I was not fully recovered, but as Hadley would be traveling with us, he felt I could safely make the trip to Riverton Park.

For too long, I'd been confined to my sickroom. Despite the monotonous surroundings and lack of fresh air, Nora's companionship was most welcome. Daily she sat near my bedside, singing or reading to me.

I convinced one of the servants to bring me a change of clothing and provide me with my shaving instruments. Hadley would likely tan my hide, but I refused to stay in bed for another moment.

I dressed and moved to a desk where the servant had placed a small mirror and washbasin. As I applied the lather, there was a light knock on the door. "Enter," I called and turned to see Nora standing with an adorable look of vexation.

"Devlin! What do you think you're doing?" she asked. "Why are you disobeying Doctor Hadley's orders? He said you are to remain in bed a few days more."

The sight of Nora vexed was a rarity. A rarity I found especially enthralling.

"Well?" she demanded, crossing her arms across her middle. "What do you have to say for yourself?"

I shrugged, and the pain pulled the grin from my face. After a measured breath, I answered. "I wanted to clean up before subjecting you to ride in a confined carriage with me."

Nora scoffed. She located a small chair and marched with it to where I stood. "If you are going to be disobedient, the least you can do is sit down and let me help."

I smiled and complied. She took the razor from my hand. "Do you know what you're doing?" I asked.

A mischievous look flashed through her blue eyes. "No, but I'm sure I can manage."

My eyebrows rose, and Nora laughed lightly. She leaned forward and slid the razor across my cheek. Her eyes evaluated her work as she wiped the blade clean and repeated the process. The metal edge glided soundlessly across my skin, and when the task was completed on one side, she continued on the other. We didn't speak. I barely breathed. Intimacy settled between us in comfortable silence.

Once the shaving was complete, Nora set the razor aside and used a towel to wipe the remaining soap from my face. "There," she whispered, and before she could step away, I wrapped my arms around her waist and stood, biting back the pain.

Nora's palms rested on my chest, and she lifted one hand and ran her fingers along my jaw. The moment her fingers connected with my skin, my eyes drifted closed. The pain left my body, replaced by a yearning desire to kiss the woman in my arms. My eyes flashed open, and with one look at Nora, I knew she wanted the same thing. I pulled her close and covered her lips with mine.

CHAPTER 50

Miss Nora Ellsworth

MY BODY RELAXED INTO DEVLIN. His arms held me, sure and steady. The intensity of his kiss shook my entire core, and I kissed him back with a passion I'd never felt before. My left hand slid around his neck, my fingers tangled through his thick black hair, and my right hand moved to his waist.

Devlin gasped, and I jumped out of his arms.

With a strained face, he said, "Sorry, my dear. I'm still a bit sore, I'm afraid."

"Then how dare you kiss me like that!" I clutched a fist on my chest, willing my frantic heartbeat to slow down.

Devlin stared at me with the most beautiful longing in his eyes. Eyes that held no regret. With an indignant sigh, I led him to the sofa. He slowly sat, and his face split into a wide smile as he began to chuckle.

"What?" I asked.

"I'd do it all again," he said with a roguish look in his eye.

"Do what again?" I asked.

"Get shot."

"Devlin!" I chided, and he chuckled again.

"If the result is getting that kiss from you, I'd do it a thousand times."

"You, sir, are shameless."

"No, my dear. I'm lucky. Very, very lucky, for I do believe you were kissing me back."

The evening before our departure, I obtained Doctor Hadley's permission for Devlin to walk with me outside in the gardens. His wound was healing well, and Doctor Hadley no longer feared infection would set in, but Devlin's steps were still slow. I held on to his arm, and excitement for my surprise bounded through me as I led him to the west side of the estate.

"Are you anxious to depart tomorrow?" I asked.

He glanced at me then focused again on his steps. "I'm anxious to see Brumley and his wife. The Brownings have been gracious, especially in their recent attentions, but I admit, I'm ready to leave this place." Devlin lifted my hand from his arm and pressed a kiss to the back of my knuckles. "More importantly, I'm anxious to call you Mrs. Nora Fausett."

"It is a lovely name." I could not suppress my grin as I turned him back towards the path and continued walking. "I worry the journey won't be easy for you."

"And you find that amusing?" he asked, glancing down at me.

"Not at all!" I said, with a culpable smile. I placed my free hand on his arm. We were almost there. "I only hoped I could make the trip more pleasant." I held my breath, and we rounded the corner of the house just as a groom led Raven to where we stood. "She belongs to you now," I said, releasing Devlin's arm and stepping back.

Raven tossed her head, and Devlin's gray eyes turned to me in confusion.

"Father bought her back for you. I mean, I guess he did it for me because I asked him to. But the reason I asked him to was—for you. And Father was so grateful for everything you did for us, for him . . ."

Devlin looked at his horse and reached forward to place his hand on Raven's muzzle. "There, girl," he whispered.

"Consider it an early wedding present," I said.

Devlin dropped his hand from Raven's face, and, with surprising agility, he turned and pulled me into his arms. "I don't deserve you, Nora Ellsworth."

"That's soon to be Nora Fausett, and you'd best not forget it." Warmth trickled from my head down to my toes as Devlin held me close.

His smile slipped as he turned towards the groom and cleared his throat. The groom looked away. Devlin's smile was as bright as the sun. He looked down at me, and, though no words were exchanged, they were not needed. He understood the burning within, the desire to have him hold me, kiss me, because I knew he felt it too. When Devlin's dark eyes found mine, he leaned forward and kissed me soundly.

CHAPTER 51

Mr. Devlin Fausett

Not long after our arrival in Riverton Park, we received word that Mr. Trenton was found hanging from a sheet strung up in his jail cell. He'd left a note airing his grievances at his horrible circumstances, but his missive expressed no remorse for his actions against Nora or her father.

We stayed only briefly with the Brumleys before continuing on to Essex. I was anxious for my parents to meet my future bride. I knew Mother would be delighted but was pleasantly surprised with Father's reaction to my fiancée. While his acceptance of me was reluctant, he wholly welcomed Nora to the family.

I believe Father recognized Nora's tender heart and devotion, and perhaps he realized that if Nora could love me, I wasn't a complete waste of a child. One word from Nora, coupled with the fact that she would be the mother of his grandchildren, wrought wonders upon Father's countenance.

We were wed in the parish near Ellsworth Meadows in July and opted for a simple wedding trip to Brighton so that I might fully recover from my injury.

We walked arm in arm along the secluded seashore, while the waves washed over the tops of our feet. The sun slipped lower in the sky, providing a beautiful sunset, but my attention was drawn to my lovely wife.

"You know if I dive in, you'd have to save me because of my injury." I dramatically pressed my free hand against my scarred stomach.

Nora's lips twisted into a feisty smile. "I've told you, I don't care to swim. I'm quite content to watch the ocean from the comfort of the sand."

"You'd make a lovely mermaid," I teased.

Nora swatted my arm, and I grabbed her fingers and pulled them to my lips. I dropped my hands to her waist and swung her around, as if I would toss her into the waves. She squealed until I set her safely back on the shore. "Devlin, be careful!" she said, her beautiful blue eyes widened with concern. "You'll hurt yourself."

"I'll take my chances." I leaned forward and grinned while I kissed her lips. "Definitely worth the gamble."

She pulled back and clasped the lapels of my jacket. "You've promised no more gambling."

"And I will remain true to that promise." With a portion of Nora's dowry, I paid off the remaining debt to Higgins, anxious to leave my past behind and begin a wonderful new adventure. "My last wager cleared me from the habit entirely. I bet the largest stakes and came off victor. What further temptation could there be?"

Nora straightened. "Last wager? What are you talking about?"

"You, my dear. By far the best bet I've ever made." I gathered her in my arms again.

"Really?" Nora asked, tilting her head so I could see her eyes. She was a temptation I could not resist. Rather than answer, I kissed her again.

Nora pulled back. "What were the stakes?"

"My heart and soul." I raised one hand to her face and stroked my thumb across her cheek.

Her lips turned up in a delightful smile. "Then thank goodness you won."

"Thank goodness, indeed," I agreed. And then I kissed my wife again.

ABOUT THE AUTHOR

CHALON LINTON WAS FIRST INTRODUCED to the Regency era by a dear friend, and now she can't get enough of handsome men in tailcoats. Chalon's intrigue in the genre stems from a nostalgic longing for manners, wit, and true love. Fortunately, she found her dashing gentleman, married him, and now lives happily ever after in Southern California.